LOVE IN NUMBERS

Love Distilled, Book One

SCARLETT COLE

Published By: Kadelo Group Ltd.

Edited by Angela James

Cover design by Letitia Hasser at RBA Design

Photo by Wander Aguiar Photography

Formatting by DJW Formatting

E-book ISBN: 978-1-8382469-1-4

Paperback ISBN: 978-1-8382469-0-7

Connor isn't in the market for messy.

His life is going completely according to plan. He's set to become CEO of his family's company, his Ironman time is better than ever, and his regular poker nights with the guys are his one night a month he can stop worrying about counting macros and indulge himself. What he doesn't need is a relationship with Emerson Dyer—daughter of his father's lifelong enemy and most-hated rival.

Emerson's life is nothing but messy.

Since her father died, leaving her CEO of their gin distillery, everything that could go wrong has gone wrong. Emerson is barely holding it together—what she doesn't need is a complication like Connor Finch. Sure, his abs do look like they've been photoshopped, but she has no time to spend counting them. It's her company's numbers she should be worrying about. Still, there's something about the way he makes her feel.

Together, they're perfect.

Connor knows he and Emerson don't make sense on paper. Too many differences between them—and one big secret that could destroy Emerson's family business tells him to cut and run. But for once in his life, Connor doesn't care about messy or imperfect—because the fact is, Emerson is the one perfect thing he needs in his life. Now if he can only convince her . . .

Dear You,
You made it.
You aren't the you that you were.
But this you is joyful.
May this dedication always remind you of that.

Acknowledgments

To my readers. I'm sorry I took so long, and I'm beyond grateful that you waited while I took the time I needed. The fact you are all still here is a miracle. I hope you love Connor and Emerson as much as I do.

To the bloggers, reviewers, and influencers of the romance community. Thank you for showing up to support me. I keep saying don't call this a comeback, but we all know it is. It would be impossible without each and every one of you.

To Angela James. This was the first time we worked together, and it was magic. I loved every moment of the process and this book is so much better for your input.

To Isabel Ngo. I know you are reading this at the start of the copy edits, but I want you to know how grateful I am for the care you've shown me and this book.

To Nicole Bailey and Olivia Kalb. Thank you for your keen eyes in making sure this book was perfect.

To Letitia Hasser and Wander Aguiar. Thank you so much for providing me with such a wonderful cover and inspiring photograph. Your creativity has no bounds. Thank you for sharing it with me.

To Lucas Loyola. Thank you for helping to bring Connor Finch to life!

To Claire and Wendy. Thank you for stepping in at the last minute and saving my butt. You are life savers.

To Cindy Kirk, Robin Covington, and Avery Flynn. Thank you as always for your friendship and words of wisdom. Writing can be a solitary occupation, but the three of you have never let me feel alone.

To Vi Keeland. For reminding me what it looks like when another woman helps you lift the weight of your crown.

To Antonia Aitken. Thank you for the joy you bring to my life, for being my opposite node, for being the Barbara to my Margo. I'll meet you in the middle. With wine.

To Lola and Finley. A pandemic forced us all to sit at the same table every day . . . but your patience and focus gave me the space and quiet to write this. I love your faces.

To Tim. You remain my greatest cheerleader in work, life, and love. I love you.

Chapter One

E merson Dyer reached the door of her father's office in their family-run gin distillery. She ran her fingertips across the brass plate with his name on it. He'd regaled her a thousand times with the story of how her mother had hung it when they'd first bought the place. "I miss you, Dad," she murmured before pushing the door open.

The office was still her father's. His raincoat still hung on the back of the door. The Denver Broncos mug she'd gotten him for Father's Day when she was fifteen sat on his desk. Her mind returned to those frantic moments of finding him on the floor two months earlier. Of screaming for her younger brother, Jake, who as master distiller had just started the next batch of Dyer's Medallion gin for the day. She'd frantically dialed 911 and balanced her phone beneath her ear while trying her best to deliver CPR to the man who had loved them so fiercely—who had been there for them ever since the accident happened fifteen years ago, when their mother had died a week after Emerson's fifteenth birthday.

It hadn't been enough.

The doctors had tried to reassure her there was nothing she could have done that would have saved him.

It had been eight weeks yet thinking about that day still had the ability to take her breath away. She'd never get to hear another one of his ridiculous dad jokes, tease him for his vast collection of blue shirts, or plant seeds with him in his greenhouse.

She swallowed deeply and tried to shake the image from her head. She'd barely stepped into his office since then, beyond grabbing the occasional piece of paperwork. Piles of unopened envelopes sat on the desk, and her stomach lurched at the thought of dealing with them. While it was hard to admit it to others, she knew she was overwhelmed. But the letter in her father's will left her with no choice but to step into his shoes, shoes that were impossible to fill.

My darling Emerson, he'd written.

If you are reading this letter, it means I've gone exactly when I was meant to and way sooner than I hoped. I hope you know how proud I am of you. You have been my rock since your mom died, and now I have to ask you to be the glue once more. Jake and Olivia are going to need you more than ever. They'll drift without you. You'll all drift without each other. You have to run the distillery and keep everyone together. You are all each other has got. I have faith in you, Emsie-bobs.

With all my love,

Dad xxx

Her father had never realized it, but his belief in not owing anybody anything had put the family-owned distillery at risk without any savings net or loans to pad their expenses. Ever since their mother had died, her father had been terrified that something unexpected was going to happen to him. And the idea of the three of them being left with a business in debt was more than he could process. As a result, they had been running month to month because her father had remained entrenched in his position.

Every day was a struggle to balance it all.

"Knock, knock." Jake burst through the door, running his hand through his shoulder-length, dark hair that matched her own. She envied the natural waves he'd been blessed with compared to her own pin-straight locks. "Wanted to catch you before you head out to the airport. Have you got the preliminary production schedule for the month?"

"It's on my desk next door. I can't believe it's the start of October already," she replied. "Are you sure you don't want to switch places and go to the liquor awards in my place? You know you love San Francisco."

Jake looked down at his gray jeans with holes in them and his black-and-red plaid shirt. "Not exactly dressed for it. And unless you want to do a twelve-hour production shift every day for the next three days, you're the only one who can go."

Emerson slipped her purse off her shoulder and pulled out the large black bags she brought with her. "I wish Liv felt better so she could go."

At the beginning of June, a violent storm had ravaged the distillery's events hall, leaving it partially roofless and flooded. They had been forced to close it and had done everything they could to accommodate all the weddings they had booked. The tasting room and bar in the main building had the same rustic ambience—red brick, faded wood, and a hint of contemporary in the bar and seating area, but it was designed for something a lot more intimate. Private tours, tastings, even the occasional book club. There had only been so many wedding parties that had been small enough to fit. They'd had to cancel the majority of weddings for the summer months. Losing out on peak season weddings had been ruinous to their cash flow. As damage control, her father, just before he'd died, had offered cancellations without loss of deposits to wedding parties as far out as March the following year, a decision that had exasperated Emerson.

As the distillery's event planner, social media manager, and all-around administrator, Olivia had carried the brunt of informing all the wedding parties about the flood. They'd ranted, sworn at her, and even made threats against Olivia and the company. One groom had taken to stalking Olivia on her personal social media profiles. Dyer's Gin Distillery's social media pages had been flooded with hateful comments, fueling online trolls until it became too much for Liv. The deep depression and frightening levels of anxiety had shown signs of lifting as of late, but it was still too early to expect their youngest sibling to return to work.

"Me too. But we can keep it together until she gets back, right? You starting on Dad's office?" he asked.

"I was going to, but now that I'm here, I don't know if I can face it."

In the past, when she'd thought about how her father would have handed over the reins to the three of them, she'd always imagined it would be at least a decade away and involve a big cake wishing her father a happy retirement. They would cut it on the production floor instead of in the office so everyone could be involved. They'd talk through her plans—the ones that included turning the distillery into a state of the art environmentally friendly masterpiece. He'd have tidied his office, removing the personal debris built up over a lifetime. The pictures of her parents' wedding, of Jake holding a glass of his first distillation, of Olivia's first wedding event, of Emerson's graduation.

But now it was up to her, and she didn't feel even close to being ready. She put her hands on her hips and looked at the piles of papers, the tchotchkes.

Jake threw his arm over her shoulder. "I have faith in you, Em."

Her father's letter had assured her the same. But somehow, she didn't feel as though she *deserved* the faith placed in her.

Four hours later, Emerson was at the airport ready to board. "Ms. Dyer, there was a problem with seating a family together, so with your permission, I'd like to give you an upgrade," said the attendant.

Doing a mental high five, Emerson smiled. "That would be wonderful, thank you."

The flight was only two and a half hours, long enough to have a drink to calm her nerves and perhaps watch a movie—anything to take her mind off the thousands of feet between her butt and the ground. Plus, she fully intended to embrace the time as her first period of enforced relaxation in months. Two and a half hours without calls, interruptions, or emails. Any work could wait until she was safely ensconced in her hotel that evening. She placed her laptop bag in the overhead compartment and slid her purse under the aisle seat in front of her.

"Wine?" asked the flight attendant.

Emerson took a glass from the tray. "Thank you." She took a sip, acidulous flavors exploding on her tongue. It was a touch fruity for her personal tastes, but it was free and available. She switched her cellphone off and let her head fall back, eyes closed, on the headrest. Two and a half perfect hours without being bothered by a soul.

"Excuse me, you're in my seat."

Emerson opened her eyes with a start. A tall man, looking way too handsome for his own good in a fitted navy suit, stared at her like a rather deliciously imperious Clark Kent with his black hair a little on the long side and most definitely ruffled. He looked down at her through glasses that quite possibly made him even hotter.

"I'm sorry." Emerson placed her glass down and pulled the ticket out of her purse. "I was upgraded; they gave me a new ticket as I boarded. Perhaps they made a mistake," she said, wondering why she felt the need to apologize to the ungracious man glaring at her.

She looked at the ticket, then up again at the numbers above the row of seats. 3B. The aisle seat. She was in the right spot. "There must be some mistake," she said, showing him her ticket.

The man growled. It was low and quiet, but it was most definitely a growl. "I so don't need this today," he muttered under his breath, before leaning over her to press the buzzer for the flight attendant.

In spite of his rude behavior, he smelled delicious. Nothing floral. Decidedly woodsy. And the move revealed a shirt that fit his taut frame as if it had been painted on.

"Are you sure you aren't in *A*?" Emerson offered quietly, pointing toward the empty seat next to her, not that the jerk was worth any of her time. But other passengers were looking, and she'd rather fix the problem than continue to cause a scene.

"I never sit by the window," he said, as if that explained everything.

A flight attendant arrived and smiled so hard Emerson's jaw ached at the sight. Perhaps, Emerson thought, she was the only one immune to Mr. Grumpy's style of charm. "How can I help?"

Mr. Grumpy explained. Emerson offered her ticket as proof.

"I see the problem," said the flight attendant, taking a look at both their tickets before placing her hand on Mr. Grumpy's arm. "You've both been given the same seat. It'll just be a moment while I figure this out. Please, take a seat."

Mr. Grumpy looked at her expectantly. Emerson scoffed. He wanted her to move. And while she half expected she'd have to move back to the economy cabin any moment, she wasn't going to make this easy for some smooth-talking idiot. Even if he did have the bluest eyes she'd ever seen.

"It would make more sense for you to move over," Mr. Grumpy said.

Emerson tucked her legs up against the seat. "There's plenty of room for you to get by."

"I can't work if I sit by the window, too much light on my laptop screen," he said, pointedly.

"What, so a woman on a plane can't possibly be wanting to work because…?" She let the words hang.

Mr. Grumpy's jaw twitched, and for a moment, she thought she saw a flicker of his dimple. "That wasn't what I was implying."

"Oh, so you just want it to be more convenient for *you* to work than me?" Damn. She hadn't intended to work, but if she ended up staying in the aisle seat and not back in 34E, she would need to work just to make her point.

Now it was Mr. Grumpy's turn to scoff. His glacial eyes looked toward her glass of wine for a moment, then back at Emerson. "I can only imagine how focused you'll be."

Standing, she quickly realized that there was still a good six inches in height between them. "Are you honestly trying to shame me and my ability to work because of one minuscule glass of wine, taken because I happen to be terrified of flying? Which, by the way, is the reason I don't want to sit next to the goddamn window. First, you get mad because of an administrative error that I did not cause. Then, you invade my personal space to call for assistance…assistance you could have gained had you walked ten feet to the cabin crew. Judgmental *and* rude is really not a good look for you."

Mr. Grumpy raised his hands in mock surrender. "Hmm. That's a lot to tackle in one go. You want me to take them one by one, or—"

"Problem solved," said the flight attendant brightly. "There's another aisle seat that's empty over there." She pointed to the other side of the cabin a few rows back. "Or one of you can take the window. Which would you prefer, Mr. Finch?"

Feeling somewhat embarrassed yet unapologetic over her outburst, Emerson reached for her purse. "Look, I can go back—"

"I'll go," Mr. *Finch* said, although he'd always be Mr. Grumpy to her.

"Thank you," the flight attendant said, casting a look in Emerson's direction, as if she'd been the problem all along. "We're grateful for your cooperation."

Silently seething and mortified, Emerson sat back down.

"Thanks for taking your seat, Ms. Dyer. Mr. Finch, if you'd like to go and take your seat, we'll be departing shortly."

Mr. Grumpy's demeanor shifted. His spine straightened, and his pale eyes glared at Emerson. He spun on his heel and marched up the aisle without another word.

It was the oddest part of their whole encounter.

Emerson raised the wine to her lips, but it tasted sour on her tongue. The enjoyment taken away by a man she didn't know and shouldn't possibly care about.

In an attempt to reclaim the positive mood she'd been

embracing just before Mr. Grumpy's arrival, she forced herself to sip the wine anyway.

But she couldn't resist one last look in his direction, and when she glanced over her shoulder, she found him staring right back at her.

C atch. Power. Recovery.

Catch. Power. Recovery.

Connor Finch focused on the repetition. He kicked his legs, propelling himself forward, turning his head every second stroke to gulp for air. When the end of the pool came into view, he tucked his head and turned, kicking off the edge of the pool to gain momentum.

Catch. Power. Recovery.

His arms burned, muscles already tired from an hour spent in the gym. His mind was empty of any thought other than lap count and form.

The hotel pool was less than ideal, but thankfully it wasn't busy enough to stop him from achieving his goal. Five kilometers. Six days a week.

As he finished the final lap, he reached for the side of the pool, holding tight as he sucked in large gulps of air. While his body screamed for rest, his mind calmed and he savored the sacred moments of peace. He pulled himself from the pool and removed his cap and goggles.

Connor checked his Rolex Submariner, a gift from his father for graduating Harvard with his MBA eight years earlier and joining him at his firm, Finch Liquor Distribution.

Sixty-seven minutes. Damn, he was slipping.

Once he'd showered, he slipped into gray sweats and a T-shirt and returned to his room to get formally dressed.

The swim made getting to the event that evening a little tight, but he felt better for the exertion.

His mother had once remarked that he lacked spontaneity. But he'd whittled his routine down to a fine art. Habits were stacked. Performance measured. Results recorded. Why anyone would waste their time without a solid routine was beyond him.

Back in his room, he caught sight of his dark hair in the mirror. He needed a haircut. Taming the ends was an episode in futility. Bristles met his hand as he ran his palm over his jaw.

He dressed in his suit, one custom-made to fit him. With his tall height and swimmer's shoulders, it was hard to find anything off the rack. Deep navy blue. White dress shirt. Silver cuff links that had belonged to his grandfather. Bowtie because it was expected. Black shoes he'd polished to perfection before he'd left home.

With a final check that he had his wallet in his back pocket and his phone and room key in his suit jacket, he stepped out into the hallway. Moments later, he was inside the elevator heading for the ballroom. What were the chances, Connor thought, that the Ms. Dyer he'd met on the aircraft was the one and only Emerson Dyer, CEO of Dyer's Gin?

Donovan Finch, his father, had dreamed of creating an empire like the Bacardi family, a rags-to-riches story. He'd wanted to build a product and establish a world-class distillery and brand. From there, he'd aspired to forge an empire that had global reach.

But over three decades before, Donovan's business partner, Paul Dyer, had screwed him over. Just when the distillery they'd built together was about to open, his business partner pulled the company out from beneath him, leaving him penniless with nothing but a vengeful ambition to become the most successful liquor business in North America.

The previous evening, on the way to the hotel, Connor had looked up the Dyer family as soon as he'd gotten into the cab. His father's constant ranting about the company had piqued Connor's levels of curiosity enough to form a periodic check-in to see how the company was performing. He'd already done a cursory study of Paul Dyer several years before. Dyer's Gin Distillery had never done well enough for Connor to understand why his father's anger had lasted this long. There had been other deals that hadn't worked out over the years, and he doubted his father could remember half of them. Perhaps it was because Dyer's Gin Distillery had been his first major loss, and that made it so…personal.

But now, as Connor studied the liquor market, he could see a shift toward artisanal brands and an opportunity to acquire a portion of the market.

Making Dyer's Gin Distillery a potential target.

Connor's cab-ride search had been about the people, not the numbers. Especially the former operations manager, now CEO, known as Emerson Dyer.

Emerson.

The name suited her, and the thought irritated him.

He'd noticed her as soon as he'd boarded. Attractive, with thick brown hair, her delicate gold earring catching the light from somewhere.

But after the shitty morning he had in argumentative meetings with his Uncle Cameron, the company's Chief Financial Officer, and the evening's pending deadline for a new contract he was working on, he'd just wanted to get seated and get on with his work, so his uncle had one less thing to complain to his father about.

When she'd finally lost her cool, those syrup-brown eyes of hers heated, he'd been distracted…momentarily entertained. She was a flash fire when provoked but was quick to quench it, and he liked it. He'd even considered taking the window seat so he could get to know her a little bit more.

Until he heard the attendant say her name, and he realized who she was.

And while taking his seat was not on the same level as stealing a company, Connor guessed that the genetics of taking whatever you wanted had been passed from father to daughter. He guessed she was headed for the same event he was and wondered how he should handle meeting her again.

A part of him wanted to tell her where she could get off. Ask her whether her father had been able to live with the shady decisions he'd made. A part of him wondered if he should play nice, get to know more about the woman— or rather, get to know more of her distillery. It wasn't unthinkable that Dyer's *could* be their first acquisition of a successful small-batch distillery, once he convinced his father. But perhaps he didn't need to. His father was due to retire, the company becoming Connor's on the first day of January. Perhaps it could be his first decision. No, the first decision was already made—to get rid of his uncle.

And another part of him, a small part he wasn't overly proud of right now, wanted to know a little more about the attractive firecracker who had set him in his place.

To do all but one of those things, he'd need to use some charm. The idea of apologizing flashed in his brain. On the one hand, it felt almost disloyal to his father to apologize to any Dyer. But on the other, as a man who held himself to a high moral standard, he knew he'd been a dick.

Fuck it.

Why was he so concerned about what Emerson Dyer thought?

He shook his head to clear thoughts of the woman from his mind.

The ballroom was filled with tables covered in blue damask cloths with large white floral arrangements in the center. A DJ played gratingly cheery pop songs as servers circulated the room with trays of glasses filled with champagne, and he immediately thought of Emerson again.

She'd been as good as her word. She'd worked damned hard on the flight, poring over spreadsheet after spreadsheet at speeds even he felt were impressive.

His thoughts were restless, and he needed some air before the ceremony began. The ballroom had large doors along one side that appeared to open out to a patio, and he wandered outside. He followed the steps into the lit gardens.

A warm breeze ruffled Connor's hair, blowing through his suit and white dress shirt. The bright lights of the ballroom flickered in his peripheral vision, but for now he simply wanted to breathe.

"Goddamn stupid heels," a voice muttered behind him near the stairs.

The frustration made him smile, and he turned to offer his assistance. All he could see was the top of a chestnut brown updo, and a woman with a heel seemingly stuck in the hem of her full skirt.

"Here," he said, walking to her side. "Take my elbow."

A pair of familiar almond eyes the color of dark maple syrup looked up at him. "You," Emerson said, taking his elbow with a scowl. Her fingers were slender and unadorned, nails short and painted in a pale pink.

"A pleasure to see you again," he said curtly. "Do you always like to make a scene?"

She released the heel from the hem and stood. The black dress was simple, fitted to the waist and falling in voluminous waves to her calves. Only a fool would have missed the way it skimmed her body to perfection.

Her body was trim, her breasts pressed delightfully against the scooping neckline of the dress.

"I didn't make a scene earlier." She appeared to be unaware that her hand was still on his arm. Her eyes were focused on him, and he found that he liked it. "I merely responded to your rude behavior. And lamenting my decision to wear heels with a low hem dress is a wardrobe malfunction, not a scene."

"That sounds a lot like semantics."

"That sounds a lot like avoidance of your role in the earlier matter."

Connor sighed. "You are right. I was in a foul mood when I stepped on the airplane. I apologize for the way I handled finding you in my seat."

Emerson rolled her eyes. "*My* seat."

"I suppose that technically it was our seat. It's called the 'And Stance.' You were in my seat, *and* I was in your seat. Both of us are correct. Both statements are true."

Emerson paused for a moment, then cocked her head slightly. "I can agree with that. But seeing as I was there first and possession being nine-tenths of the law and all that…"

Now Connor grinned. "Are you always this friendly with people you don't know?"

Emerson smiled, and he was taken aback by how it completely changed her face. "In this case, *you* are right. I'm being rude. Sorry. I told my sister, Olivia, I would have been better in flats, but she assured me flats would look stupid with this dress."

"If I told you that your shoes aren't what people will be looking at, would that be offensive?" he asked, before mentally kicking himself.

"Urgh. Not offended. And I knew it. I could have saved

myself three hours of agony in these torture devices." She removed her hand from his arm. He felt the loss of the warmth immediately. Perhaps it had been too long since he'd last dated if he was lamenting the loss of Emerson Dyer's touch. His father would be appalled at what he was thinking. And he loved the way she'd glossed over his compliment without acknowledging it.

"Connor Finch," he said, offering her his hand. "We got off on the wrong foot. Can I suggest a temporary cessation of hostilities? At least for this evening?"

She reached for his hand, and he could feel the calluses on her palm. "Emerson Dyer. Are we late?"

They both looked to the stairs that had begun to empty of people. Connor reluctantly let go of her hand and checked his watch. "Right on time by my estimate. Not a minute sooner than we need to be."

He shifted his elbow in her direction for the second time that evening. "To avoid further hem and heel mergers, let me assist you up the stairs."

Emerson grimaced. "I feel like that's a good idea." She reached for him again. He placed his hand over the top of hers. Her skin was soft and warm.

"So, Emerson, what brings you here tonight?" For some reason, he wanted to slow their ascent of the stairs, take a few extra moments to get to know the annoying woman who smelled like summer evenings.

"Oh, you know these things," she said, casually. "Network, socialize, enjoy some overcooked chicken and house white."

"You enjoy overcooked chicken and house white?"

Emerson laughed, and the sound made him grin in response. "Lord, no. But sometimes you've got to eat crap chicken to remind you to enjoy it when it's stuffed and cooked to perfection. You know, when it tastes a little of tart lemon mixed with the smoothness of rich butter all melted together."

Her description made his mouth water. They reached the top of the stairs, and Emerson's hand suddenly flew into the air to wave to someone she knew.

"One second," she said in the direction of the man she had waved at, and Connor felt a twinge of envy. The woman in his presence was quite the dichotomy, and he wanted to know more about her.

He didn't know much beyond her quick temper and her hatred of heels, which actually made her toned calves look delicious. Even her description of chicken had him hanging onto her every word.

"I'm sorry," she said, breaking his curiously errant thoughts. "I've got to go. I was supposed to be seated by now. It was nice talking with you, Connor. I hope you have fun this evening."

And before he had time to say anything in return, she was gone. He smiled as she hurried to her friend with the occasional wobble on the paving stones. She was right, she really didn't look comfortable in heels, but she looked kind of cute trying.

He was just about to step toward the doors to the ball-room when she turned to look at him, a soft smile dancing on her lips.

He held her gaze, as curious about their encounter as he imagined she was.

That was it. His decision made.

Before the night was over, he was going to find out more about the woman.

And her distillery.

And figure out if there was a way to have both.

E merson tried to listen as Sven, a botanicals trader who had assisted with the sourcing and procurement of some of the rarer ingredients Jake had required, explained his latest thought on growing unique botanicals for the distillery in heated greenhouses.

But her thoughts were on Connor Finch. Who'd told her that nobody would be looking at her shoes. She'd felt a flutter of excitement at his appreciative comments and glances that had left her unable to come up with anything remotely flirty to say in response.

When she'd seen him the day before on the plane, he'd looked like the consummate businessman. But in a dark navy suit and bowtie, he looked debonair.

A little bit Gatsby.

Emerson smiled at the reference. When she'd placed her hand on his arm, he'd felt so...*solid*. Like an unmovable rock.

"Where are you seated?" Sven asked, interrupting her thoughts.

"Table three," she replied. "Over there." She pointed toward the stage, grateful to be seated near the front, meaning there was less carpet to maneuver if by some miracle Dyer's did win a medal. Less chance to fall flat on her face.

"Cool, well, good luck. I'll see you later?" It sounded like a question, and there was a hint of hope in Sven's eyes that she hadn't seen before. Her father had instilled in her that business and pleasure did not mix, but Emerson certainly didn't think of Sven in any other way than a man who was able to supply seaweed from the Welsh coast for Jake's latest inspiration.

"I'm sure I'll see you around," she said noncommittally.

There were two seats left when she arrived at her

rather crowded table, and she took one of them, placing her purse next to her wine glass.

"Emerson Dyer, Dyer's Gin Distillery," she said, offering her hand to the matronly looking woman next to her.

"Mary-Anne Dowler," the woman replied with a Texan accent. "Editor for *Liquor and Spirits* magazine. Good luck tonight. We've a review of Dyer's Medallion coming up in our quarterly issue."

"Oh, that's very generous of you. Wait, did you like it?" she asked before mentally berating herself for such an impolite question. She was certain Olivia or her father would have come up with a more suitable response than she was capable of.

Fortunately, Mary-Anne laughed. "It was a very favorable review. If you give me one of your business cards, I'll send you a link to it when it goes live."

Emerson rummaged in her purse, pulled out a card, and handed it to Mary-Anne. "That would be very kind, thank you."

The lights dimmed, and a presenter appeared on the stage at the front of the room.

"We must stop meeting like this," a familiar voice whispered in her ear. His breath was warm, and his scent familiar with tones of frankincense and neroli.

She turned and came face-to-face with Connor. Those pale blue eyes of his revealed nothing as they held her gaze.

Words would be really good, but she couldn't think of any.

"Ladies and gentlemen," the presenter began.

The corner of Connor's mouth lifted in a smile as he shifted away to his chair and sat up straight, as if the speaker on the podium were sharing the secrets of the universe rather than explaining the order of ceremony.

As the speaker droned on about cellphones and exits, she couldn't help but glance at Connor. His wide shoulders filled the seat, his thighs strong and firm. And he never moved, sitting still as a statue until the introductory formalities were over and food was being delivered to their table.

"So, what is it you do, Connor?" she asked, finally coming up with some safe ground she could talk to him on.

"I manage strategy and M&A, mergers and acquisitions, for a liquor distributor."

"Ah," she said. "Mass market quantities then?"

His eyes narrowed as he turned to face her. "Was that scorn I heard?"

Emerson bit her lip. She hadn't meant to be so…forthright. "No. Honestly. There's certainly room in the market for artisan and mass products with the inevitable quality and quantity tradeoffs."

Connor laughed. "Would you like to borrow my spade so you can dig that hole a little deeper?"

Emerson put her palm to her face. "I think that maybe I should stop trying to talk to you."

He reached for her wrist and playfully pulled her hand away, and Emerson was certain he could feel her elevated pulse. When he let go to reach for his silverware, she was a highly contradictory mix of relieved and disappointed.

"No, please. I find you thoroughly entertaining." They both took a bite of their food. "You were right," he said. "Overcooked chicken and what I'm guessing is a mediocre house white."

Emerson noticed the swift change of subject but decided not to push further. It wasn't like Dyer's gin needed distribution help right now, and she hadn't meant to sound so darn snooty about it. She leaned toward him conspiratorially. "Wait until dessert…it'll be dry chocolate brownie with melty ice cream on top, I'll bet."

Connor glanced at her. There was something about his

gaze that caused her heart to flip-flop. "You sound almost excited."

"Are you kidding? It's second on my crap-but-delicious food list."

Connor laughed. "You have a crap-but-delicious food list?"

"Doesn't everybody?" Unable to resist, she leaned a little closer. "You know, food that you can get great quality of, but somehow the lower quality food tastes just as good?" She knew that she should quite possibly be smooth-talking the other people at the table, but she glanced around quickly to find them either eating or having private conversations.

"I'm intrigued, Em. Tell me more."

"It's Emerson. Please don't shorten it."

"My apologies."

She paused and took a sip of wine. A shortened name was a sign of friendship, occasionally affection. The idea of Connor using her name in that manner was more than she wanted to deal with. Plus, the sound of it rolling off his tongue made her shiver in the best of ways, something she really should work on suppressing.

"So, my friend prefers the giant dollar store white chocolate Easter rabbits to a Belgian chocolate egg, for example. It's packed with stuff that's borderline fit for human consumption, but she loves it anyway."

Connor leaned back and folded his arms across his chest, and, sweet baby Jesus, his arms bulged. "That's gross."

Emerson took a sip of wine and noticed his had gone untouched. She admired his discipline. "But that's only because you look like a guy who probably meal plans with sweet potatoes every Sunday and counts your macros. The rest of us humans like to combine the luxurious with the glutinous...the five stars with the…well, whatever the opposite of a fancy restaurant is."

"Have you been checking me out, Emerson?"

Gah. She had. "It would be hard not to," she replied truthfully.

Connor's laughter was rich and deep. "Do you always speak this bluntly?"

Did she? Or was it just him making her ramble? She tried to remember the asshole on the airplane. The guy who had glared at her more than once. The guy who had accused her of being a lush over one teeny-tiny measure of wine. Perhaps he'd been having a bad day. Lord knew she'd had enough of them the last three months.

"You seem to bring out the worst in me," she admitted honestly.

Connor unfolded his arms, and she couldn't help but follow the movement. He placed his hand on her knee beneath the table and squeezed it gently before removing it. "Apparently, you do the same to me. So, what's number one on your list?"

She could still feel the imprint of his warmth on her skin, making it hard to focus on the question. "I was once in a mall in Cleveland, and I had the most amazing food court General Tso's Chicken. One day, I'm going back to see if it tastes as good as I remember it."

Laughter burst from Connor. "You want to revisit a Chinese stall in a mall?"

"I do. Don't tell me there's no food you crave. Like, ever done a midnight run for a dirty burger?"

Connor appeared to think for a moment. "Swim meet I went to in Toronto once. Got me hooked on shawarma until I realized I'd put on four pounds over the course of the four-day event."

This time it was her turn to laugh. Connor Finch looked as though he carried the same percent body fat as a coat hanger. She couldn't imagine him splurging and was proven right when the dry chocolate brownie with melty ice cream came out and he lifted a hand to signal to the server that he wasn't having any.

As dessert came to an end, the awarding of the medals began, starting with tequila. Two bronze medals, two silver medals, and one gold were handed out to enthusiastic recipients. The same happened for whiskey, only this time a double gold was issued, meaning every judge in the panel had awarded the whiskey a gold medal. Emerson made a note in her phone to contact the distillery and congratulate them.

Then it came to gin.

"Good luck," Connor whispered in her ear, and for a moment she was struck with the question of how he knew this was the category she had entered. She racked her brain to recall if she'd told him.

But Dyer's was reasonably well known in Denver, and if that was where Connor actually lived rather than just where he'd caught the plane, he might have heard of the family and put two and two together.

She ran her tongue nervously along her lower lip, wishing she'd checked that there were no bits in her teeth from dinner.

"And the bronze medals go to…"

Emerson paid attention, her heart raced, and her vision began to blur. When they didn't call out Dyer's name, she experienced a simultaneous rush of hope that they might get a silver medal and a downpour of reality that it was unlikely.

"And the silver medals go to…"

There was a hope the gin was good enough for silver. The bronze medals had been awarded in alphabetical order, and when Ginevere Distilleries won silver, disappointment began to take root.

The disappointment flourished and bloomed when the gold medals were announced. Only two of them, and neither were Dyer's. In the grand scheme of things, it didn't even matter. But winning one would have pepped up the morale of everyone working their butts off to keep the distillery afloat. Now she had to go back to work and tell everyone they didn't win a medal, and the thought was depressing.

The enjoyment she'd felt at the start of the night, from chatting with Connor, began to drain from her bones, leaving her tired and even more resentful that she'd have to make her way up to her room in the heels she'd borrowed from Olivia.

It was hard to admit that it was pure ego preventing her from looking in Connor's direction. The last thing she needed was commiseration from a man she'd just met. Even though she'd bet he'd dish out nice sympathy. Perhaps he'd buy her a drink and whisper sweet nothings in her ear. They could sit close on those bar stools, arm grazing arm, a hand placed on a thigh. She'd give him an hour before she went back to her room to lick her wounds.

"And finally, we have a double gold medal in gin this year."

Emerson grabbed her phone, ready to make a note of who won the prestigious award. The award that meant *every* judge, not just the majority, had rated the liquor as a gold medal standard. Perhaps they could learn something from the winner, from their distilling process.

"Dyer's Medallion, from Dyer's Gin Distillery in Denver."

Emerson started to type it before she realized that it was her. It was them. It was Jake and his stupid process that took five times longer than it should and drove her to distraction every week. It was her father and his obsession of ensuring the business stayed in the family. It was Olivia. And her. And everyone else who kept the place running.

"Holy shit," she muttered, then louder. "Holy shit."

When she returned to her seat in what felt like milliseconds later with a statue in her hands and a certificate proving their double gold status, Emerson could barely hear the applause over the beating of her heart. Somehow, she'd successfully navigated the steps, made a speech that she prayed was coherent, and walked back to their table without tripping.

She needed to message her father and…the thought of her dad made her chest tighten. He'd missed the distillery's greatest moment.

Emerson shook her head to clear her thoughts. Jake and Liv would help her celebrate. This was huge.

A waiter appeared almost as soon as she sat down, holding an ice bucket and a bottle of champagne.

"I figured this deserved something a little more special than house white," Connor said with a grin.

"Thank you," she said, placing the statue on the table in front of her. "That was really thoughtful of you."

She double-checked the name on the statue.

Yup. Dyer's Medallion was right there. Connor offered her a glass, and she reached for it, their fingers touching briefly. Her heart raced, and she couldn't tell where adrenaline from the win and heat from his touch met. Instead, she took a sip. "Mmm," she said, closing her eyes as the bubbles fluttered over her tongue, her full palette enjoying the experience. "As much as I love cheap food, you can't beat quality over quantity sometimes."

"I'm guessing it tastes better than the wine you had on the plane yesterday."

Considering the brand name on the bottle and its probable cost, it was a given. She leaned closer to Connor. "That was incredibly judgy of you."

Connor's shoulder met hers. "You were in my seat," he whispered, the warmth of his breath causing the hairs on the back of her neck to stand on end.

She was certain he saw her slight shiver. "I thought we agreed it was ours." Emerson tried not to focus on the way his leg brushed up against hers. The way the warmth of his skin seeped through the thin layers of clothing between them.

For a moment, she wondered if he might close the gap between their lips and kiss her because if he did, she—

"Congratulations," said Mary-Anne, thrusting her hand towards Emerson.

Emerson jumped slightly, while Connor smirked. The presenter had temporarily left the stage. There was obviously a break in proceedings.

"Thank you," Emerson blurted, unable to transition from the intimate moment with Connor smoothly. She turned to Mary-Anne and realized the whole table had been waiting to congratulate her. Then there were the people at neighboring tables. And she hadn't even messaged her family.

One attractive, blue-eyed, black-haired man had taken her common sense away.

Shaking off the feelings Connor had stirred up inside her, she pulled her work face on and smiled and shook hands, fending off questions on availability of product, exclusive distribution deals, and interviews. This was so much Olivia's bag, and she'd do a great job handling them. It made her miss her sister's presence even more.

She found herself relieved to see Sven waiting to congratulate her because it was safe ground. Discussions about how the win might affect sales and tonnage of botanicals was so much more her jam.

By the time she was finished, and the next round of

awards announced, she turned to take her chair and found the seat next to hers was empty.

It remained that way when she texted her family.

It remained that way when Dyer's Medallion won Best in Class for unaged white spirits.

And it remained that way when Emerson left the ballroom with her trophies.

Connor Finch had disappeared as smoothly as he'd appeared.

The only downside to an otherwise perfect night.

Chapter Two

I *thought we agreed it was ours.*

Ours.

The word kept reverberating through Connor in Emerson's husky voice as he placed his work bag on his office desk and packed it up for the evening. The last words Emerson had whispered to him before his father had messaged in a rage, ruining Connor's evening.

His father had been following the event online and had seen Dyer's Gin Distillery win.

While he would never admit it to the woman herself, Connor had been disappointed the previous day to scan the boarding area of his flight home and not see her. He'd held out hope she would board until the airplane was actually in the air. But even then, he'd thought about her. The way her smile reached her eyes, so genuinely happy. And the way she'd leaned toward him conspiratorially when they whispered to each other. It had been a bonus that she'd filled out that dress the way she had, leaving him wondering what she'd look like without it.

Yet, the only person she'd seemed even remotely comfortable with besides himself had been the guy she'd waved to on the stairs, Sven. They'd joked about increasing her botanicals orders for the next few weeks. Then she'd gone off talking about tonnage and capacities and the like. Her ability to do complex math in between sips of the champagne he'd bought her on a whim impressed him.

The way she'd spoken, suggesting of constrained production rates for what appeared to be a highly successful product, was a problem. A best-in-class medal winner needed unconstrained production rates to see just how far it could go, how much it could sell.

With investment, the company could do well.

With *his* investment and oversight, it could be a gold mine.

After Paul Dyer had shafted his father, his dad had persevered and worked multiple jobs until he'd saved enough to create a small liquor import and export business. It had taken over a decade of back-breaking work to build the success they now enjoyed. But it was a long stretch from the premium products his father aspired to. Without a distinctive family-owned brand, he had nothing to build on. There wasn't a premium product in their lineup. They were good old cheap and cheerful liquor.

Connor locked his office door at seven p.m. exactly, as usual, and walked to the exit. He planned to walk to Charles's apartment where he was meeting Charles, Ben, and Blake for poker...just what he needed to blow off some steam.

His father and Uncle Cameron were already at the elevator. He knew people viewed his position as Senior Vice President of Corporate Strategy at thirty-two as nepotism. Yes, Finch Liquor Distribution was his father's company. But he'd worked hard to prove his worth. While his father dined out on the fact Connor, his heir apparent, had garnered the best grades possible at Harvard, in real life they hadn't proved anything to his father beyond the fact that education was expensive. Every day since he'd joined, his father and uncle had attempted to extract the proverbial pound of flesh they felt he owed for the expense.

"You got a second, Dad?" he said, wanting to share his thoughts about acquisition.

"I'm heading over to Cameron's for dinner, can we chat in the elevator?"

"Sure." The doors closed once the three of them were inside. "I've been giving some thought to the next five years. We're going to see continued growth in the small batch premium products. The artisanal flare that has revived products such as gin and vodka. Average alcohol consumption is decreasing, but the expectation is, especially in the twenty-one to twenty-nine segment, that if they aren't drinking often, it had better be the best quality when they do. Nobody is going on social media celebrating drinking middle-of-the-road price points."

"And?" Cameron said drolly.

Connor raised his eyebrow in impatience and looked at his father. "To keep pace with that change, I think we need to shift part of our portfolio from the B-class and mass market brands to capture this market. We need to innovate, find the best labels, and bring them in-house. We might even need to buy some of them, help invest in their businesses to increase volume without messing with what makes their spirits unique. It's going to take quite a pivot, but I believe we can, and need to, do it."

Cameron attempted to hide a smirk behind his hand. Fuck, the man wasn't even subtle anymore. "I feel like this is a stretch, fueled by your own personal objectives for when you take over," he said, his nasal tone highlighting his boredom. "Your father has successfully steered us for decades. I know you want to make your own mark, Connor, but this is not the time or way to do it."

"And that's why I'm bringing it to my father, not you,

for consideration. This is a long-game play and won't fuel any immediate success. But it's a move to protect us in the long term. Look, I know how you feel about Dyer's, and it doesn't need to be them, although we'd be foolish to ignore them," Connor said, trying to get them back on track. "But if we don't tap into this market, we're going to see a significant drop in our sales with nothing to plug the gap."

"You don't need to play catch up, Donovan," Cameron advised. "It feels like a lot of outlay."

"Says the guy with moth-balled purse strings. Dad, it won't be. We have underperforming assets we can let go of. We research the leading up-and-coming brands and make a bet on those we believe can make it to the big leagues. We do our homework. Casamigos Tequila went from an idea George Clooney had to a billion-dollar sale in four years. It's doable."

"I'm not totally adverse to the idea," his father said. "Come see me tomorrow, and we'll discuss."

"I'll do that." Connor made a mental note to ensure the meeting took place at a time Cameron was busy so he couldn't invite himself.

When the elevator reached the ground floor, Connor stepped out before it headed down to the parking garage. He'd left his car at home and was grateful his father hadn't asked what was in his bag. He probably would've lost his shit in the elevator to learn there was a bottle of Dyer's Medallion gin in it.

A cool breeze blew on the walk to Charles's apartment as he thought back to Saturday night. It had hit him, somewhere between saying goodbye to his father and drinking his mediocre room-service beer, that he envied Emerson— that she and her family had actually built something worthy of an award. It was the reason he'd bought a bottle to take to poker night so he could try it.

"Hello, loser," Charles said, opening the apartment

door and allowing a waft of something garlicky and delicious to filter into the hallway. Charles's Asian fusion restaurant had opened the previous year with a financial helping hand from Connor, but as the smaller, silent, and culinarily incapable partner, he left the running to Charles. And the Brit hadn't let him down. The restaurant opening had been met with rave reviews and a booking list that went out for months.

Connor raised an eyebrow. "Nice to see you, too. Ben and Blake here?" He'd gone to high school with the two of them, and they'd introduced him to Charles at one of their poker nights four years earlier.

"Already eating. Wild mushroom risotto, rocket salad, and I'll even make you a poached egg on top to offset all the carbs and butter involved in making food that tastes like food instead of the shit that you eat."

"Not going to argue," Connor replied. "I'll take the eggs. Make it two, thanks." Connor headed into the open plan apartment and found his friends. "Ben, how'd the IPO go?"

Ben had just taken the company he'd built over the last six years from private to public. The green energy provider was now listed on the stock exchange.

Redheaded Ben looked up from his plate. "It did okay. Institutional investors were slow to respond, but the price jumped and helped postlaunch, so the valuation was obviously conservative."

Connor grinned as he emptied his bag of the gin he'd brought. Ben was a pessimist, a glass-half-empty kind of guy currently sitting on a hundred-million-dollar payday.

He turned to Blake. "How's the new apartment?" He loaded up his plate with salad and what he hoped was a reasonable portion of the buttery risotto.

Blake stood and rinsed his plate in the sink. "Talia went overboard with the fucking plants. They're everywhere.

Can't even take a shit in peace without tendrils of this thing hanging from the ceiling tickling the back of your head. But otherwise, cohabiting is better than I hoped, to be honest. Can highly recommend."

"Did you need a pass to get out tonight?" Charles asked, dropping two poached eggs on Connor's risotto.

Blake laughed and shook his head. "No, because we're both grown adults with our own lives and respect that. What about you, Connor? Cameron still being a dick?"

Connor shrugged, chewing a mouthful of food. "He knows that once Dad retires at the end of the year, he's out. He was a decent head of finance about fifteen years ago, before the company grew to the size it has, but I'm going to need someone a lot more dynamic." He told them about the ride in the elevator. "He hates change. Wants everything status quo. He's risk averse and prefers the company to be cash risk instead of having a balanced portfolio."

"You played the long game well, Connor," Ben said. "You deserve to take over. I don't know how you've stuck with it all these years."

"Every day is like playing chess, strategizing moves. I just stay focused on the shit that matters to me. It sucks balls to let some things slide, but I realize that while Dad wants me to take over, Cameron still has a certain amount of sway with him. So keep your friends close and your enemies closer and all that."

Charles placed a sparkling water next to Connor's plate. "Thanks," Connor said.

"No worries," Charles replied. "Donovan has always listened to Cameron. Are you worried your dad is going to spring some last-minute surprise in your new contract saying you have to keep Cameron on?"

Connor's gut tightened. He'd had the exact same thought. "The draft CEO contract I've seen doesn't have a clause in it. But I'll triple-check it before I sign it. I'm more concerned Cameron is going to influence Dad into looking externally for a CEO replacement, leaving me where I am, or perhaps he'll even offer to be the CEO himself." He was sick of his uncle and needed to get off the topic before it soured his mood.

"Anybody want to try this?" he said, holding up the gin.

Blake nodded. "You're drinking on a school night?"

Connor grinned. "Was one of the medal winners the other night. Wanted to try it. Figured sharing it with you guys was better than sitting in my apartment drinking alone."

Charles slapped him on the back. "Told you you were a loser. What did it win?"

"Best in Class. The packaging is crisp and bright, totally stands out on the shelf...a smart touch by whoever created the design. If it tastes as good as it looks, which the medals suggest it does, then the distillery is onto a winner."

"Is this one of the distilleries you're thinking of buying?" Ben asked.

"Undecided. Meeting with Dad tomorrow to discuss." His friends didn't know his father's history with the distillery; there had never been reason to share his dad's business with them. They took his comment at face value.

And he certainly wasn't ready to tell them about Emerson Dyer. He looked at the gin bottle. Should he find a way to contact Emerson and tell her what he thought?

If his father could get set off by simply knowing Connor had drunk Dyer's gin, he could only imagine what his father would say if he knew about the thoughts Connor had harbored about Emerson Dyer.

He'd spent several frustrated hours reminding himself it was none of his business if she'd gone back to Sven's room to geek out on the tonnage of seaweed required for ten thousand bottles of gin. Or perhaps to slip out of that black dress to reveal the body Connor had lost sleep imagining. He'd eavesdropped as they'd spoken to one another after her win, only to be interrupted by his father's call. Not knowing what Emerson had done after he'd left was gnawing at him.

He rubbed his hand along his cheek and grimaced.

The woman had him in knots, and she didn't even know it.

Needing to change the topic from Dyer's Gin Distillery and distract himself, he reached for the poker set and placed it on the dining table.

"Who's ready to play?" he said.

And attempted to push Emerson Dyer to the back of his mind.

E merson groaned. "Why did I decide to do this? And how was I able to convince you to join me?" she asked Ali, her patient best friend, as she sweated through every available pore.

"Because it's the only way I get to see you," Ali replied, the sentence punctuated by gasping breaths as they finished their final set of burpees before the trainer allowed them to collapse on their mat.

When Emerson's father had died, it was Ali who'd stayed with her that first week. It was Ali who made sure she functioned enough to keep the distillery going. And Emerson had thanked her by diving headfirst into running a business she was barely capable of, leaving little time for her friend.

"I'm sorry. It's been a lot."

Ali sat up on her mat and crossed her legs, her long,

blonde ponytail swinging. "I know it has. I was only teasing."

Emerson wiped the sweat from her forehead. "I'm serious. I've got to get on top of all this, but I still feel like I'm drowning in stuff I didn't do yet." She stretched her legs out and reached for her toes. "I'm like a novice skier heading down a double diamond on their first day out."

Ali stood and pulled her foot to her butt. "What can I do to help?"

"Meet me at the six a.m. class for the foreseeable future?"

Laughter bubbled from Ali. "I can do that. Outside of the amazing medal wins, how was your trip?"

Connor's face flashed in Emerson's mind. "Interesting."

"The way you drew the word out says there was something *specifically* interesting. Care to elaborate?"

Emerson changed to a different cooldown exercise. "There was this guy—"

"Oh, the best stories start with that. Tell me."

As they finished their stretches, Emerson found herself telling Ali everything that had happened.

"And you didn't get his number?" Ali practically yelled as they walked to the showers.

Emerson shouldered her friend gently. "What part of he disappeared from the ballroom did you not understand?"

"Urgh. You are useless. You could have called down to the hotel desk, asked for his room, and spoken with him."

"And even if I'd thought of that, I wouldn't have done it because that is spectacularly creepy. If a guy did that to me at an event, I'd have to change hotels!"

"Fine. You're right. It would be weird. But a quick search online would tell you where his office is, and I'm sure you could come up with something to say."

Perhaps she could.

After she showered and went to the distillery, the thought kept rattling around in her mind.

"Hey, Emerson," Jake said, sticking his pen behind his ear as he popped his head into her office. "Cash flow. I'm placing a botanicals order. It's a big one. Am I good to go?"

She shook the thought of Connor from her mind. "You're fine."

"I don't suppose there's any sign of the insurance check for the events hall yet, is there?"

Shit. Did she notify them about the change of ownership? Abruptly, she stood. "Not yet. But I can't even remember if they were contacted. I'll check my list. There were so many documents to sign and names to change over the last two months. I know Dad said it would take a while before we heard anything from them."

Once they had that check, she wouldn't need to worry about cash flow to place orders or pay overtime.

"Em, relax. If you didn't, then we need to fix it, that's all. It shouldn't stop them from processing the claim in the meantime."

Emerson sighed, the tightness in her chest was replaced with low-grade anger. It was easy for Jake to tell her to relax. Liv hadn't been in any state to help, and Jake was needed on the production floor. She'd already been carrying her own job and Liv's. And then she took on the burden of her father's work. Basic math said that was untenable. "I'll get on it. They won't tell me the status until they have my name on the forms."

Jake threw his arm over her shoulder. "It's okay for us to make mistakes, you know."

Emerson shrugged. "Not when there's a lot of money at stake."

Jake let her go and ran his fingers over the award statuettes that stood on the newly cleared top of the filing cabinet. "I can't believe we pulled it off."

Emerson cheered a little. "*You* pulled if off, Jake. You. Dad always said you had talent. Remember how when we were little, Mom always used to play that game over dinner? What did she call it?"

"Guess the Ingredients," Jake said with a grin. "I always crushed it."

"It was always some stupid herb or something. Like she'd sneak chopped, fresh oregano leaves into pasta. You could always taste them or smell them."

"So, what you're saying is that there's finally a place for my talents."

Emerson smacked his arm playfully. "You know what I mean."

"Yeah, pity it counted for shit at school."

Jake hadn't gone to college. He'd left school with less than stellar grades and gone to work directly for their father. "But look at you now, Double Gold and Best in Class medal winner."

"Let's hope I'm not a one-trick pony. Dad only won one medal in his career."

She could hear the doubt in Jake's voice. They all had fears about stepping into their father's shoes to drive the business forward. "You're off to a strong start, Jake. I'm sure you'll keep the momentum going. I have faith in you."

Jake looked at her intensely for a moment. "That's exactly what Dad used to say to me."

The loss had affected all of them deeply, but Jake rarely shared his emotions about it.

"He used to say it to me too."

Jake squeezed her hand, gave her a sad smile, and left the office.

Her gaze returned to their trophies. For a moment, she

wished her father had been the one to bring them home. Instead, it had been her.

And then there was Connor.

Wait. Why was she still thinking about a man who'd simply disappeared?

It had been rude.

It had been expected based on his behavior on the airplane.

But it still hurt.

Damn it.

Emerson pulled up her hair into an elastic and turned on a focus playlist. Within the hour, she'd reviewed all the new order requests. She'd had to quietly remind herself that having too many orders was a good problem to have. Only then had she been able to make a plan for production that would see them hit at least eighty percent of it for the month.

She opened the presentation she'd started during her enforced airplane working session.

Thoughts of Connor's eyes on her had spurred her on until she'd not only forgotten about her fear of flying, but also had the most productive two hours she could remember in months.

Gah!

Why did he keep appearing in her thoughts? It had been three freaking days.

She focused on the presentation. When the insurance came in, she was going to suggest putting the money into expanding the distillery with additional stills and labor, so Jake could have time away from the stills to develop the new line of products. The additional production would quickly translate into sales, and the resulting profit could be used to reopen the reception venue.

Her father had already cancelled weddings for the next few months, and then there was the lighter spell before they hit spring and summer weddings. It wouldn't require much risk. It could work.

Emerson looked at the numbers again. It was tight, but it was doable. And then they wouldn't even need a loan for the expansion. They'd use the insurance to pay for the expansion, and the expansion to pay for the renovation. It was a win-win.

With a sigh, she flopped back into her chair. Knowing her luck, there was some clause that you had to use insurance money to repair the thing you claimed for, or they'd recall it all or something. She'd have to double-check before she proposed this to Jake and Olivia.

The idea of calling the insurance company made her feel a little sick inside. She hated phone calls. Hated the flood of paperwork that would inevitably follow. And while she knew she sounded like an overtired, pouty toddler, she just wanted to be left alone for a little while.

By eight, the factory was dark. Jake preferred starting his days early and had just completed another fourteen-hour production run.

Emerson was confident she had the framework of a solid plan that built on what she had started on the plane. There had been something about Connor's energy and antagonism and her own stubbornness that had merged together to stimulate her problem-solving skills, with just enough alcohol to stop her from censoring or second-guessing herself as she wrote.

Connor.

Had it been ridiculous to think that after their bumpy start, they might have been able to create a friendship, or perhaps a flirtation out of it?

She thought they had.

But he hadn't, obviously.

Her fingers were on the keyboard before she could stop

herself. She typed Connor's name into the search engine as Ali had suggested and pressed Enter.

A trade journal article popped up with his name. She hadn't known much about Finch Liquor Distribution beyond their existence. Dyer's never made the volumes a company like Connor's dealt in, so their paths had never crossed. She hadn't been aware it was still family owned, like her company.

See, another thing we have in common. Both in the liquor trade, both in family business.

She clicked on a photograph of Connor, this time in a wetsuit and swimming cap. So, he competed in the Iron-man. There were facts and figures, which by her deduction meant that, for an amateur, he was quite good.

Really good, according to one of the races he'd done. Some Norwegian Ironman that involved jumping off the bow of a ship into borderline frigid waters for the swim.

Emerson shuddered. *Dear Lord.* The closest she came to swimming was hanging out on the back of an inflated, pink flamingo sipping cocktails while on vacation. And though she did run, it was highly unlikely her three-mile circuit would impress Mr. I-Can-Run-A-Marathon-After-Cycling-A-Billion-Miles.

After twenty embarrassing-to-admit minutes, she found herself on Connor's company profile. When she had turned into a cyber stalker was unclear, and she'd likely have to have a large gin when she got home to absolve her sins. But here she was. Sitting in the dark, reading his professional bio.

This image was a straight-up corporate headshot. He stood in a white corridor with chrome details, his arms folded, just as she remembered them, feet forty-five degrees to the photographer, with his head tilted in the direction of the lens.

It looked like a cardboard cutout.

It lacked personality.

But the page didn't lack his email address.

She hovered over the link, then copied it.

Perhaps she should email him. She could make it friendly. Polite.

The champagne.

That was it. She could email him about the champagne. Thank him for the wonderful celebration. And she wouldn't ask him where he had disappeared to. Nope. She wouldn't ask.

But she wanted to know.

She pasted Connor's address into a new email.

Dear Connor,

No. Too familiar.

Connor.

Better.

Thank you so much for keeping me company on Saturday evening. It was such a huge day for our distillery, and I really appreciate the champagne you bought presented provided

Urgh.

Ask her to write a report on the production requirements to fill orders in the first quarter, and she'd be all over it. Ask her to write something personal, something to foster connection, and she'd be as useful as the weak head of a new distillation.

Emerson slammed the lid of her laptop shut.

Oh my gosh. What if it accidentally sent?

She opened her laptop and quickly deleted the message, but not before copying the email address into her contacts.

There might be a time when she'd need it.

Like when?

With a burst of energy, she jumped from her seat and shoved the laptop into her bag before she got any more bright ideas that might include calling the company switchboard to get his voicemail. If she couldn't write him an email under pressure, the chances of her doing better on the phone were slim to none.

Emerson grabbed her purse, set the alarms for the distillery and stepped out into the cool Denver evening air. Perhaps she'd call Ali to go out for a drink.

Anything to avoid the temptation of contacting Connor Finch.

F*uck, that's hot.*

Connor juggled the plastic container out of the microwave, switching between fingers and thumbs, and dropped it on the concrete countertop. The sweet potato, broccoli, rice, and chicken steamed as he nudged the lid off. He fought off the urge to cover the stuff in soy sauce or chili sauce or something that would make the food just a touch more interesting. Emerson had judged him correctly in her assessment of his eating habits.

Macros mattered, even if they sometimes tasted bland.

While it cooled a little, he grabbed a fork from the cutlery drawer and topped up his glass of water.

He pulled the leather stool from under the counter and perched on it. Fork in hand, he opened his laptop to study his latest project.

Dyer's Gin Distillery.

Their Medallion gin was just as good as it was reported to be. So good, in fact, he'd had one more drink than intended yet he'd woken up with a head as clear as if he'd not taken a sip.

Emerson Dyer was already encouraging him to break his own habits.

From his first sip while playing poker, he was committed to learning more about the distillery, and he'd spent the last twenty-four hours doing as much research as he could about the private family-owned company.

Except there wasn't much to find.

His father had always suggested he was heavily involved in the beginnings of Dyer's Gin Distillery, but Connor couldn't find a trace of his father's name in connection with the distillery anywhere. Paul Dyer had completely erased his father from the narrative. Even in old online newspaper reports of the time, he couldn't find any reference. Every source said the same thing, that it had been started by Paul and Rebecca Dyer. He assumed Rebecca was Emerson's mother because not only did they share the same last name, they shared the same warm brown hair and cute smile.

Thoughts of Emerson onstage, laughing her way through her speech, made him grin. There had been pure joy in her words when she thanked everyone on behalf of her family.

In-between bites of food, Connor returned to Dyer's social media pages, looking at photographs of the distillery. They'd obviously begun some kind of social media campaign at the start of the year. It was clear and consistently on brand. He wondered what firm they hired to do it.

But then the campaign had stopped. News articles revealed there had been significant damage to an on-site event venue that resulted in a significant amount of negative press, but that seemed to have eased up over the past couple of months.

Stopping social media presence was a mistake, one he'd fix when…

When? When he bought the damn thing? He needed to stop thinking like he already owned it. Dyer's Gin Distillery had floated to the top of his proposed acquisition list even though he knew his father would have strong issues with it.

Videos from within the distillery gave him a sense of scale, but he wasn't definite on the kind of volumes they produced. From his assumptions on the number of stills, the size of the warehouse, and their distribution channels, he would put them in the midsize distillery range.

The recipes were attributed to Emerson's brother, Jake, a master distiller with an obvious palette and nose for botanicals. If he came up with these formulas, he could come up with others. And others meant growth. Especially if he could parlay his skills into other spirits, like a standout rye or a homegrown tequila or vodka. But it also meant that the success of the recipes hung on one person. Dyer's was definitely more secure than other companies given Jake was a family member. But even family members could be convinced to leave and go to other enterprises, depending on the size of the paycheck.

Yet, in spite of not having all the information or a secure innovation strategy, he felt the usual rush of excitement in his stomach that came when he was onto something and closing in on the target.

Except he wasn't certain whether his target was the distillery or the woman who ran it.

He pushed his finished dinner aside and reached for his wallet. He opened the smooth leather and pulled out Emerson's business card from the slot in the middle. When people had started to crowd her, she'd reached for her purse to pull out some business cards. One of them had landed on the table next to his champagne glass, and he'd picked it up.

Her cellphone number was listed on it.

Connor tapped the corner of the card on the countertop.

There was so much he should be doing instead of sitting in his kitchen and debating the merits of messaging Emerson. There were sales projections to go over and an urgent last-minute request from Cameron for the third quarter review. His uncle was so predictable, feigning urgency in an attempt to trip up Connor in front of his father. He'd done it so reliably for the last six quarters in a row that much of what Cameron had asked for was already complete, but Connor had no intention of sending it until one minute before his deadline. Two could play that game.

Hell, perhaps he should watch the replay of tonight's basketball game on his new TV.

He looked over the open-plan living space of his newly purchased and renovated condo toward the large TV he'd mounted on the wall. He'd simply slid his own furniture straight into the place, and made orders for the rest. A custom tall dining table, thick slabs of wood that Derek, his stepdad, had polished to a shine and turned into side tables. There were a handful of boxes in his new home office that needed unpacking and filing. The restful shades of blue and ivory reminded him of the surf even though he lived in Denver.

Connor took another look at the card, studying it intently for any clues as to what he should do next.

Fuck.

He was stuck between a rock and a hard place. Interest in a woman his father would likely disown him over. Interest in a distillery, a business opportunity that his father would not back, which would probably make him lose the woman.

Uncertainty was not one of his usual traits. Outcomes of decisions were usually crystal clear to him. But in this instance, it was difficult to separate Emerson from her business.

Perhaps he should just cast both lines, the woman and the distillery, and see which took the bait faster.

But why did the idea upset his gut?

Normally, he had no issues with messy lines, big deals, and consequences.

Connor got up, business card in hand, and paced to the window.

Make a decision, Finch.

He pulled his phone from out of his back pocket and added Emerson's number to his contacts. Then he began to type.

Hey, how was your trip back from San Francisco?

It wasn't the greatest opening line in history, but what the heck was he supposed to say? That she'd been on his mind constantly for the last few days and did she want to come over to his apartment and talk about a takeover while perhaps making out on his sofa? He didn't think he'd ever thought a more wrong sentence.

Connor rubbed his hand along his jaw and walked to the kitchen to clean up the mess. He made a point of putting his phone on the side table next to the sofa to resist the urge to check it again.

When the kitchen was pristine, his coffee maker set for morning, and his pre-workout snack prepped into containers, he grabbed another glass of water and made his way to the sofa.

She'd replied. *Who's this?*

Obviously, she didn't know it was him. Why was he acting so dumb?

Connor. Owner of the seat. Buyer of the champagne. Table mate for the medal win.

There was a pause. *Oh, right. You forgot Mr. Grumpy from the flight and leaver of the evening.*

Okay, so no "Hello, great to hear from you, I was thinking of you." He couldn't help but grin.

Sorry. Urgent family business came up. I didn't leave deliberately. And only Mr. Grumpy because you're a thief.

Better a thief than a liar, she replied.

I tried Dyer's Medallion.

Emojis of hands clapping filled his screen. *And, what did you think of it?*

It's good. Really good. You deserved the Best in Class.

He regretted not being there in person when it had been announced, but he'd been delighted for her when he'd seen the announcement on social media. The best in all of the white spirits was a massive accomplishment.

Thanks, Connor. I'll pass your comment on to my brother. He's the genius. I just get the stuff made.

It was interesting how she was happy to assume the behind-the-scenes role. She'd said as much in her speech, suggesting that as a family of three, she was the third pick for being there.

Well, I think you're being humble. Running a distillery is probably challenging. There was a beat where the conversation could diverge. If it went toward details of the company, he'd be happy. If it focused on her, he would be happy. It was a win-win for him, his preferred kind of outcome.

So, Ironman, huh?

Wait. What? Okay, so unexpected response. But that meant she'd checked him out. That shouldn't make him feel as good as he did. *You looked me up online?*

I did. I was going to send you a message to say thank you for the champagne. Your athletic feats popped up before your business profile.

Damn. For a minute, he thought it was because she was interested. *I get bored if I sit still for too long.*

He waited for her response.

There's a lot of gray between sitting still being bored and throwing yourself off the bow of a boat. Ever considered squash?

Connor laughed. *I happen to be good at squash. And tennis. And golf.*

Color me surprised, she replied. *I prefer to do quality over quantity. A three-miler run well, rather than twenty-six miles run feeling as though I were dying.* She followed it with crying laughter emojis.

Quality over quantity. The second time she'd mentioned it. And while he fully understood she was just joking, he wondered for a moment if she felt that way about his company. The gin they distributed was very drinkable, reasonable quality for its price point, but nowhere near the quality of Dyer's. If that was how she felt, he'd completely understand it.

Before he thought of a response, another message appeared. *I'm off to bed. Super early start tomorrow. Thanks for your kind words about the gin. I'm pleased you liked it.*

No. He didn't want their conversation to end. He wasn't ready to be left alone with his thoughts.

Have dinner with me on Friday.

Nothing.

No answer.

Had she turned her phone off without waiting for a response from him? Was it a clear no? He watched the end of the game, brushed his teeth, did his evening meditation, and set his alarm.

With one last check to see if there were any messages, he turned his phone to silent.

And as he placed it on the side table, the screen lit up again.

I'd love to.

Chapter Three

"Constance isn't getting up to temperature."

Emerson looked at the copper pot still and then back to Jake. "What do you mean she's not getting up to temperature?"

They named their stills. Constance, because she was most reliable. Patience, because she had an odd temperament that appreciated soft handling. And Melody, because of the assortment of whistles and hisses she'd make over the course of a run.

Jake shrugged and threw his arm around her, a grim smile on his lips. "You know what I mean, Em. You just don't like the implications."

Emerson pushed his arm off her shoulders and grabbed a hair tie from the pocket of her overalls. She pulled her hair up in a messy bun and stepped closer to study the dials on the panel next to the bright copper kettle. The vapor temperature dial had barely flickered away from room temperature. There was no heat in the still.

"Okay, smart-ass," she replied, unable to resist a grin despite the dire situation. Her brother had always been able to make her smile. "Is anything getting through to the helmet and cooler?" She tilted her head back so she could look up the long column that rose out of the kettle.

Jake shook his head. "No. I've done everything I can think of. I didn't even get enough to get the head off."

Urgh. The head was the first part of the distillation, the gin that was all over the map with regards to concentration. Jake would often make a call to either add it back into the start of the distillation process or simply discard it.

Which meant this batch hadn't even gotten started before the kettle had given up the ghost.

Emerson thought through the production schedule and momentarily cursed Jake's style of distilling each botanical separately rather than together. It took so much time. They could produce so much more if they distilled everything at once.

But then...it was the reason Dyer's Medallion was winning medals. The oils of the botanicals vaporized at different rates, with the citrus generally coming off first. Instead of hovering in the super dry end of gin that came from trying to get the best out of the orange while getting the worst out of the juniper due to distilling the lot together, Jake's approach made sure the notes of all the botanicals were crisp and clear. The spirit became rounder, richer. The flavors, fresher. They rarely lost focus. It was the reason the brand had done so well. That, and Jake's nose for botanicals. His latest additions, Vietnamese black peppercorns and Thai lemongrass, had been well worth the increased supply costs.

Interest in orders had increased since the Best in Class medal. There was no doubt in her mind that it was the volume they had been pushing hard for since the gin had hit the market that had killed their still. There was barely a moment to rest or service machines between batches. As a family-owned business, the distillery was operating more often than not on the weekends.

And while she knew everyone in the building was rooting for the volume, she needed to get more familiar with the financials of the company. Her father had held the purse strings ridiculously tight.

Emerson sighed. "I'll go make a call to get a service engineer in, then I'll take a better look at the financials. I started something on the plane the other day that I wanted to go over with you and Liv. Let me get to work."

Jake glanced up at the mezzanine and their father's office. *Her* office. "Good luck."

Emerson walked through the distillery and looked toward the high, beamed roof as rain lashed against it. The old Denver millhouse was the perfect size and location, but boy, did it need renovation. It was the one thing she and her father had disagreed on. It needed investment. With the distillery as collateral, if needs be. They could invest in a more environmentally friendly production process by purchasing sustainable biomass boilers to power the distillations.

Perhaps now was the time to clean up her presentation for the bank. With a broken still and the threat of reduced production of a medal winner, perhaps the bank would help. Emerson sat down at her desk and opened her laptop.

They needed this last run of the day to go smoothly. *She* needed it to go smoothly so she could get ready for her date with Connor. The last thing she wanted was to cancel because, heck, it had been two years since her last serious boyfriend. Since then, there had been a few casual things here and there, but she actually wanted to spend time with Connor.

She had a thought and quickly dialed Jake. "Can we

manage on the two stills this weekend?" she asked when he answered.

"Only if you want to cancel orders. We already had weekend runs planned for all three stills. Dyer's Medallion is flying off the shelves, especially since that trade review last month. Add that to the usual Thanksgiving and Christmas sales bump, I was even hoping to try and get ahead."

Emerson ran her fingers over her brow. "Can it wait until Monday at least? So we don't have to pay them extra for a weekend callout."

"Nice try, Em. But I think you know the answer to that. Can we take a chance and not run anything? Sure. But is it advisable? No."

Emerson groaned. "I know. I guess I was just hoping for a different answer. I know how full the schedule is. Would you consider an option to distill some of the ingredients together to save time?"

"Emerson," her brother said slowly. "We've had this discussion. It will affect the product and—"

"Okay. I get it. I was just thinking out loud with you. I'll figure something out."

She put her phone down and recalled her last conversation with her father.

"I'm sorry, Emerson. You made your point clear. I thought I'd made mine," Paul said, folding his arms on the desk. "We need to manage. We need to see some of the returns from Dyer's Medallion, give it a little bit longer than three months. What if it's a flash in the pan? Plenty of good gins have peaked and then flopped. What if that's what happens here, and then we've spent the insurance and still have no venue?"

"We might just win a medal at one of the most prestigious liquor festivals in the US. How much proof do you need? Dad, listen, if it flops, it's because we can't make enough."

Emerson leaned forward, frustration bubbling in her chest. "We'll be sensible. Not overextend. Although, if we did take out a loan at the same time, we could do a faster renovation . . . perhaps take a loan out over a longer term. We'd increase production immediately, there would be a significant bump in sales. Dad, we're turning away orders."

"And scarcity helps build—"

"Please don't tell me scarcity drives interest and prices, Dad," she begged. "We could have prices and volume. Enough businesses want the product. We even got an inquiry from a pub chain in the UK."

"Emerson," her dad said with a tone she was familiar with. Exasperation. He'd used it when she'd begged him for six months for a dog. He'd used it when she'd desperately wanted to go to Disneyland instead of camping in Yosemite. He'd used it when she'd insisted that the distillery should continue to be a family concern and hence she was skipping college. Skip, their golden lab, had been a loyal friend for ten years. Disneyland had been the trip of a lifetime. The diploma from her degree in economics hung in her office down the hallway. Two out of three was a good success rate, but she knew when her father wasn't going to budge.

Her temples had begun to pulse. He'd died of a heart attack less than twenty-four hours later. Thankfully, they'd made their peace, but the knowledge of that argument being one of their last conversations sat in her gut like lead.

Channeling the upset that thinking about her father had caused, she opened the company's most recent bank statement. They had enough to call the service engineer out, but not enough to buy a new still. That would require the insurance or a loan.

The phone weighed heavy in her hand. She hated making phone calls. Hated the way they asked questions she didn't have the answer to, making her feel inept.

Just get it done, Em!

She dialed the number and made the call, hanging up quickly once she'd arranged for an engineer to come.

Not feeling remotely sociable, she debated messaging Connor to let him know something had come up at the distillery and she couldn't make it. But the idea of doing that made her feel even worse. Connor had been the one little spark of joy that had made her feel human again.

As she considered, a message popped up on her screen from Ali.

Wear the green dress...makes your boobs look good! Have fun. Ax

It made her laugh, and maudlin thoughts weren't going to achieve anything. Emerson set a timer for an hour and threw herself into the weekly distillery orders.

And when the sixty minutes were done, she intended to drive home and get dressed up, promising herself that once she'd left the building, she'd do everything she could to find the old Emerson and have fun.

With Connor Finch.

Connor sat at the bar and sipped on ice water. Tonight was about getting to know Emerson as a woman, not as a Dyer. He knew his reasons were complex. Sure, he was curious about the family that had the ability to send his father into a spiral of despair. But he was also curious about the playful, witty woman he'd sparred with. In his mind, he managed to compartmentalize the two.

Catching sight of himself in the mirror that hung behind the bar, he straightened the collar of his black shirt. He'd offered to pick Emerson up, but she'd been adamant about meeting him there. She'd dismissed his chivalrous attempts with a simple *No, thank you*, and he admired her straight-talking ways.

When the door finally opened and Emerson walked in, his gut relaxed. For some reason, he'd been nervous she was going to bail, and he was sure it was some throwback from his father's conditioning that anything with the name *Dyer* attached to it was incredibly unreliable. It was almost as if he expected her to let him down right off the bat.

She wore a sundress in dark green, with thin straps and a skirt that flowed just above her knees. Long, gold earrings reached her toned shoulders. Connor watched as the greeter pointed in Connor's direction.

A momentary tug of guilt fluttered through him at the deceit of knowing a lot more about her than she knew about him. When her eyes found his, her smile was so genuine and bright it almost burned, and for a second, he felt like confessing.

"Hey, Connor." She leaned forward to kiss him on the cheek, a kiss so brief he wondered if he imagined the contact of her lips against his skin.

"I'm so glad you could make it," he said, pulling out the bar stool next to his. "Please, take a seat that isn't mine."

Emerson laughed. "I thought we agreed that technically the seat was ours."

"Well, you are more than welcome to come sit on my lap and share this one," he replied, wiggling his eyebrows.

"I think I'd have to know you a lot better before I try that. I don't just sit on anyone's lap." Emerson threw her denim jacket over the back of the stool and climbed up.

Connor tried to be a gentleman, but his eyes still travelled the length of her legs as her dress hitched up her thighs. He fought the urge to follow its path with his fingers to see if her skin was as soft as it looked.

"I've been looking forward to this since you suggested it. Have you eaten here before?" she asked, looking around the restaurant.

"I have, and I can highly recommend the All-In Burger, or the tuna if you like it rare. What can I get you to drink?" The bartender walked toward them. "Gin?"

Emerson looked along the modest gin selection before scrunching her nose slightly. "I'd love a cosmopolitan, and would you mind switching the triple sec for Cointreau and keep the lime juice to a little shy of half an ounce please?"

Gins he represented were on the shelf, and it bothered him a little that she hadn't seemed to find any of them appealing. Not that he was mad at her, more that for the first time in his life, he was aware of just where his products stood in the quality pecking order.

He ordered a beer for himself. "You know your way around your cocktails," he said in admiration. "What's the secret with the Cointreau?"

"Triple sec can be…sharp. And since bars tend to use a lot of cheaper, really sharp limes, it can be too much. But switch it out for Cointreau and it's smoother. More nuanced. There's a hint of delicious orange that comes through."

Connor couldn't help but watch her mouth as she spoke. She was wearing a deceptively nude gloss, and he wondered what it would taste like, what she would taste like without it. He turned his stool to face her properly.

"How was your week?" he asked.

"A masterclass in how to keep your head just above water. I graduated as an expert."

Connor leaned forward and took the hand that was in her lap, relieved when she clasped her fingers around his. "Some weeks are like that, I guess."

Emerson shrugged. "I suppose. I've only been doing this for two months, but it's a steep learning curve."

Her fingers were warm and soft. "Give it time. Is there anyone in your organization you can rely on to help out?"

"Not really. Everyone else is tapped out, too. I think it's the double-edged sword of working in a smaller company, especially a family-owned one. It's a tightly controlled structure, but it struggles when someone is absent."

"Ours is still a family business, but it's a multi-hundred-million-dollar business, so we have a bigger structure. More people who think they need to be involved in every decision." Thoughts of his uncle flitted into his mind, and he quickly dismissed them.

Emerson grimaced. "Right now, I feel like I'd benefit from a few more people. My dad—"

"Here are your drinks, folks." The bartender placed their drinks on coasters in front of them. Connor squeezed her hand one last time before letting go.

"Thank you," Emerson said, reaching for her drink. "Anyway. Cheers. And thank you for asking me to dinner. I'm so glad you did."

Connor tapped his glass to hers. "Cheers. And I'm happy you're here."

They sipped their drinks for a moment, and Emerson moaned. The sound reverberated through his chest. "Oh my. That's so good." Emerson offered the glass to him. "Try it."

His eyes were locked on her as her tongue ran its way slowly across her lower lip. *Lucky fucking tongue.*

He took the glass she offered and took a sip. "Better than I expected," he answered honestly. "I tend to stick to whiskey for a spirit. You were about to say something about your dad before the drinks arrived."

"If you remember, I mentioned in my speech how my dad passed away recently."

Connor nodded. That flutter of guilt that he already knew so much about her family returned.

"Well, because it's a family business, the share is split equally between the three of us, but my father requested in his will that I take it over. I'm the oldest. Jake and Olivia both have their thing. It's what I always wanted, but…"

"It's hard?" Connor filled in.

"No, it's not even that. I don't mind the hard work. It's

just…lonely. And decisions that my dad made every day seem huge to me. Like I might break something precious if I don't make the right call."

Connor was struck by the way she viewed her family business. Precious. Finch Liquor Distribution was just a company to him. A hugely profitable one, but still just a company.

"And you had some of those issues to grapple with today?" Connor asked because he was concerned for her *and* because he couldn't help being curious about what possible difficulties the distillery could be facing.

"Yes, but nothing I can't handle…get through… manage. Whatever. You know what I mean. But I thought I'd have so much more time with my father to learn; I'm not sure I'm ready."

If he pressed her now, he could get the kind of information that would help him make a better offer should the time ever arise. Vulnerability was always a weakness when it came to a negotiation. But the truth was he didn't *want* to manipulate her. He'd done shady things to get the deal he wanted before. And yes, he wasn't proud to admit that at least one deal he could remember had taken advantage of a grieving family who couldn't decide what was best for their business.

Yet as Emerson looked at him with growing trust in her eyes, he couldn't do it.

"I'm sure you are doing an admirable job." He reached for her hand again and squeezed it tightly.

"I hope so," she said, straightening on her bar stool. "Nobody wants to go down in family lore as the person who destroyed the family business."

The server arrived and ushered them to their table, where they finished their drinks while checking out the menu. After they'd ordered, the burger for him and the seared tuna for her, Emerson placed her forearms on the table and leaned toward him. "Tell me more about yourself, Connor."

He couldn't help but notice the way the move pushed her breasts high beneath the cut of the sundress. Round and full. Wait, she'd asked about himself. "What would you like to know?"

"What's the first movie you remember watching as a child?" Emerson took a sip of her drink.

"Easy. *Star Wars*. My stepdad, Derek, couldn't wait to watch it with me. I'm sure there were others before it, but I loved *Star Wars*."

Emerson grinned. "Me too. Which character did you want to be?"

Connor thought for a moment. "Luke, obviously. What about you?"

"You're going to laugh."

"Princess Leia?" he asked. "Got one of those cosplay bikinis in your closet?"

She shook her head. "Nothing so predictable. Chewie."

"You wanted to be Chewbacca?" Connor began to laugh.

"All the way. My mom got this brown fur material and made the costume. I had a mask. I even had the gun belt thing. I learned everything about the Wookiee warrior…I learned about his planet Kashyyyk…and sometime, which isn't now, I'll show you my amazing impersonation."

Connor grinned. "You speak Wookiee?"

"I speak Shyriiwook. There are many Wookiee dialects."

Connor tried to reconcile the beautiful and slightly bohemian woman sitting opposite him letting out the guttural groan of a nearly seven-foot-tall, aggressive ball of fur. "Are you still into the whole"—he waved his hand as he grasped for the word, but it didn't come—"thing?"

Emerson shook her head. "Cooper Clark from two

doors down made fun of me one day while I was riding my bike in my costume, and seeing I had an epic crush on him, it was the last day I wore it."

His heart squeezed for the little freewheeling girl and her love of Wookiees. "That's so sad."

Emerson shrugged. "In fairness, it had started to smell a little, and it was getting kind of hot in there in July."

When their meals were placed in front of them, they tucked in. Connor offered another round of drinks but Emerson decided to wait, considering she would need to drive home later, which led to a longer conversation about their homes—hers in Morrison, his in The Coloradan next to Union Station.

Every conversation took a twist or turn he didn't anticipate. She asked questions that, at first glance, were so off topic, yet weren't. While he had hoped their dinner would be friendly, he hadn't expected to be so intrigued by the woman sitting opposite him. She was in turns a gentle summer breeze and then a bracing breath of winter air.

What started out as curiosity had turned into so much more. And he suddenly had the urge to learn everything about her.

E merson had fought to pay the bill with Connor and lost. But his promise that she could pay next time, if she really felt she needed to, was the sign she'd been hoping for.

That he intended to see her again.

Taking one last check of her lipstick, Emerson washed her hands, dried them, and left the bathroom. Connor was engrossed in something on his phone, and she had a moment to study his profile. Eye candy was an understatement, and while she wasn't usually one to tear her own reflection apart, she did have a fleeting moment of insecurity as to what he saw in her.

Their conversation had been wide, varied, deep at times, and honest. More importantly, they'd laughed.

It was safe to say she wanted another date with Connor as much as she wanted to walk into the distillery tomorrow and find the gin-loving elves had fixed Constance for free overnight.

"Ready?" Connor said as she approached him. He smiled at her as he slid his phone into his pocket.

"Of course."

He held the door open, placing his hand in the small of her back as she passed by. The heat and pressure from his touch caused her to shiver slightly.

"Cold?" he asked. "Would you like my jacket?"

Emerson smiled. "That's a very swoony gesture, but I'm fine in my own. Thank you."

"Well, I wouldn't lay it down in a puddle for you or anything. You're sweet, but you are no Queen Elizabeth I." Connor took her hand, and she linked her fingers with his. "I'd like to spend some more time with you if you're okay with that. A walk, maybe. Another drink somewhere?"

There were times for intrigue, for playing coy. But at thirty years of age, standing in front of the first man in a long while who made her feel a spark of something, now wasn't it. "I'd like that very much."

She wrapped her other hand around his incredibly solid bicep and leaned against him.

They wandered along Larimer Square, one of the most historic spots in Denver. Between the sparkling lights hanging across the street and the bustling excitement of people out of work for the weekend, Emerson's previously fading spirit became completely energized.

"The Crimson Room?" Connor suggested, pointing to the famous red door.

Umm. A night of jazz, perhaps a glass of red wine, and more time with Connor. "Sounds perfect."

He did that thing again, where he opened the door and placed a hand on her back, and this time she just managed to control the shivers it gave her.

Just.

They found a spot in a cozy corner. A sofa in red velour with a small table tucked deep in the shadows of the club. A jazz trio was playing a sultry piece across the room. Connor slipped his jacket off and rolled up the cuffs of his shirt. The action was so damn masculine that Emerson crossed her legs to ease the ache between them as she took a seat. He took the seat next to her and turned to face her again, placing his hand on her knee, allowing it to drift to the hem of her skirt.

His fingers were warm and gentle, and Emerson bit down a grin and turned to watch the trio for a moment to allow her heartbeat to return to normal.

The waitress arrived, and Connor ordered her choice of red wine, a perfect pinot, a small glass seeing she had to drive home, and a single malt whiskey for himself.

He leaned closer, the scent of his cologne reminding her of one of the candles she liked to burn. Not a floral note to be had. "I have to be honest," he said, his breath tickling her ear and sending a shiver down her spine. "You aren't what I expected, Emerson."

She turned her head slightly, looking directly into his eyes. In the dark, they looked even brighter than normal. "What were you expecting?"

Their lips were so close, it would only take a fraction of a movement for them to touch.

"I may keep that to myself. But it's very safe to say that, whatever expectations I had, you've surpassed them." The breath of his words fluttered over her skin, leaving her a little breathless.

Then he smiled and leaned back a little in his chair, but his fingers teased the ends of her hair. "So, you like jazz?" he asked.

The interaction had left her feeling stirred like a good martini…and perhaps a little like a dirty one. She bit back her grin at the connotation. "I do," she said, relaxing as he had. "And rock. And classical music. And rap. A bit of an all-rounder. Tell me about your family? Do you have any siblings?"

Connor shook his head. "Only child right here. My mom and dad split up when I was really young, so I don't have a lot of memories of them together. My mom remarried my stepdad. Derek has been a part of our lives since I was four. They get along okay. Just weren't meant to be and all that. Mom and Derek couldn't have kids, so there's just me. You might have heard of my dad, Donovan Finch…"

Connor was looking at her expectantly, but while she wished she could say she had, she hadn't. "I'm sorry. I know of your company by name. There aren't many large liquor distributors based in Denver, so I knew your company existed. It's funny how our paths have never really crossed before. Well, apart from the whole I-don't-like-going-to-networking-type-things phobia I have going on."

Connor studied her for a second longer and then relaxed. "So, what's with that? You were a natural at the awards."

"It's not that I hate them. And I don't think I get any more nervous than the average person. But I find the whole thing a little…tacky. Fake. Lots of smiles and feigned interest in you as a person, when all the while they are trying to figure out what they could do for your business or what you could do for theirs."

Connor placed his arm on the back of the sofa, his fingertips playing with the ends of her hair. "Isn't that what all relationships are about? Give and take? Getting to learn how you can be of service."

Thoughts of what giving and taking might look like with Connor made her core tighten. "That might be what *business* relationships are built on. But personal ones rely on honesty, loyalty, compassion, love. If you only think how the other person can be of use, you're missing the whole point."

His lips brushed the soft spot behind her ear. "Love doesn't pay the bills."

Emerson tilted her head a little to the right to give him more access, feeling prickles of excitement as his lips skated along her skin. "Money doesn't keep you warm at night."

"Fair point," he said, sliding his hand beneath her hair, his thumb brushing her cheek. "Can we agree with both? Call it a draw."

She pursed her lips, pretended to be thinking about the question, which was almost impossible with Connor so close to her, her stomach feeling as though someone had popped a bottle of champagne inside…after shaking it. "For now," she said teasingly. "I feel this deserves a richer debate."

Connor studied her face for a moment before running his thumb across her lip. "You are infinitely entertaining with that smart mouth of yours." He moved closer, his face inches away from hers.

"Are you going to kiss me?" she asked hoarsely.

"In a moment, and only if you're okay with that. You can't take back the first kiss," he said, before running his tongue over his lower lip. "You have to give yourself the opportunity to think about how it's going to feel, how…"

"How what?"

"How even though it's just one kiss, there's a whisper of a chance that everything you thought you knew was going to change, no matter what the consequences," he said resolutely. "Are you ready, Emerson?"

Unable to form a coherent sentence in response, she simply nodded.

And with that, he pressed his lips to hers. They were soft. Tender. She felt a surge of warmth from him as his arm went around the back of her neck to pull her closer.

There was a certainty, a control to it, and yet a deep unbinding passion as he took them both deeper. His tongue sought hers, and she tasted the earthy flavor of the whiskey he'd drunk.

Connor pulled back for a moment and placed his forehead on hers. "As I said, you most definitely weren't what I expected." The look of longing in his eyes reassured her he'd meant it as a compliment.

He released her, and Emerson couldn't help but smile. It was all she seemed to be able to do around him. She knew it was the first flush of something new, something that seemed to have some potential and momentum to propel them forward. And she was reassured that Connor felt the same.

She'd tried online dating, but she wasn't a big fan of getting skeevy messages at two in the morning asking in all kinds of creative ways if she was available for sex. And so what if she occasionally had been?

But this…

This was the start of something.

And unless she was completely misreading the signals, Connor felt the same.

As the hours of the evening slipped by, they discussed their lives in Denver, their friends, their hobbies. And Emerson ordered dessert…to share.

She eyed Connor carefully. "It's not going to kill you," she said, grinning at his indecision.

He sat with his arms folded and stared at her. Granted,

those eyes were hooded and telling her he was well aware she was teasing him.

"Not even a little taste?" she said innocently.

"Emerson," he growled.

"Yes, Connor?" She took one of the two spoons, scooped a small bite of the delicious dessert involving chocolate and salted caramel, and slowly put it in her mouth, groaning as the sweetness hit her tongue. Then she opened her eyes and laughed. "It's only chocolate."

She scooped another spoonful of dessert, but his hand gripped her wrist on the way to her mouth. "With you, I don't think anything is *only* chocolate." He steered the spoon to his own mouth and ate it. "And see, I can do dessert."

Emerson laughed and took another scoop for herself while Connor released her wrist and reached for the other spoon. "There aren't many people I'd break my habits for, but I feel you might be one of them, Emerson."

His softly spoken words warmed her heart.

"I want to see you again," Connor said as he walked her to her car. "Soon. If you'd like to."

Emerson pointed to her car pulled up along the sidewalk before grabbing the keys out of her purse. "I had fun with you tonight, Connor. And I don't see the point in playing games. So, yes, I'd love to see you again."

Connor wrapped his arms around her waist, and as she'd hoped, he kissed her. This time the kiss went deeper, his tongue brushed against hers, the sweet taste of chocolate and Connor filled her taste buds.

Her body ran flush against his, her nipples straining against the lace of her bra as Connor held her.

A younger Emerson would be shy about kissing a man on a street corner in Downtown Denver, but the world went on around them as she slid her hands inside his jacket. Jesus on a freaking bicycle, his body was firm to the touch. She was right about the macro counting and felt the tiniest bit of remorse for tempting him to eat dessert. And while her body had none of the firmness that his did, Connor seemed to appreciate her just the way she was.

"Damn, Dyer," Connor said with a grin as he pulled away from her. "You drive a hard bargain. Kiss me like that and I'll go on a date with you every night of the week and twice on Sundays."

He pulled her car door open and waited as she climbed inside before shutting her in. Emerson started the car and lowered the window.

"Sunday, any day next week. I don't want to wait for next weekend," Connor said.

"I'd like that," she said.

"Message me when you get home, and drive safe," he said, tapping the roof of her car.

The gravel of the driveway crunched as she pulled up in front of her home twenty minutes later. She stepped out of the car and took a deep breath of fresh air. She loved the vibrancy of the city. The noise and hustle and bustle. But she preferred it here, where she had room to breathe, wide-open spaces to hike, and a less polluted sky.

Quietly, she let herself into the house and dropped her keys and purse on the bench. She pulled out her phone and pondered what to say as she walked to her bedroom.

It was too late to come up with something super inspiring...something flirtatious. Instead, she stuck with simple and straight forward.

Dear Connor. Thanks for a wonderful evening. I really enjoyed your company. Have a great weekend.

She completed her bedtime routine as quickly as she could and climbed into bed, fresh-faced and thoroughly moisturized. There was a message on her phone.

Me too. I'm going to fall asleep to the thoughts of your hands on my body again and mine on yours, even if that doesn't happen for a while. Sleep tight.

How on earth did he expect her to sleep tight with thoughts of what *his* hands would feel like racing through her mind?

Chapter Four

Connor placed his father's sixtieth birthday gift on the table just inside the doors of the opulent hotel ballroom they'd booked for the celebration. It was momentous. Not just because of his father's milestone, but because it marked the start of his father's handover of the business to him. In eighty days, on the first day in January, the business would be officially his.

The gold theme was ostentatious. Gold cloths, gold balloons, and more white flowers than the state was capable of growing.

While he knew his father would expect him to join his table, he couldn't face an afternoon of work talk with his father and constant opposition from his uncle just yet. He needed some space from their opinions and his uncle's overinflated sense of self-importance. On a table to the left of the stage, he found his mother, Alyssa, and stepdad, Derek. Derek wore a short-sleeved shirt and a black tie, the mechanic's token gesture to the black-tie dress code.

Connor opened the button on his favorite black custom Tom Ford suit jacket.

"Connor." His mother's face lit up when she saw him.

"Come, come." She pulled out the empty chair next to her. "Derek will get you a drink."

"Beer?" asked Derek.

"G and T, please. Dyer's Medallion if they have it," Connor replied.

His mother raised an eyebrow. "Living dangerously?" She looked around for her ex-husband to ensure he couldn't overhear. "Your dad would give birth to a cow right now if he found out you were drinking the enemy."

Connor grinned, wondering what his father would say if he knew Connor's thoughts were more in line with sleeping with the enemy. He'd likely have a heart attack if he found out that Connor had jerked off in the shower before coming here. Overwhelmed with memories of Emerson's lips on his and the way their bodies had fit together, it hadn't taken long. "I was persuaded to try it and really liked it. Plus, Dad is pissing me off."

"What did he do now?"

Connor shook his head. It wasn't worth getting into. "He's clinging on to the business until the bitter end."

Alyssa placed her hand on his arm. "It's just a few more months, sweetheart. What's that after all these years?"

Derek placed the gin next to his elbow. "There you go, kid."

The use of the familiar term touched Connor more than anything his real father ever did. The majority of his child-hood had been spent in Derek's split-level. Despite his father's wealth, he'd never paid Connor's mother a nickel more than he was legally obligated to. While she'd looked after Connor and tried to build a home while his father forged his business, there had been little profit to go around by the time of their divorce. It had taken time for Finch Liquor Distribution to take off and become the success it now was.

Only after Donovan's profile increased, only after people asked about the son he had, did his father realize he wanted Connor to follow in his footsteps, to keep the business in the family like the Bacardi family had. Connor kept that in mind every time he renegotiated his salary with his father.

The dinner came and went. Connor hid a smile when brownies and ice cream arrived for dessert. Sure, they were some high-end brownies with sea salt from the ends of the earth and vanilla bean-infused ice cream in perfectly as of yet unmelted spheres, but they were still brownies and soon-to-be melty ice cream. He wondered what Emerson Dyer would have to say about it. He refused the plate, thinking of the way her eyes had fluttered closed as she'd eaten the chocolate dessert.

Shortly after the last plate was cleared, his Uncle Cameron clinked the edge of his glass to get everyone's attention as his father stepped up on the stage.

Donovan tapped the microphone. "Is this thing on? Can you hear me in the back?"

A few whistles and cheers went up around the room.

"Great," his father said. "First, I want to thank you all for coming out. You know, the funny thing about turning sixty is that you still feel like a twenty-two-year-old trapped in an old man's body."

The audience laughed, a few people nodded in agreement. "Does it ever," murmured his mom.

"You don't look a day over forty," Connor whispered, making her laugh.

His father went on, sharing humorous anecdotes with the occasional name drop. "So you see," his father concluded, "I thought I knew where I'd be at sixty. I had a plan that I'd sail off into a life of boats and sunsets. I had Connor, the son you all know I respect, ready to take the helm of Finch Liquor Distribution. But now that I'm here, it's not what I want."

It's not what I want.

Connor's heart skipped a beat. It skipped another when his father looked right at him.

"I've spoken with my brother and have come to a decision. I'm not ready for a life of retirement."

The words ripped right through Connor. He couldn't be about to say what Connor was imagining. His father couldn't have made him commit the last eight years to the family business with the promise of the head job only to rip it away.

"In discussion with Cameron, I've decided that I'm going to remain the CEO of Finch Liquor Distribution for the next five years."

The cheers and clapping echoed the roar between Connor's ears. He looked over to his uncle's table where Cameron, who was staring right back at him, raised his glass and nodded. The movement was barely noticeable. But the grin was.

Cameron knew his days were numbered under Connor's leadership. And by encouraging Donovan to stay on for another five years, he had secured his own future.

A hand held his arm down firmly on the table. "Smile," his mother encouraged. "Fake it. Pretend it doesn't bother you," she said through her own hard smile. "Get through the next ten minutes."

Connor did as she suggested. He plastered a smile on his face and raised his glass in a toast to his father. The asshole who had told him the company was his.

He watched as his father stepped down from the stage and circled the room. Silently, Connor fumed as he ran through scenarios of what to say to his father when he finally made it to their table. What he should say was that his father and uncle could go fuck themselves, but the frag-

72

ment of his measured self that was left knew there was nothing to be gained beyond an immediate release of anger.

A part of Connor wanted to simply grab his jacket from the back of his chair and storm out of the room. He didn't give a fuck who saw it.

But the business would still be his someday. Perhaps he could change his father's mind, shorten it to two years. Part-time. A partial handover of responsibility. Perhaps he could find a way to convince his father to fire Cameron, find an approach he hadn't tried.

No matter how badly he wanted to walk out of there, he'd stay and pretend he was fine. To help with the illusion, he knocked back two doubles in quick succession. Slowly, he managed to get his feet back under him.

By his strategic estimates, the business would decline by at least twenty percent if his father didn't change his path by the time Connor took control in five years.

There would, God willing, still be the assets he needed to rebuild the business. The next five years would be about protecting the assets they had and preventing his father from making any large acquisitions that were out of line with his plans.

It would be a battle of wills. A silent fucking war. He was smarter than the two of them. While his father had relied on strong gut instinct, one that had been pretty damn accurate, he was growing out of touch. He relied on insight from Connor. From now on, Connor would shape that intel to meet his own aspirations, and if that didn't work, he'd consider leaving. He could make huge progress elsewhere in five years. He wasn't prepared to let his uncle and father stall his career.

If they wanted to fuck around with his future, he'd fuck with theirs.

By the time his father reached Connor's table, his

shield was up, his brain clear, and his plan formulated.

"Connor, son," his father said, his words ever so slightly slurred. "You know how important you are to me, to the business. I'm sure this is a bit of a shock, but I'm sure you can see it's for the best."

Connor looked around before he stood up to shake his father's hand. He pulled him close for the appearance of a son congratulating his father. "This is not the time or place for this discussion," he whispered through clenched teeth, while slapping his father soundly on the back. "In fact, this is unprofessional as fuck. And we both know it was Cameron's decision to spring this announcement here without consulting me first."

"He had a point. You had a vested interest in the outcome."

"And so did he. He knew I'd fire him, and he didn't want that to happen. Arguably, he is more vested than I am." Connor whispered, before stepping back and forcing himself to smile. "I'm sure there is still plenty we can learn from each other," he said loudly for those waiting to see his response. He wouldn't give them, or Cameron, the satisfaction of being anything other than professional.

His father's eyes betrayed his ebullient posture. There was a hint of something akin to remorse. He couldn't pin it down. Was it recognition that he had handled it wrong? Was it the realization that Cameron had played them both? Or was it fear that he'd entered a five-year battle with his son?

One thing was for sure, Connor's place was only as secure as his father's desire for his son to take over the family business. But the battle lines were drawn.

Now was the time to get closer to his father than ever. To prevent Cameron from driving an unrecoverable wedge between the two of them.

Which meant that for now, his father was going to hear

a lot more from his son.

After their morning workout, Emerson and Ali had grabbed smoothies from the juice bar. Emerson had sipped hers while Ali gave her own version of a pep talk involving several cuss words and a hokey slap on the ass. But it had worked. She had arrived at the distillery ready to tackle the things she *really* didn't want to.

The bookkeeper had called to remind her that all the paperwork and receipts were due to him by the end of tomorrow, before he took off on a two-week vacation to hike to Machu Picchu. She'd gathered all the bank statements, unopened letters, and everything else ready to drop off on her way to work the next day.

Now there was just one thing left to do. Deal with the insurance company. It was six days since she'd realized they hadn't been notified of the change of owner. Six days where she'd ruminated tackling it while she'd simultaneously berated herself for not doing it. Before she could talk herself out of it, she dialed the number.

At first, she was passed from pillar to post, explaining her reason for calling only to be told she was speaking to the wrong department. Finally, exasperation overwhelmed her.

"As I just told your colleague Jennifer, I simply need to change the contact details on the insurance policy," Emerson said, her patience stretched tighter than the vapors in the heads of the gin. She rested her forehead in her hand and shook her head.

Yet again, she'd been hit with a wall of bureaucracy. Official papers needed to be filed to show that the person named as the representative of the company had changed.

"All I need to do is change one name…from Paul Dyer to Emerson Dyer. Same last name. I'm his daughter and have taken over the company."

She listened as Andrew, the person on the end of the line, rattled off scripted lines about protection of private information, which she knew well and understood. What she needed was instructions on how to prove she was who she said she was, so she could get on with negotiating the claim soon.

"Look, please just tell me what documentation you need, and where I need to send it," she said, cutting Andrew off. When she had what she needed, she thanked them curtly and hung up.

"Problems?" Jake asked, walking into her office, holding two cups. He handed one to her, and she took a sip of the scalding hot tea, wincing as it hit her tongue.

"The frigging insurance company was giving me the run around. All I want to know is when we can expect the check for the hall. I'm not asking them for the serial number of the dollar bills they'll pay it with."

Jake scoffed. "You know it'll just be a bank transfer, right? You're a CEO, not a stripper."

"Funny. And so typical men think a dollar is a good enough tip for titillation. If I ever ran a strip club, there'd be a ten-dollar minimum tip. Holy fudge nuggets. I had no idea Dad had to deal with all this stuff."

She blew on her cup of tea to cool it a little before taking another sip.

"Anyway, the service engineer for Constance just arrived," Jake said. "I'll let you know what he says." He was gone as quickly as he'd arrived.

Happy thoughts. Happy thoughts. Happy thoughts.

Instead of her usual memory of a family trip to the Adirondacks where she and her father had sat and watched the sunset one evening, Connor's face came to mind.

They'd messaged occasionally over the weekend. She'd been concerned on Saturday evening...he'd not seemed quite like his usual ebullient self. He'd assured her it was a work problem that was on his mind, and boy, did she know how that went.

Four hours later, she knew two things. The first was that Constance would be out of order for three more days due to the part required to fix her being unavailable. The second was that she had a meeting on Friday with the business manager at the bank to ask for a loan.

"I'm out," Jake said, walking into her office and taking a seat.

"If you're out, why are you sitting down?" Emerson replied.

Jake took his beanie off and ran his hand through his hair. Worry creased the corners of his eyes. "I wanted to see how you're doing. Handling your old job, taking on Dad's job. And I know a lot of it is new to you. Plus, Constance being off-line for so long. Are you doing okay?"

Emerson thought through the question before answering. "Not going to lie, I feel like I've bounced from task to task the last couple of months. I try to make a plan each morning, but by eleven it's in the trash."

Jake leaned back in the chair. "Do you remember what we agreed the day after the funeral?"

Memories of the three of them standing in their father's living room, experiencing the silence that came after loss.

"We agreed that for six months, we'd just keep the company going, right?" Jake said.

Emerson shrugged slightly. "I know, but—"

"There is no *but*, Em. Anxiety and depression have swallowed Liv whole and spit out a shell of the girl she used to be. I don't want to see that happen to you, too. The six months was for us to grieve. For us to take mental health days any time we needed them. Is it great that Dyer's Medallion is doing so well? Yes. Will the distillery still be here next year if we have to turn down an order or two? Yes."

Jake ran his hand through his hair again, something he'd done since he was little when he was worried. She wanted to reassure him. He hadn't seen the books like she had, not in the detail she had. They were busting their butt, and yes, they were able to pay everyone's salaries, and all the procurement orders, and all the bills, but the cash flow wasn't there for their plans. So, no, the distillery might not be there next year, but she didn't share any of that with him. Not when he was obviously worrying about her and Liv.

"You know, as younger brothers go, you do not suck," she said softly.

"Well, as older sisters go, you're not always a jerk. You will talk to me if it gets too much, right?"

Emerson nodded. "I will."

Jake patted the desk and stood. "You going to be okay locking the place down?"

"I got it. You go home."

About twenty minutes after Jake left, her phone buzzed.

I'm in the neighborhood. You still at work?

Connor.

Just a text from him had the power to brighten her day. It was ridiculous that a guy she hadn't known two weeks ago could mean so much to her already.

I'm hoping to leave soon. Did you want to meet up? We don't have to wait for our official date.

I'm glad you said that, he replied. *I'm in Dyer's visitor parking lot.*

I'll come down and let you in. Give me a minute.

A minute. What the hell. She needed at least five. She

ran to the bathroom and quickly brushed her teeth, wishing she'd not had onions in her salad at lunch. After a long day at the distillery, she looked like she'd fought a battle with a hedge and lost. Running a brush through her hair took thirty seconds. A quick swipe of lip gloss took five.

She jogged to the visitor's entrance and unlocked it. Connor, dressed impeccably in a dark gray suit with his white shirt unbuttoned at the neck, leaned against the brickwork of the entrance archway. He had his foot up against the wall and his head down in his phone. By his feet was a beautiful arrangement of bright gerbera daisies.

"Hi," she said as he looked up. His eyes ran a trail up her body from her feet to her face, and she could feel the heat of his gaze.

"Is it cheesy if I said I really wanted to see you?" he asked, picking up the flowers and handing them to her.

She pressed her nose to them and inhaled deeply. "Thank you. And not cheesy at all. In fact, that's very good verbalization of your emotions. I'm impressed."

Connor placed his hand on her neck, his thumb on her cheek, and pulled her to him. His lips were tender when they met hers, his tongue playful as he kissed her deeply and all too briefly. Butterflies fluttered from her stomach to her toes and back again. "I'm so glad I caught you," he said gruffly.

"Me too. Would you like a tour?" she asked, tipping her head in the direction of the production facility.

"I'd love one." Connor stepped inside.

Emerson locked the door. "Precaution from intruders rather than an attempt to hold you hostage in here."

Connor's laugh echoed off the brick walls and concrete floor. "Funnily enough, that hadn't crossed my mind until you put the thought there."

She flicked the lights on to the main production floor

and left the flowers on the stairs. "Thank you so much for the flowers. I can't decide whether to take them home or leave them here on my desk, seeing as I spend most of my time there."

"You're welcome. I left work and was on my way back to my condo when I decided to take a detour. Don't let me distract you, though, if you have things you need to be doing. I get that sometimes the work just has to get done."

Emerson shook her head. While it was thoughtful of him to come by and bring flowers, it was even more considerate to realize she might not have time to see him.

"I'm pleased to see you," she said, taking the hand he offered. "And I wouldn't have offered to meet up if I couldn't make it. I tend to be quite plain with what I'm thinking."

Connor kissed her chastely, then grinned. "I've noticed that about you. Didn't you call me Mr. Grumpy?"

Emerson laughed. "I only call it as I see it," she said. "You want to see who's being grumpy in here?" She led him toward the stills. "This is Constance. I would say this is where the magic happens, but Constance doesn't have much magic in her at the moment." Emerson ran her hand along the surface of the copper still affectionately.

"Is this the equipment you make Dyer's Medallion on?" Connor asked, and she noticed he ran his hand across the still, too.

"We tend to, just because Constance is the most reliable and biggest. But we can swap and change between stills really easily."

She walked him through the preparation area where lemons were hand peeled. The scent of lemon and juniper berries still lingered in the air, zesty and fresh. When they entered the bottling area, it became clear Connor knew his way through a liquor production plant. He asked about bottling rates and automated labelling equipment.

"As a distributor, you must have been through plenty of facilities like this," she said, before leading him in the direction of the tasting rooms. "I'd love to pick your brain on what you've seen."

"Any time. I've been through a fair few. With Medallion doing so well, do you intend to expand?"

Emerson laughed. "To answer that would take the rest of the night. Yes, I have plans. Right now, I don't have the capital to back those plans up."

"What are your estimates for the costs versus the yield improvement?"

Tired after hours of thinking about it, she needed a break from talking numbers. "It's been a long day working out the very thing you are asking. I'd love to talk it through with you, and I'm really grateful you're actually interested in all of this," she said, waving her arm around her, "but if it's alright with you, a really cute guy just showed up with flowers, and I want to fix him a drink and make him dinner."

"Here?" Connor said, looking surprised.

"The tasting rooms are open every day. We do light lunches and flights of gin. We have cocktail classes, book clubs." She pushed the door open to the tasting rooms. They were her favorite part of the distillery.

A long, rustic wood bar stood in the middle of the room with twelve chrome high-back stools in ivory leather flanking each side. One of the walls had been left as red brick, the others were smooth cream. The floor was a terracotta-colored tile, offset by low hanging lights with burnt orange blown glass shades. Floor-to-ceiling windows lined one wall, and the trees in the courtyard outside were hung with thousands of fairy lights, giving the whole place a magical feel.

She turned to Connor. "Take a seat, and let me take care of you."

L ord, if she only knew just how willing he was to let her take care of him.

He wanted her hands on him, and his on her body. Seeing her, kissing her again, no matter how briefly, only fueled that.

From the moment Connor had pulled his dark gray Mercedes into the Dyer's Gin Distillery parking lot and turned off the engine, he'd had to cool his heels.

He'd forced himself to study the sign on the wall of the distillery. In shades of sage, white, and gold, it gave the impression of something timeless, something traditional yet with a contemporary flair.

But even as he forced himself to absorb his first impression of a distillery he still considered a potential asset or investment, his mind had wandered to Emerson of the pretty brown eyes and soft hands, who appeared in his thoughts when he least expected it.

He'd thought of her when he was grocery shopping. Buying a steak for one had seemed almost pitiful when he could have been following his father's retro Steak Diane recipe for two. He'd thought of her while he swam laps in an attempt to assuage some of the anger from his father's announcement.

And it was the reason he was here. He'd spent the afternoon responding to his father's bombshell seventy-two hours earlier. Cameron had lost his shit when Connor removed his access to Connor's team of analysts. It was a petty but painful slap to Cameron, who ran his own P&L and had his own staff. If Cameron thought he was so smart, let him wrap up the quarter without any assistance from Connor's team.

He'd cancelled his own attendance at any meeting his uncle was in, leading to his father's intervention. In the end, he'd given his father two alternatives. Either it was okay for him and his uncle to never be in the same room again, or his father had four weeks to figure out whether he wanted to keep Cameron or Connor.

His father let the meeting cancellations stand.

At first, Connor had plans to go to the gym or the pool again to work the frustration out of his system. He'd even been on his way there. But then he'd thought of Emerson and his world had temporarily righted itself.

And watching Emerson as she slipped behind the bar and leaned toward him, he knew he'd made the right call. Her smile had already brightened his mood.

Her long hair fell over her shoulder. "Do you have to drive home? I can lock your car in the owners' lot with mine."

He reached forward and tucked it behind her ear, taking a moment to trail his fingers along the smooth expanse of skin. The rest of her skin would be that smooth, he knew it. The dip of her back, the valley between her breasts. And fuck, if the idea didn't make his dick start to harden.

"Are you propositioning me?"

"Oh," Emerson said, her cheeks going pink. "No. I just…well, alcohol and all that."

Connor laughed. "I was just teasing, Emerson. I'm in no rush…for dinner or anything else. I'm happy to go with whatever pace you are at. Yes, I can leave my car."

Her shoulders relaxed. "Phew. Okay. Good. Right, menu," she said, pulling up a short menu attached to a brown clipboard. "What do you feel like? I can do pretty much anything on there, except the risotto."

He scanned the list quickly, more interested in Emerson than his stomach. "How easy is the pizza?" Sure, it would fuck up his macros for a few days, but the idea of pizza and Emerson was the perfect combination for the mood he was in.

"Simple, give me twenty minutes to pop them in the oven and make a salad."

"Can I come help?"

"Let me do this," she said. "I'll be back before you know it."

He watched her as she walked toward what he assumed was the kitchen. The jeans she wore fitted her to perfection and watching her ass wasn't going to do anything to ease the ache.

Instead, he focused on what she'd told him about the distillery and their need for investment. Usually it was easy for him to make a decision, to see a path. And he could certainly see several avenues the distillery could take to grow and be successful.

His brain told him a woman he'd only known for ten days shouldn't even be in the equation. But the more he got to know her, the more his gut told him Dyer's shouldn't be involved in his acquisition plans at all if he wanted the two of *them* to work.

For once, he was conflicted by the morality of his thoughts.

And it didn't sit well.

He'd always been a business-first guy. Hate the game, not the player. But the idea of doing something that affected Emerson curdled his gut. The idea that she could already be affecting him was equally unsettling, but when she reappeared from the kitchen twenty minutes later, he couldn't deny it.

They ate their food, discussing innocuous things. And when the plates were cleared, Emerson resumed her place behind the bar.

"Do you always put ice in whiskey?" she asked as she

pulled out a number of glasses and placed them in front of him.

The way she asked made him assume there was a correct answer, and his competitive streak wanted to get it right. "Mostly, yes. On the rocks."

"Hmm. Okay. Do you ever drink gin neat, or always with a mixer?"

He'd obviously failed the first one. "A splash of mixer, unless I'm considering doing business with the producer. Then I'll try samples without."

Emerson bit her lip. "Okay." The words were drawn out slowly...every syllable sounded out.

He reached for her hand and lifted it to his lips, kissing each of her fingertips. "You going to tell me where I'm going wrong?"

She studied where his lips touched her skin. He put the tip of her finger into his mouth and sucked on it, watching her bite her lip.

"Emerson?"

"Urgh, you're distracting me. Focus, Finch." She whipped her hand out of his and turned to select a gin. He could see her thought process as she worked, her fingers tapping, reaching for, and then discarding bottle after bottle before she settled on one.

"This is a classic London Dry Gin, which, as you probably already know, is a type of gin which originated in London but can be made anywhere. It's all about the juniper berries. This glass," she said, holding up the wide-bowled wine glass, "is a Copa de Balon-style glass from Spain." She ran her fingers down the stem gently, and he could only imagine her caressing his dick in the same way. "It gives the gin room to simply be."

He placed his fingers over hers and raised an eyebrow to let her know he knew she was teasing him. When she bit her lip in response, he almost tugged her over the bar so he could enjoy the taste of her again.

Emerson poured a splash of gin in each wine glass and offered a glass to him. "Swirl it gently and then put your nose to the glass. Sniff it, but don't inhale aggressively. It's easy to lose the differentiation of the scents with gin, so you need to breathe easy."

Connor followed her lead. He'd been to tastings before, but not any conducted in the altogether sultry manner that Emerson was carrying out this one.

She closed her eyes and inhaled gently, letting out a small moan of appreciation. Then her eyes snapped forward. "Go ahead," she instructed, and Connor was suddenly aware that Emerson had mesmerized him into inaction.

He did as he'd been instructed, inhaling gently. The fresh piney, almost sappy scent of juniper hit him first. But with the slower, shorter inhale, he could pick out something else. "What's the earthier scent?"

"Angelica. Juniper and angelica can often be difficult to separate, but we have a secret way of distilling them that allows both flavors to come through. Now the fun part. Take a sip, and before you swallow, let it roll right around your mouth. Over your tongue. Under it. Coat the inside of your mouth with it."

Fuck. The words from her mouth, from those full lips. Swallowing. Tongues. Coating their mouths. She looked at him from beneath long eyelashes. Prolonged foreplay had never felt so damn satisfying.

Connor took a sip and let the bite of ethanol and burst of flavors swish around his mouth, watching as Emerson did the same.

Lemons, maybe…*dear god, the way her lips pursed and cheeks moved*…no, maybe orange, definitely citrus…*and the moan she made when she swallowed.*

He swallowed, too. The gin was great, the foreplay better.

Connor wished the bar wasn't between them. He wanted to pull her into his arms, but he settled for leaning across the bar, sliding his hands into her hair, and pulling him to her. When they kissed, he could taste the gin on her lips. Her tongue met his as boldly as the gin had done, bursting with life and flavor.

Her hand went around his neck, tugging him toward her, and he had half a mind to take her on the bar. Only the recollection that they were in her workplace stopped him from acting upon it.

When they finally broke for air, Emerson grinned. "When I said let it roll over the tongue, I meant yours, not mine."

"It tasted better on yours," he said. "I needed a second opinion on the citrus."

Emerson laughed, a sound he'd already come to adore. "You could have just asked. *Citrus aurantium*, bitter orange peel."

"And where would the fun be in that?" He reached for her hand again, seemingly unable to stop touching her. "I look forward to doing that again many more times this evening."

They were silent for a moment, eyes fixed on each other.

"I'd like that, too," she said at last. "Ready for another?" she said, tilting her head in the direction of the bottles of gin behind the bar.

Connor nodded discretely and adjusted himself below the bar. The woman was effervescent as tonic and as deep as gin. And there was no place he would rather be—no matter how much it would anger his father—than right here with Emerson.

"I'd love one."

Chapter Five

Three days after her wonderful evening at the distillery with Connor, Emerson unbuttoned her overcoat, ran her palms along the flare of her dress, and stood straight.

It was fine. She wasn't doing anything wrong. She wasn't committing to anything by investigating loan options. Her father had hated the idea of a loan so badly, it felt as though she were going behind his back somehow. And there was the nagging concern that Olivia or Jake may feel the same way. But she needed to know what their options were before she presented the idea to them. After learning more details on repayment costs, she might be able to persuade them.

She'd resisted the urge to run her presentation by Connor. Lying in bed that morning, she'd concluded that in the absence of her father, she simply wanted someone credible, someone with industry experience, to tell her that it was a solid proposal she planned to share with the bank. She had to consider why she felt she needed someone's approval other than her own, and why she felt Connor was the right man for the job.

Taking a deep breath, she pushed the bank doors open.

She made herself known at the information desk and waited a few moments before she saw the person she was waiting for.

"Emerson," said Dawson Allen, the business banking manager and her former high school classmate. "Great to see you. I was so sorry to hear about your dad."

"Thank you, Dawson. I'd be lying if I said things hadn't been rough, but we're muddling through it."

Dawson led Emerson to his office, where he gestured toward the chair opposite his desk. Once they were both seated, he pulled out a notepad.

"So, how can I help, Emerson?"

She offered him a copy of the presentation she'd created to make sure she mentioned everything in the pitch. "We're stuck in a catch-22. We have more orders than we can keep up with, but we don't have the capacity to fill them. I estimate that we could sell at least a half million more units this year if we had the capacity. But without the wedding venue revenue and all the fallout that came with it, we don't have the cash to do the kind of expansion we need to. Any renovation needs to be fast and simultaneous to reduce disruption to our supply chain. The venue and the distillery will need flipping at the same time."

Dawson looked confused. "You want money to renovate?"

Emerson nodded. Why did it seem like such an odd question?

Dawson tapped something on the keyboard and looked carefully at whatever was on the screen.

"Is something wrong?" Emerson asked.

When Dawson looked at her, his features were as perplexed as she felt.

"Your dad was approved for and received a quarter-of-a-million-dollar loan thirteen weeks ago. It was a five-year loan. See the monthly payments here?"

He turned the screen towards her, and there was the deposit, just as Dawson explained. A deposit and a monthly automatic repayment of just under five thousand dollars a month.

Her stomach lurched as her eyes flitted over the screen. The distillery name was on the screen, and the account number matched, but there was no way her father was sitting on that kind of money. When she'd taken over immediately after he died, she hadn't looked that far back in the business accounts. And in the muddle of grief and sudden shift in her responsibilities, she must have missed the loan repayment or mistaken it for a company credit card payment or something.

Shit. The piles of envelopes in Dad's office. She'd ignored them, assuming they were simply bank statements, but perhaps they contained information about the loan. It suddenly felt too warm in Dawson's office. She needed air.

"Can we look through the transactions to see where that money went?" Emerson asked, because it certainly wasn't in the account right now.

Numbers began to blur together, but less than a week after the money had been deposited, cash began to leak from the account. Twenty-five thousand dollars here. Fifty thousand dollars there. Round amounts, no invoice numbers.

What the hell had her father done?

"Emerson," Dawson said. "I hate to say this, but if this money hasn't been used to upgrade the distillery, the bank would take issue with that."

Her chest felt as though it were in a vise. A vise that was being tightened at an aggressive rate. She needed to think on her feet. To come up with something.

"I wonder if Dad had arranged for the repairs. Those look like contractor deposits, don't they?" she asked breezily.

Dawson didn't look convinced, and she realized he could just check who the money had been sent to.

"Look, Dawson," she said, deciding to come clean. "I don't know what Dad planned. But please, can you give me some time to sort this out? I need to go back to the office and figure out what happened. Are you able to tell me who the money went to? That would help me hugely."

"We can, but not from this screen. Leave it to me."

"Thank you, Dawson. Look, I'm not asking you for any favors, but if you're unhappy with what we find out, I hope you give us some time to respond appropriately."

Dawson nodded. "I'll do the best I can. But Emerson, I couldn't possibly approve another loan without clearing this issue up first."

"I understand," Emerson said, grabbing her purse. "Thank you, Dawson."

She rose, her palms damp, and left the office.

The cool air was a welcome balm to her nervous sweating. What the hell had her father done? Where had all that money gone? She'd seen the amounts but still couldn't believe her father hadn't told them about such a large loan. Why had he kept it quiet? None of it made sense.

She needed to get back to the distillery, to start going through the office, her dad's laptop, the invoices, through anything that might help her find the money. But if she went back right now, Jake would see straight through her, and she didn't want to worry him yet.

She ran her fingers through her hair, then straightened the skirt of her dress. How was she going to explain this to Jake and Olivia? Especially Olivia. Emerson had hoped that by fixing up the venue and getting as many weddings as possible back on track, they could permanently erase some of the damage the hostility toward the distillery had caused. And if it died down, it would be safer for Olivia to be back at work.

An hour ago, she thought she had a plan. A plan to save the distillery with a loan. Now she had no loan. Worse, she had no possibility of a loan. *And* the distillery was a quarter of a million more in debt than she'd known about. The renovations now seemed even further away.

Her best intentions to understand what loan options were available had put the distillery at even more risk. Best case, they had to meet the monthly repayments, but worst case, the bank would foreclose on the loan, and they'd have to find a way to pay it back. They'd go bankrupt trying to fund such a huge sum.

Perhaps the only option would be to sell, and even then, the distillery would be devalued because of the pending loan repayment.

The nausea came again in a giant wave.

Perhaps she should call their bookkeeper. Shit, he was in Machu fucking Picchu. She could go through the books online thanks to the software package the bookkeeper used, see if there were any notations there as to what the checks were for.

On autopilot, she walked to her car and got inside. She rolled the windows down, the only thing she could do to ease the trapped feeling constricting her chest like iron around a barrel. The drive took her half an hour, longer than usual due to traffic, and she had only fleeting memories of the thirty minutes when she parked in front of her home and stepped into the house at five o'clock.

With what was left of her energy, she collapsed on the couch. Her head had started to pound, but the painkillers were in the kitchen, which was a step too far away.

Closing her eyes, she breathed deeply, letting the scent of the lavender from the planter on the side table soothe her, the peace and quiet drift over her. The throbbing started to subside, a blessed relief. Emerson pulled on the throw from the back of the sofa and snuggled beneath it.

It was wrong to act like an ostrich, to bury her head in the sand. But for a moment she needed to feel scared, to feel uncertain of what to do next. Certainly, there was a risk she would fall asleep and wake up at some ungodly hour with her hair stuck to the side of her face, but she couldn't bring herself to move.

When she finally opened her eyes, it took Emerson a moment to figure out where she was. Wrapped in the crocheted blankets like a mummy, she fought to get her arms free and push the blanket from her head.

Her head.

Oh, *halle-fucking-lujia*. The pounding had gone, leaving her with a dry mouth and a rumbling stomach.

Once free of the blanket, she stood, wobbling a little at first, as her body fought the decision to move, and then went to grab her phone from her purse.

7:45 p.m.

No wonder she felt as groggy as all heck.

With squinting eyes, she scrolled through her notifications as she wandered to the kitchen. While a part of her wanted to just stumble to bed, now that she was awake, she became aware of just how hungry she was.

Brazil nuts, that's what she could—

Her heart skipped a beat.

A message from Connor.

Hey. I'm at the restaurant. We said 7:30, right? Is everything okay?

Shit. She caught a glimpse of herself in the mirror. Her hair was everything she'd expected it to be. Slightly sweaty and stuck to the side of her head. It would take ages to get herself cleaned up, and then the drive.

She couldn't face it. Even for Connor.

I'm really sorry, but I'm not going to make it. Can we rain check?

Dots bounced on her screen, then stopped.

Her phone rang.

Connor.

For a moment, she debated letting it go to voicemail, but he knew she had her phone with her, so she answered.

"Hey, Connor."

"Are you okay? What's wrong?" he asked immediately.

He could tell. Why hadn't she thought of a response before she'd answered? She should have let the damn call go to voicemail. "I'm fine, I just…you know, work. And things came up and—"

"Where are you? Still at the distillery?" His voice was a mix of stern and concern. It warmed her otherwise chilled heart.

"No. I'm at home. I got some news I wasn't expecting. It was…"

"I'm on my way."

There had been a waver to her voice. An uncertainty that didn't belong there and had him worried. He was secure enough in the way they had left things on Tuesday and the messages in between that she wasn't trying to blow him off.

And he wanted to fix whatever was wrong as a result.

She'd given him her address when he'd insisted on getting a ride for her when they'd left the distillery on Tuesday. He'd decided to walk home, partly because it had been a lovely evening and he'd spent most of the day inside, and partly because liquor and pizza wasn't really a part of his fitness plan, certainly not on a Tuesday.

But he'd loved every minute of it.

He left his seat at the bar of the restaurant and wandered into the kitchens.

"Finch. What do you want? I'm working. Thought you were front of house tonight with some bird."

Connor watched Charles check off an order against the dishes waiting to be served and laughed at the gruff anglophile tones and turn of phrase of one of his closest friends.

"Delighted to chat with you, Charles. I need a favor."

"I said finely diced, not fucking macerated," Charles yelled at a junior chef opposite. "Sorry, I seem to be surrounded by idiots. What do you need?"

"Remember that salad you make...the one with the beef and crispy noodles and peanuts and shit?" Connor asked.

Charles pointed his knife in the direction of the macerating chef. "Make up the batch of the mango ponzu dressing if you've got nothing better to do...Yeah, what of it?"

"I need two servings of it tonight to go."

"Your date bailed?" Charles said with a laugh. "Never known you to have that problem before."

"No, she didn't. Work came up," he said, thinking on the fly. "I'm going to drive it over to her so she at least gets to eat."

"Let me get this straight. You're asking me to make a meal for a woman because..."

"Because she's balancing a bunch of shit and didn't have time to eat. So, don't be a dick, and don't ask any more questions," Connor said with a hint of humor.

"Don't need to," replied Charlie. "You just told me

everything I need to know. Let me make it in peace. I'll have someone bring it out."

"Poker night again soon?" Connor asked.

"Sounds good to me. Now fuck off."

Half an hour later, after doing speeds that would have landed him with some serious tickets, he pulled up outside Emerson's house. It was a pretty timber-and-stone-fronted single story on a decent-sized lot. There were several apexes to the roof and a large bay window to what he assumed was the living room. The living room appeared to be lit by the flickering light of candles.

He knocked on the door and looked to the sky while he waited. Dark clouds skittered across the moon. When Emerson answered, he was glad he'd made the trip. She was dressed in navy sweatpants and a gray T-shirt that had the faded look of a top well-worn. It was impossible to miss the fact she wasn't wearing a bra, but he forced the thought to the back of his mind. Her damp hair was up in a messy bun.

"I brought us dinner," he said, lifting the bag.

A sad smile graced her lips for a moment. "I'm not really good company."

Connor knew she was giving him an out, and he'd be the first to admit that in the past he might have taken it. Comfort and care were not his specialties. But this was Emerson, and he really wanted to be there for her. "You don't have to be good company. I brought food. We can eat in front of the television. Or read. Or nap on the sofa. Or we can talk if you want to tell me what is going on."

Emerson sighed and let him pass. He pressed a kiss to her cheek as he walked by.

From the wide cream hallway crammed with plants, he could see the kitchen. The cabinets were old and in need of updating, but Emerson had decorated it with old farmhouse-style tin jugs and red-and-white polka dot fabrics. The cast iron oven looked brand new. He placed the food and bottle of wine he'd added to the order on the kitchen island.

"Thank you," Emerson said quietly as she walked into his arms. Her body pressed up against his, her head pressed into his shoulder. It felt right...it felt perfect. She sighed, and he felt her body relax, as if a coiled spring had been released.

He ran one of his hands along her back and pressed a kiss to the top of her head.

Silence filled the room.

Emerson's hands gripped his shirt.

Neither of them moved. Connor felt more grounded, more present, than any of his daily meditations made him feel. He was aware of her body pressed against his in comfort, rather than anything sexual.

Finally, Emerson lifted her head. "I'm glad you came, Connor."

The softness around her eyes told him she was telling the truth. The tension he'd seen in them when he'd arrived had concerned him.

"I meant what I said. We can eat, we can chat, we can nap. Whatever you want."

Emerson bit her lip. "Is there anything else on offer?" she asked, her voice softer, huskier than normal.

His dick got with the plan before his brain kicked into gear. He placed his hand on her cheek, his thumb caressing her smooth skin.

Hell, yes, she could have whatever she needed from him, and as her hand slid just an inch beneath the waist of his jeans, her meaning became crystal clear.

"Emerson, I meant what I said. We can do whatever you want. I came here because I was concerned about you.

And if us taking it a step further is what you need from me, I'm here for that. But I don't want you to think I came here for sex."

Expectation glittered in her eyes. "I know. And I didn't think it was what I wanted, either. But you. Coming here, caring about me, caring about how I am. Even the feel of you against me, right now, does something to me."

He lined her body up against his before spinning them around so her back was against the island. Slowly, he ground his dick against her as he pressed his lips to hers for a moment that was too intoxicating. "You do something to me too," he growled. "But before I continue, I need you to understand two things. The first is I don't need to know what happened today before we do this, but I expect you to talk to me after. And the second is I'm not doing this if you tell me that I'm just a distraction, even though my cock will not forgive me tonight. Our first time together needs to mean more to you, to *us*, than that."

The words were out of his mouth before he could stop them. Fuck. Where had this responsible grown-ass man come from? Why did he suddenly have to be the knight in shining fucking armor when he had a willing woman...no, a willing Emerson...ready to ride his dick into the sunset?

Emerson reached for the buttons on his shirt, her eyes on his. Slowly, she opened every one and tugged the edge of his shirt from his jeans. "I promise to talk with you if you stay. And you *are* a distraction. How could you not be, Connor? Just your presence is a distraction."

She ran her fingertips over the ridges of his abs, and he tightened them in automatic response. He daren't watch her hands' trajectory, knowing it would threaten his control and good intentions.

"*This* is a distraction," she said, pressing a kiss to one pec, followed by the other. Her hand slid lower, running her fingers over his rock-solid dick. "And *this* is most definitely a distraction."

He watched her lips as she spoke, full and soft, taking in every word. For a moment, he'd let her think she was in control, but once they got into her bedroom...

"But it's more than all that. I just want you, Connor. I've been thinking about this since the night at The Crimson Room, perhaps even sooner if I'm honest."

"So, we're doing this?" he asked, reaching for the hem of her T-shirt. "You're going to let me be with you for the rest of the night, however I want to."

"Please, Connor," she begged, as he ran his hands beneath the soft fabric to cup her breasts. He began to knead them gently, playing with their weight, running his thumbs over her nipples.

Connor slid the T-shirt over her head and, just as quickly, slid her sweatpants down her legs, helping her slip each foot free. When she stood before him in her underwear, hands on the counter behind her, dusky pink nipples just waiting for his lips, his dick pulsed. The woman had him wound up tight.

He picked her up, savoring the feel of her nearly naked body in his arms, as she wrapped her legs around him. Kiss after kiss was planted behind his ear and down his neck. The sensation drove him as wild as it tickled.

"Bedroom?" he asked.

"Second left off the hall."

Connor kicked the door open to her bedroom and laid her down on the bed before switching on the small lamp next to the bed. The room was cast in a warm glow as Emerson wiggled back on the soft white bedding.

She watched him through hooded eyes as he removed the shirt she'd already unbuttoned, as he unfastened his jeans and slid off his shoes.

Wearing only his boxer briefs, he climbed onto the bed,

bracing his weight over Emerson, before bowing his head to kiss her. Knowing they were both on the same page as to where this was headed, he kissed her as he'd wanted to at the distillery.

Passionately. Messily. Desperately.

Emerson responded. Her tongue searching for his, her hand threading through his hair and the other tracing the contour of his back, pulling him closer to her. When he settled between her legs, they both groaned.

Seriously, was there a better feeling than skin pressed up against skin?

Connor savored kissing her, the way her body fit against his, and the way they moved in sync. He moved down her body, kissing her collarbone, her shoulder. He indulged himself, licking the tip of her nipples before blowing on them as they reached firm peaks.

He sucked one into his mouth, absorbing the way her body arched against his as she gripped the bedsheet with one hand. Emerson was so responsive, and he couldn't get enough.

He kissed her hip bone, nipping it gently with his teeth, before sliding his fingers beneath the waistband of her underwear.

Slowly, he stood and slid them over her hips, down her smooth long legs, and when done, he removed his boxer briefs.

"You're quite the fucking view, Emerson," he said. Her chest rose up and down as if she were already breathless.

Emerson's eyes tracked a lazy trail down his chest, focusing for a moment on his dick. And damn, if she didn't flick her tongue across her lip. "Impressive is the word I might have chosen."

"Yes, you are." His finger traced the seam of her pussy, finding it delightfully wet.

"I meant you, Connor," she gasped.

"I know." Bending forward, he pressed a kiss to her clit, and then, using his tongue, set out to demolish Emerson Dyer.

Emerson groaned as his tongue ravaged the deepest parts of her. One moment, he'd circle her clit, teasing her until she grabbed his hair, holding him where she needed him. Then he'd slide his tongue inside her, slowly easing in, then out.

The pace confused her and set her on edge, heightening the anticipation.

When he returned to his knees, she groaned. Hovering on the edge of orgasm, she needed more. She looked up at his body, his muscles were taut. The discipline he had to look so utterly perfect was apparent in their sinuous movement.

"The first time you come, Emerson, will be around my cock," Connor said gruffly. "But that doesn't mean I'm done playing with you. Yet." He stroked her gently with his finger. Far less pressure than she needed to get off, but enough to keep her close. "How does that feel?"

Connor must know she was writhing beneath him. How could he not see the effect he was having on her? She reached for him, pulling him back down on top of her. He pressed against her, so hard. So firm.

"How does it feel?" she repeated. She kissed him, nipping at his lip. "Do you really need me to tell you what you're doing to my body? How ready it feels for you? How much I want you in me?"

Sliding her hand between them, she gripped him. Lord, he was so wide.

Connor groaned. "Fuck, Emerson."

He was hot and firm to the touch, and she could feel

the steady beat of his pulse. The idea that he was about to slide into her, stretch her and fill her, caused her clit to throb.

His hands traced every inch of her body, and for a moment, Emerson understood what it was to feel thoroughly desired by the man she was with. The idea that he had driven to her home because he was concerned about her, that he hadn't planned a booty call or intended to stay added to the need she felt for him. The promise she'd made to talk to him scared her slightly, but at the same time fueled the feeling inside her that she wasn't alone. That he would be there for her no matter what difficulty she was in.

His kiss took her out of her head. His touch took her out of her body. She was at the heady precipice of coming apart.

"Are you ready for me, Emerson?" Connor asked. She felt the absence of his warmth and solid weight as he pushed himself off the bed in one fluid motion. He grabbed something from his jeans.

Condom.

She had her own, but the fact he was prepared and brought one reassured her he took such things seriously.

Connor rolled the condom on as Emerson watched. The light of the lamp cast shadows on his body, casting the muscles in stark relief. Every part of his body revealed the discipline he must live by.

As he crawled back on the bed, he kissed her foot, her shin, her knee, her thigh. She flinched when he kissed the ticklish spot on her hip, and Connor smiled, as though he knew exactly what he was doing.

When he settled between her thighs, he pressed his lips to hers, gently.

Softly.

His pale blue eyes burned with intensity. "Are you ready for this, Emerson? Are you ready for us?"

Unable to verbalize everything swirling inside, she simply nodded.

Connor reached between them and guided himself into her slowly, groaning as he inched forward, his eyes never leaving hers.

The feeling was so intense her head spun. She hadn't realized how wet she had gotten for him, and she opened her legs wider, allowing him to move more freely.

"Connor," she moaned as she reached around his back, pulling him against her, arching upward to meet him. The movement allowed Connor to press deeper until he was fully inside her, stretching her, the sweet sensation of being held in place removing any anxieties she felt.

He stopped moving. "Fuck, Emerson. You feel so good," he gasped.

Emerson ground her clit against him, desperate to chase the orgasm that hovered just out of reach.

"If you keep doing that, you know I'm going to come, right?" he muttered, his face pressed against the side of her neck, the warmth of his breath heating her shoulder. Connor slid his hand beneath her ass, lifting her, opening her.

She felt safe in his grip as he began to move again, the steady back-and-forth increasing in pace.

Pressure began to build deep inside her. The telltale sign that she was riding the right wave.

"Connor, I'm close."

She grasped for him, wrapped her legs around him as best she could to allow him to sink deeper and deeper, faster and faster. The man had more stamina than anyone she'd ever met. The pace, the delicious friction, the absolute control he had over her body.

"Me too," he grunted. "Fuck, yeah. Me too."

The sound of his voice, the lack of control in his words, was the push she needed.

As his thrusts became almost frantic, Emerson exploded around him. "Oh, God," she cried as she lost all sense of self or rhythm. Every muscle clenched. Warmth flooded her.

"Em," Connor groaned as he thrust hard into her, his body jerking against her as he came, pulsing, within her.

His movements slowed as Emerson came back down to earth. Connor lay on her, his breathing heavy, their bodies damp and sweating. Neither of them said anything, neither of them moved.

Energy raced through her, but her mind was finally clear, absent of worry.

Connor pressed a kiss to the side of her neck, and she ran her fingers through his hair. When he finally lifted his head to look at her, he looked relaxed, more youthful. "That was incredible," he said. "*You* were incredible."

He rolled to one side and tucked her against him, wrapping his arm around her. For a moment, Emerson considered leaving to get cleaned up. But Connor didn't seem to care and was quite content to simply lie there with her in his arms.

"Thank you," she said, kissing his smooth chest.

They fell silent, and Emerson was close to falling asleep when she heard Connor's stomach rumble. They hadn't eaten, and there was food sitting on the kitchen island. She looked over at the clock on the bedside table. It was nearly nine. If they were going to eat, they should do it now.

And with the stress out of her system, perhaps she could finally relax and enjoy her food.

"How do you feel about dinner?" she asked, aware his breathing had dropped to an almost frighteningly slow pace.

"Do I have to move to eat it?" he mumbled, and then finally opened his eyes to look at her.

Emerson thought for a moment. "I could always pop it on trays and bring it in here."

Connor slipped his arm from beneath her and ran a hand across his face before running it through his rumpled hair. "It's okay. Let's make a move so I can get cleaned up and perhaps open the wine if you feel like it."

Emerson sat up and pulled the sheet up to cover herself. Yes, she might have just let the man screw her into oblivion, but she was suddenly aware she was naked.

As Connor climbed out of the bed, he kissed her shoulder. "You're beautiful," he said, as if reading her worries.

He disappeared into her bathroom, and Emerson got out of bed, grabbing her robe. It wasn't flowing and sexy like one she thought Connor might appreciate. It was pale pink and fluffy. Warm and cozy. She put it on and tied it around her waist.

After cleaning up in the washroom off the hallway, she waited for him in the kitchen, busying herself getting plates and cutlery and her corkscrew for the wine.

When Connor joined her in the kitchen, he was wearing his jeans. And only his jeans.

Emerson couldn't decide if it was the scent of the food he'd brought or the sight of the man without a shirt on that made her mouth water.

He wrapped his arms around her and kissed her softly. "Mmm…those lips," he murmured.

She couldn't help the self-satisfied smile.

"Let's get some food," he said, letting her go before he opened the bag. "I'm so glad I got cold salads. I didn't think hot food would last the drive here."

"Honestly, I could eat a horse." Emerson opened the takeout boxes to see a delicious salad. Thin glass noodles, strips of medium-rare beef, slivers of peppers and carrots, and the scent of freshly chopped cilantro.

"Wait until you try the dressing. It's all the good stuff… soy sauce, sesame oil, loads of lime." Connor tackled the wine. She watched the muscles in his arms flex as he removed the cork. Damn, even the way he sniffed the cork was giving her sensations in places that shouldn't yet be ready for action.

As he poured the wine into glasses, she tipped the salads onto their plates.

"Cheers," Connor said, handing her a glass.

Emerson took it and clinked the edge of the glass against his. "A pinot noir?" she asked, after she'd taken a delicious sip.

"It was what you ordered in The Crimson Room the other night, so I knew it was a safe bet."

They sat down at the island. One of the things she had loved most about the property was the quiet at night, and beyond the odd scrape of the fork or clink of the glass, they ate in a comfortable, companionable silence.

As she came to the end of her meal, worry started to creep in. He was going to expect her to talk to him, to tell him what had her so wound up. But she wanted to simply exist in the happy silence between the two of them.

"Connor. I know I owe you an explanation. But do you think, just for tonight, we could just go to sleep?"

Connor turned on his stool to face her. He opened the hem of the dressing gown, placing his hands on her knees. The warmth of them grounded her. "As long as you aren't blowing me off."

"I'm not," she assured him. "I want to talk to you about it, I really do. For the first time all day, I don't feel so stressed…and just thinking about how to explain what's going on at work is starting to make me feel anxious. I need some sleep and some perspective, that's all."

He studied her face for a moment, before nodding. "You go climb into bed. I'll rinse these off before I join you."

She should clear up the dishes in her own kitchen, but suddenly her body was bone-tired. Emerson walked to the bedroom, and after a few minutes in her bathroom, climbed into bed.

She was already asleep by the time Connor joined her.

Chapter Six

The *rat-a-tat-tat* sound infiltrated Connor's dream, rousing him from sleep.

Was someone hammering something in his building? Was someone trying to bust down a door?

He couldn't open his eyes. Wherever he was, it was a hell of a lot brighter than his bedroom.

Connor tried to move, only to find his arms were wrapped around a woman.

Emerson.

With a sigh of relief, he pulled her closer, her back to his chest. The sound, he realized, was a woodpecker somewhere outside the open window. They'd fallen asleep before closing the curtains, exhausted from great sex and delicious food.

Sex. Was that all it was to him?

The idea that it meant more unnerved him a little, yet he couldn't deny the fact that it did. The way she felt as he slid inside her, as she moved and opened up for him. It was so much more than sex. It was the connection he'd felt, the way she'd held his gaze, the way she'd asked him for what she wanted, the fact that for once he felt like he was building something with Emerson, and that feeling had pushed him over the edge.

His dick stirred at the idea of a repeat, especially with that ripe ass of hers pressing against him. And while he hoped that could happen before he left for the day, they needed to talk first.

Trying his best to not disturb Emerson, he pulled his arm from beneath her, grabbed his jeans, and left the room. There was a bag full of workout clothes in the trunk of his car that he could pull clean stuff from later. But for now, he needed coffee.

The kitchen was bright, and from the window he could see what looked like a vegetable garden. There were rows of beds, some with plants still thriving. A greenhouse was positioned off to one side. The rest of the garden was planted simply in shades of green and white. On the patio just outside the door sat a small bistro table.

Thankfully, he noticed a coffeemaker on the counter, and Connor set about making an espresso. He was just making his second shot when Emerson shuffled into the kitchen.

"You scared the crap out of me." Emerson squinted in the daylight. She pushed her hair off her face. "It took me a minute to figure out what kind of home intruder breaks in to make coffee."

Emerson made her way to him and stepped into his arms before placing her head against his chest and closing her eyes. "It's too early to be doing morning yet."

Connor glanced at the clock on the microwave as he pulled her in close. It was a little after eight. "Believe it or not, usually I'd be up at least three hours by now. I feel like I had an epic sleep-in."

Sure, he'd be late getting off on his usual Saturday seventy-five-mile bike ride, but his energy level felt boundless. Add in the double-espresso and he'd be good to go.

Emerson lifted her face to his. "We need to talk, don't we?" she said.

He kissed the tip of her nose and smiled as she scrunched up her face. "We do."

"Have a seat in the front room while I make myself a coffee."

Connor wandered into the living room. It was warm and inviting, if a little cluttered for his more minimal tastes. A soft green sofa was stacked with cushions in different fabrics and sizes, but all black or white. White walls were covered in artwork and photographs. And plants hung and sat on every available surface. He thought of Blake and Talia's plant-filled apartment. Evidently, Emerson and Talia would get along.

Emerson also liked to read...widely. Books on economics and business theories sat next to thrillers, horrors, and books with titles that caught him off guard.

"*Best American Erotica?*" he asked when Emerson walked into the living room.

"Nothing wrong with reading about sex, Connor," she said, pulling her knees beneath her on the sofa.

Connor was the opposite of offended. "I never said there was. I'd be more than happy to spend a night on this sofa with you, taking turns reading and possibly reenacting everything between those covers."

Emerson grinned. "I'd like that, too. We could do that now," she said, raising an eyebrow.

His dick twitched in agreement. Now would be a great time to push that robe open and try something new with the lovely Emerson Dyer. "As much as that idea just took top spot on the list of ways I'd like to spend my day, we need to talk first."

"You and your talking," she said, but her tone was playful. Emerson sighed and took a sip of her coffee. "Listen, I'm fine, really. It's a business thing…and after sleeping on it, I feel much better about things."

Connor reached for her hand, and she let him take it. He hoped it felt solid to her. Grounded her. Showed her that he wanted to be there for her. He ducked slightly to look straight into her eyes, and damn, if those big brown eyes weren't trying to hide something.

"If you're fine, then I just got drafted to the Nuggets," he replied. "Look, I'm not going to push you. If you want to talk, I'm here. If you just want to sit and drink coffee together, I'm game. If you'd rather I just gave you some space today, I can be on my way. But I guess I'm kind of hoping we might be working toward something more than friends with benefits. I can't make myself clearer than that."

Emerson was silent for a moment before squeezing his hand. "I hope that, too. I've got a business problem. But I need to know that you're serious…no, not that…that you won't share any of the information I share with you."

Connor held her gaze. "I deal with confidential mergers and business acquisitions. You can trust me."

Trust me. He considered for a moment his father's preoccupation with the Dyers and the circumstances of their first meeting. Unease crept through him. Sometime soon, he'd need to tell her about his father.

But looking at Emerson now, he wanted her to know she *could* trust him. Any ideas he might have had to purchase Dyer's Gin Distillery were put to rest. He'd remove them from his acquisition list, unless Emerson decided to sell. There were plenty of other distilleries to buy.

His father's obsession with her company would never be anything more than that. It had been an uphill battle to convince him to even consider buying Dyer's. And it only served to give him and his uncle something else to disagree over.

"We've got a very real cash flow problem. Dyer's Medallion is selling really well, which is a great thing. But at the start of the summer, we lost the events hall during that freak storm we had. The insurance hasn't paid out yet. We got a lot of bad press because we had to cancel so many weddings. It got so bad that my sister had a mental health emergency."

"That must have been really tough for you all. And then with your father…" He didn't need to say more.

"Yeah," Emerson said sadly. "Even before all this, it's been a lot."

"Is your sister okay now, though?"

Emerson nodded. "She's not back at work, but she's doing so much better. I fear this new issue will cause regression for her, though."

"What else has happened?"

They sipped their coffee, as Emerson explained.

"The distillery is in an *okay* state."

Connor listened as she explained Medallion's demand, the equipment working flat out, and Jake being too busy to come up with a new product for the Medallion line.

"Your assets are just about keeping up?"

"Yes," Emerson agreed. "So, yesterday, I went to the bank to see what options we had to get a loan for some improvements, only to find Dad took out a loan and spent it in round figures over the next few days, and I don't know why. And because I naively went to the bank to talk to them about a loan for something my father apparently already asked for money for, the bank is suspicious."

"Shit," Connor said. A million thoughts flitted to mind, the main one being that the bank could recall the loan any day they wanted if Emerson couldn't prove that they used the money for its original intentions. "How much was the loan for?"

"A quarter of a million. And we most definitely don't have that money to pay back, on top of repairing the events venue, let alone starting any renovations."

"What options do you have? What are your next steps?" He wanted to know what she had already considered before speaking.

"I'm going to spend today seeing if I can find out where those payments went. I have access to Dad's old business email account, so I'll see if I can find anything there. If he paid advances on anything, that would be so helpful, but I doubt it. I think people or products would have showed up by now."

Connor thought about the situation for a moment. "What about the insurance? You mentioned you were due a payment?"

Emerson nodded. "Yeah, for the events hall. I'd asked Dad, but there seems to be a run of issues. They lost the initial claim, then took ages to send out an auditor. Dad said it could take up to ninety days to get the check just before he passed away. Then I forgot to change the business contact name after Dad died. I need to submit the paperwork before they'll even talk to me."

From what he remembered, Paul Dyer had passed away toward the end of July, which meant the check was only a few weeks or so away. "So you sit tight. Keep maxing out production like you're doing. Can you lease equipment rather than buy it?"

"I'm going to have to consider all of that. Dad hated debt. I'd talked to him about taking out a loan to refurbish the factory, but he'd always said no...that we should save for it. We never could've considered that as an option before. That's the main reason I feel so weird about the loan Dad took out. It was so unlike him."

Connor had cut ties the previous year with a vodka producer whose CEO had suddenly started dipping into the accounts, and from what his father had told him about Paul Dyer, the man had lacked scruples. "Do you think he took the money?"

"No!" Emerson cried. "Of course not. He was a good and honest man."

Connor immediately regretted asking. But Emerson's answer was so passionate, her eyes showing genuine hurt at the question, that he wanted to believe her.

"I'm sorry, but I had to ask. Stranger things have happened in business."

Emerson folded her arms across her chest. "Well, you're wrong. There must be a good explanation."

"I'm sure there is," Connor said. "For a moment, I forgot we were talking about your father."

Who also happens to be Paul Dyer.

The man had a track record of stealing what wasn't his. How could Emerson and his father's view of the man be so polarized?

He shook the thought from his head.

Emerson stood. "I need to get into the office."

Connor realized just how deeply his comment had sliced. "Emerson," he said, getting to his feet. "Thank you for telling me what happened." He placed his hands on her shoulders and ran his palms down the length of her arms until he could hold her hands.

She reluctantly let him.

"You don't know my father," she said, quietly. "He was a good man. Whatever he did was for the good of the distillery."

But even as she said the words, Connor could hear the hint of uncertainty.

"Afternoon coffee," Jake said, placing a mug next to her elbow.

Emerson closed her father's laptop. She hadn't been able to find any information about their insurance claim or the loan on it over the weekend, which was odd.

She glanced at the clock, noting it was close to five in the afternoon. "Thanks. How was the production run today?"

"Constance is like a new woman. Back in her groove after the service."

"Perfect." Relief flooded Emerson. A good Monday was helpful. A great week would be awesome.

"So, I drove over to see Liv on Friday night, and I was just passing yours when I noticed a fancy-looking Mercedes in your driveway." Jake peered at her over the top of his own mug.

"My driveway is up the end of a long track that is nowhere near the main road, so do you want to be a bit more specific with your *just passing* story?"

Jake laughed, and his eyes—the mirror of hers and their mother's—crinkled in the corners. She had a vision of him hiding beneath the very desk she was sitting at when he was about six years old. Hide-and-seek in the distillery on the weekends was not considered to be the major health and safety issue it would be now, with so many more staff operating at full tilt. She'd screamed when he jumped out at her after she found him, and she'd refused to play any more games with him.

"Remember when you pouted all day because I wouldn't play hide-and-seek with you anymore?" she asked.

"I do...and good attempt at stalling. I was going to ask to borrow your lawn mower because mine gave up the ghost, but I did a U-turn when I saw you had company and borrowed Dad's from Liv." His eyes dramatically narrowed. "Fess up. Who owns the Merc?"

She wasn't ready to share Connor with anybody yet. It was hard to believe that it was only three weeks since she'd met him. And they were already taking all the right steps toward something more intimate, more permanent.

At least they had been until he'd so easily and naturally suggested that her father might have been on some embezzling scam to screw his own company, and ergo children, out of the company. But she remembered how he'd tried to make amends over the weekend, and she was finally beginning to think she'd been too sensitive.

"New guy. Early days. His name is Connor."

Jake leaned forward, resting his elbows on his knees. His mug looked like a doll's toy in his large hands. "I don't know whether I should say something about being safe or ask if he treats you well or demand you to bring him for Thanksgiving next month."

Emerson laughed. "Or you can just remind yourself that I'm a street-smart woman who knows how to take care of herself, and that at least two of those statements were suspiciously patriarchal, and that I don't need you looking out for me in that way."

Jake grinned. "Or you can just realize that I'm simply a younger brother who cares for his older sister, and get over yourself, and still invite him for Thanksgiving."

"Fine, I'll see if he has plans. But seeing as it's a month away, I might wait awhile. See where things go for a little bit," Emerson said.

Jake stood. "Well, seeing as his car was still in your drive in the morning, I'd say things have already gone quite a way."

"Jake," she cried, launching the nearest thing to her hand, an apple, at his head. "Were you spying on me?"

He caught the apple, as she'd suspected he would, and laughed. "I swung by the bakery and got you one of those cinnamon buns you like. Saw the car was still there and figured it would be rude to drop off just one, so ate it on the way back home."

"Asshole."

"Don't I know it," he said. "Catch you later."

Emerson collected the paperwork the insurance company needed to change the contact on the policy, so they could talk to her about the claim, and sent a digital copy of everything to the email address Andrew had given her. It was six o'clock, and she was slightly mad that something so important had taken so long.

Her phone vibrated, and she picked it up.

Any chance you're free for dinner at my place tonight? Cx

For a moment, she vacillated, acknowledging that she might still be feeling overly sensitive about his comments regarding her father and the loan. Everything else, when put into the pros and cons columns, stacked mightily in Connor's favor. His questions about her father were his only misstep in an otherwise delightful, fledgling relationship.

I'd love to. What time?

I'll be home about 7:30 so any time after.

They exchanged a few more messages about logistics before Emerson got back to work.

At fifteen minutes before eight, she pulled into the parking garage and into the bay number Connor had instructed. Once parked, she grabbed her things and took the elevator to Connor's floor. It was a short walk down the contemporary, gray-and-white hallway until she reached his door and knocked.

When he answered the door, Emerson could have sworn her breath left her body. He wore a black V-neck T-shirt that fit him to perfection, setting off the color of his eyes. His jeans hugged his hips and thighs, and he was barefoot. He ran a hand through his still-damp hair.

"Hey, come in," he said, holding the door wide enough for her to pass through with her bags. Once she'd placed them all on the wooden bench and hung her jacket on one of the cute metal coat hooks above it, he spun her around, caught her in his arms, and kissed her. "I missed you," he whispered.

She'd missed his arms around her, and the scent of him, and the feel of his body against hers. She'd been a jerk to have negative thoughts about him, and she needed to fix it. "I'm sorry. I took the comments you made about Dad too seriously. I know you were just asking questions. I'm sorry I was standoffish this weekend. I just needed to reconcile it."

"I've been kicking myself for asking. I know if anybody asked questions like that about my dad, I'd be mad. My uncle, yeah, I'd let 'em pass…and likely even agree. Ask them about my mom, I'd knock someone's lights out for even suggesting it."

"So, we're good?" Emerson asked.

"Yeah, we're good. Let me give you a quick tour before I have to get back to the dinner. This is the living room."

The light wood flooring carried on through the whole apartment. Straight ahead was a luxuriously plush ivory sofa. A white media unit ran along the wall and a soft rug in navy blue rug pulled the area together. It was sparser than her own home. Every piece seemed very…deliberate. Symmetrical prints in black-and-white, a solitary plant that resembled an aloe, a side table made from an inches-thick slice of a tree trunk.

To the left was the kitchen. "Wow, this is beautiful," she said, running her hands over the contemporary square wooden table. It was tall, much taller than a normal table, and the eight chairs in crushed blue-gray fabric were part chair, part stool.

"I didn't want a predictable table. I wanted something I could eat at, or hold a poker game around, or serve food at a get-together on. I found the stools, which were perfect, but I couldn't find a table. I ended up having it custom made."

"It's stunning." Emerson continued to look around. Not that it mattered to her, but Connor appeared to be wealthy. The apartment was likely a million-dollar property, the furnishings luxurious.

The kitchen was all white with a large, industrial double-door fridge with freezer drawers.

"These things are huge." She opened it to find shelf after shelf of labelled containers. "I knew you meal-prepped," she said, laughing.

Connor grinned. "I'd like to argue it's convenience, but I'd be lying if I didn't admit to a healthy dose of both competitive spirit and vanity. Want to grab that bottle of San Pellegrino off the door there?" He bent to check on whatever was in the oven.

"Smells good," she said, placing the bottle on the counter. "What are we having? Rice and three slices of sweet potato?"

"I didn't realize you were such a comedian, Emerson. And for the record, it's sheet pan fajitas," he said, spooning a ripe avocado out of its shell.

"Is that even allowed on your plan?"

Connor grinned. "Yup."

Emerson ran her hand down his bicep, which flexed as he continued with his task. "Maybe I should try your plan."

"If that's a genuine suggestion, I'd be happy to show you how. If it's a less-than-subtle comment about my body,

I'd be happy to show you more of that, too. But tonight, let's eat dinner first, so I can build up my stamina."

Connor winked at her, and she couldn't help but laugh.

And the laughter help put her worries to one side, at least for a couple of hours.

"Stay the night," Connor said as they cleared the plates from the table. They'd spent dinner talking about their work. He'd found himself telling her a little bit about his uncle and the petty outburst he'd had the other day. Connor's father had asked him to do an organizational structure review, including of Cameron's finance department. Cameron had been furious when Connor told him he had no intention of sharing the findings with anyone other than his father. Connor and Emerson found themselves discussing the merits of working with family members and the strain that could bring to relationships.

She'd understood and that had meant everything.

Emerson could drive home—they'd stuck with water for dinner, so it was safe—and at ten thirty it was early enough for her to go. There was no other reason for her not to drive home, apart from the fact he didn't want her to leave.

He placed the last dish in the dishwasher, put a tab in the dispenser, and set it running.

Emerson was silent for a moment, and he could tell she was thinking over his suggestion. "I'd love to, but I don't have any clothes for tomorrow. I'd have to leave here super early to go home to shower and change."

Connor mentally ran through the problem. Nothing he owned would be suitable for her work, and neighboring stores were likely closed. "I have a washing machine and dryer if that helps."

Emerson laughed. "Because nothing says I didn't go home last night like showing up to work in the same outfit, no matter how nicely it smells of laundry detergent."

"Fair point." He leaned his hip against the kitchen counter. Negotiation was his strong suit, and he was determined to persuade her to stay with him in his bed. "I normally get up at four forty-five in the morning to get my workout in and then head to the pool. For an extra eight hours with you, I could ditch the workout, take you home, and bring you back with clean clothes."

As if she understood this was a bargaining game, she crossed her arms. "That's a big play, Finch. I know how much your fitness routine means to you."

"Big enough for you to stay?"

"Hmm. I'm not sure. I have my own car here, I could drive myself home."

"Where is the chivalry in that? Being equal and treated with respect does not negate the idea of being a gentleman. Plus, it's slightly mercenary. If I take you home in the morning for clothes, we could even shower together. In fact, I really like that idea."

When she bit her lip, he knew he'd won. He walked over to her and pulled her into his arms, nibbling the side of her neck. She tilted her head, allowing him access. "Fine," she said. "But I'm not getting up at a time that starts with a four to shower, no matter how hot the idea of you and soapy water sounds."

Now it was his turn to laugh. "What if I throw in a breakfast burrito?" His fingers moved to the buttons of her blouse and began to open them slowly.

"If it comes out of one of those two hundred calorie prepped meals and is solely made of egg whites, then no."

"Fine, I'll scramble eggs, you can make the toast." He

slid the blouse down her shoulders, kissing a trail along the revealed skin.

Emerson reached for the hem of his T-shirt, and he obliged by releasing her and bending forward so she could pull it over his head. "Eggs are good, but we still haven't agreed on a time. No alarm should desecrate my ears before six."

Connor nudged her backwards down the corridor toward his bedroom, taking note of the pretty lace bra she wore. The practical Ms. Dyer had surprised him. "I like this," he said, running the tip of his finger across the crest of her breast.

"I feel a six a.m. alarm call is a good price to pay for the ability to admire it." Emerson's voice wavered as she reached for his belt.

6:00 a.m. He could still squeeze in a swim.

Fuck.

He could even tolerate the congested evening swim if it meant he got to sleep in with Emerson. "Five forty-five, my last offer," he said, even though he knew he didn't mean it.

"Deal." Emerson stepped out of his reach to offer him her hand.

He took it and raised it to his lips. "Deal."

The way Emerson looked at him, standing just outside his bedroom in her bra and jeans, her dark hair down messy around her shoulders and a look of need on her face, took his breath away.

Somehow in the last three weeks, Emerson Dyer had shifted from a name his family loathed to someone he was curious about, to someone he was starting to care deeply for.

He'd wanted to solve her problems for her as they'd talked over dinner. He'd love her perspective on the industry. He admired the way she talked so freely about the people she worked with, who she appeared to think so much of—something that made him question his own relationship with the people who worked for him.

Who'd have thought that out of all the women on the planet, he'd fall for the daughter of his father's enemy.

"I really like you, Emerson."

Emerson blushed slightly, a gentle pink hue that only made her even more appealing. "I like you, too, Connor, very much."

He took her hand and led her to his room and, for a moment, wondered what she'd think of the space. Deep blues and whites to remind him of the ocean he loved to swim in. They undressed each other in silence, the act feeling almost sacrosanct. When he reached for the covers to pull them back and allow Emerson to slip inside, she kissed his shoulder, the small gesture adding to the intimacy of the moment.

Connor followed her into the bed and pulled Emerson close to him, his arm around her, the length of her body warm against his. Her skin was so smooth to his touch, and he couldn't get enough. Pressing his lips to hers, he savored the taste of her as his tongue met hers. His hand trailed the dip of her waist, the curve of her hip.

Emerson explored his body with confidence. She placed a kiss to his chest while her hand moved down his abs until it brushed the tip of his dick. When she reached for him, he gasped. "I fucking love it when you touch me," he groaned.

The firm hold made him twitch.

She moved from his grasp and began to kiss his pecs, his abs, his hip. And he prayed she was heading where he hoped. Unable to take his eyes off her, one of her hands holding the hair from her face and the other holding his dick, Connor wondered how he'd gotten so fucking lucky.

"Emerson," he warned.

"Let me," she murmured.

When she licked the tip, every muscle in his body tightened. When she took him deep into her mouth, he lost all sense of rational thought. He tried to form thoughts about ensuring the woman he was with came first, but the way Emerson sucked him gently as she moved up his dick made it impossible.

Part of him just wanted to come right then, with her perfect lips pursed around him and a fierce look of concentration and lust singing in her eyes. But he wanted a lot more than a quick orgasm. Hell, they could save that for the shower in the morning.

Stretching forward, he reached for her arms and pulled her back on his body. Emerson squealed at the action, and despite the mood, he couldn't help but laugh. "You keep doing that and you'll be going to bed unfulfilled because I swear I'd pass out straight after."

She knelt with her legs on either side of his. His dick between them. With her eyes fixed on him, she slid both hands over his length.

"Fuck," he moaned and blindly reached his arm in the direction of his bedside table, pulling the drawer open to find a condom.

Once it was on, he reached for Emerson's wrists to stop their movement. "My turn," he said, placing her palms on her thighs.

"Connor," she gasped as his finger touched her clit.

Gently, Connor eased one finger inside, watching Emerson as she began to rock against him. He added another and, with his other hand, reached for one of her breasts, teasing the nipple.

"Oh, God. Yes," she cried, her eyes closed as she lost herself in the sensations he was able to give her.

His dick ached to be inside, a throbbing distraction. Watching Emerson fall apart, watching the way she chased her own orgasm so confidently was erotic, but he was inherently a selfish man. He pulled his fingers out of her slowly, teasing her as he placed them into his mouth, sucking on them as he tasted the sweetness of her. "When you come, I want to be in you," he said gruffly. "Come here."

Emerson crawled up the bed a little, her knees on either side of his hips. He took hold of his dick, and Emerson slid slowly down on him. "Like this," she gasped.

Connor rose to meet her, the friction taking his breath away. "Yeah," he said. "Just like that." He placed his hands on her ass, encouraging her to rock against him in the same way she had against his finger. Looking down at the point where they merged, him seated deep within her, he watched her swollen lips rub the length of his dick, almost bringing him to his breaking point.

Emerson fell against his chest, her breath coming in sharp erratic breaths as she began to moan. "Yes, yes," she repeated, her actions becoming more frantic. He could feel her begin to squeeze him, and he could feel his own orgasm build.

She pressed her lips to his, a wild uninhibited look in her eyes. And then she gasped and shuddered against him, losing herself to the sensations. "Connor."

The feel of her squeezing him tightly was enough to have him thrust against her, deeper and firmer, faster and wetter. Thrust after thrust in pursuit of his own climax. "Fuck, you feel good, Em," he groaned.

He squeezed her ass, holding her in place while he took everything he wanted from her body, coming in hard jerks that ripped his soul out.

His body continued to shudder for a moment, prolonging the exquisite pleasure that coursed through his veins. Emerson, still breathless, gasped against his shoulder as he tried to control his own breathing. He'd never experienced anything quite like this with anyone else.

This was something unique.

This was something special.

And in a startling moment of clarity, he could imagine them together, permanently.

Connor reached for the sheet and pulled it up over Emerson's back. Sweat and air conditioning wasn't always pleasant, and he didn't want her to get cold. Nor did he want her to leave her comfortable position draped across his body, despite the fact he would have to deal with the condom in a minute or two.

Emerson lifted slightly, her weight on one arm. "I need to be honest," she said quietly, almost shyly. "I think I might be falling for you, Connor."

Connor pushed a piece of hair behind her ear and allowed his finger to trail her cheeks. Flushed from their lovemaking, she looked sated and less worried than she had been during dinner. "I'm glad we're on the same page," he said, honestly. "I don't know where this is headed, but it's more than a casual thing to me."

Emerson rewarded him with a smile that reached her eyes. "It's the same for me too. I'm past the point of playing games and wondering if I should text you or not. We're exclusive now, right?"

"Damn straight, I don't like to share." Connor kissed her, but a kernel of worry filtered through the otherwise perfect moment. What kind of games would his father think he was playing?

He couldn't keep Emerson a secret, not when they had just declared this was something more than a casual hookup.

But for the foreseeable future, he couldn't let him know, either.

Chapter Seven

"Liv, Jake," Emerson called out, kicking off her shoes as she set her purse on the old wooden bench in their father's hallway.

"In the kitchen," Olivia replied.

The sweet scent of apples and cinnamon greeted Emerson as she entered the craft kitchen made from pine that had taken on a yellow glow. Anxiety-baking, as Olivia called it, was her sister's way of navigating the here and now.

Perhaps I should give it a go. She'd spent the last several days going through her father's business emails and found no record as to whom the loan her father had taken out had been paid to. There was no paper trail on his company laptop or in the filing cabinets.

"Smells good in here," Emerson said.

Olivia switched from rinsing dishes in the sink to washing her hands. "Figured the least I could do for you guys is throw together a lasagna and pie."

"Lasagna? You made my favorite?" Jake said, coming in through the back door, the sleeves of his sweater dirtied with mud. Jake waved his dirty hands near Olivia's face.

She squealed and flicked tap water at him. "Your gutter is now clear, and you're welcome."

Emerson grinned at the bickering. "Apple pie's *my* favorite. You trying to butter us up for something, Liv?"

Olivia turned to face them. "It's time to get on with things. With life, work."

Emerson cast a look toward Jake, who immediately looked concerned. "You don't need to," he said. "We've got this covered." He circled the air around the kitchen, meaning they would continue to help Olivia with bills and the like.

When Olivia had been at her worst, their father had suggested Olivia give up her apartment and move back home with him. Fortunately, his house had no mortgage, and Emerson and Jake had agreed to keep paying Olivia's salary while she was off work. But the upkeep was expensive, and Olivia needed help with chores to focus on her recovery.

"I know you guys would." Olivia reached for Jake's hand and squeezed it. "But I've been speaking to my therapist. I'm finding it hard being here...without Dad. It's like a time warp. I wake at seven every morning missing the sound of the coffee grinder. I'm not like you two. The quiet drives me mad. I have zero interest in the garden. Someone else should be here. It's a family home. And I feel like moving out and working again are the first steps in getting back to normal."

Emerson listened as Olivia spoke. Her sister seemed...hopeful.

"Move in with me for a while," Jake said. "I'll tone down the farting if you promise to brush your teeth twice a day."

Emerson smacked his arm as Olivia laughed. "You are such a jerk," she muttered.

"I know I could live with either of you, but I think I'd

like to head back downtown. I know I can't do it until this place sells, but I think I'd like to buy instead of rent. Get on the property ladder like you two."

Emerson's heart stopped beating. The house. With no mortgage. It had to be worth at least five hundred thousand. With five hundred thousand, they could pay back the loan if they needed to and at least make a start on renovating the distillery. They could start with buying two new stills, even if they had to be installed in their current setup, and retire Patience to the smaller-batch runs and for new product development.

"But I started to see what I could find. Look," Liv said, opening her laptop on the kitchen counter to show them a photograph of a listed property she liked near the university. "It's only a one-bed. With the down payment, my mortgage would be so much lower than the rent. And that would be one less thing stressing me out. Knowing I'd be in a stronger financial position. Just looking and seeing a future made me feel so much better today."

Olivia linked arms with Emerson, who could barely speak. "Look, Em. Don't you think that bookcase I have in my room right now would look great in that space?"

"Yeah...fabulous," Emerson said with all the energy she could muster. How could she consider asking Olivia to punt her recovery for the distillery? Hadn't the only thing she'd wanted all along was for Olivia to be back to her happy self? This was the closest she had seen Olivia in months.

She'd intended to tell them about their father's loan but planned to wait until she knew what the bank intended. Causing them unnecessary stress wasn't the right thing to do. It hadn't occurred to her to kick Olivia out of their father's house until she was ready. But if she was ready now, they could sell, give Liv her share, and then she could see if Jake would agree to put their remaining balance to the distillery.

Emerson mentally shook her head. That wouldn't work. Olivia wouldn't stand for the two of them putting more in than she was expected to...and she couldn't do it without Olivia knowing because the split of the company would need updating, a document they'd all have to sign.

"Do you not like it, Em?" Concern etched Olivia's features.

"No, I love it," she managed to say. "If we are putting this place up for sale, we should start thinking about clearing it out and getting it staged."

There was time to figure it out. None of them wanted to see the distillery go under...and neither she nor Jake would want to save the distillery at the risk of Olivia's progress. It seemed like there could be enough money to do both.

But wouldn't it be amazing if the insurance came through, the house sale came through, and there was an explanation for her father's loan? She was expecting the details to come from the bank soon.

Emerson smiled, this time for real. Olivia and Jake had their heads in the laptop, and she had access to the funds they might need.

After dinner, filled to the brim with apple pie and ice cream, Emerson drove home and let herself into the house. She had the urge to ask Connor to come over, but it seemed pathetic that after less than forty-eight hours, she was craving his touch.

As she slipped into bed, her phone vibrated.

My bed feels pretty empty without you in it. Cx

Emerson smiled. She snapped a quick picture of the other side of her bed. *Mine, too.*

A minute later, he replied. *I don't know your limits yet, sweetheart. But want to get off with me? Virtually?*

Yes, she replied, jumping out of bed. She had no idea what he had in mind, but she bet it didn't include the Scandinavian-patterned pajamas she picked up in a sale. Whipping her top off over her head, she ran to her dresser. Black push-up bra, that would do. And the black silk slip edged in lace that she rarely wore because the lace itched her skin…she'd manage for thirty minutes.

She pulled her pajama bottoms off, put her bra and slip on, and caught sight of herself in the mirror. Tousled hair, flushed cheeks from the very idea of getting it on over the airwaves with Connor. Too bad she'd washed off her mascara already.

Hi. Connor had sent her a picture of himself sitting up in bed, his chest naked. One hand was in his hair, his muscles flexing. Damn, the man's body was something else, but it was the smile that flipped her heart.

Emerson opened her camera. She couldn't do the same pose. So, she lifted one knee and draped her arm off it, and as she did so, the strap of the lace slip fell off her shoulder, revealing her bra. Perfect. She sent it with the return greeting that matched Connor's.

Fuck me, Em. Was totally not expecting that. Will store in my spank bank for future reference. You look good in black.

His response warmed her. She didn't really have it in her to play the role of seductress. *You look good naked.*

Like this, or more? The message was accompanied by another photograph, this one taken a little farther out. He'd lowered the sheet so she could see both of those V-lines near his hips and a covered but clearly hard erection.

Her stomach clenched in anticipation, and she squeezed her knees together.

Emerson rolled onto her side, grateful that she'd shaved her legs that morning, and slid the hem of the slip up her leg until it just skimmed the top of her thigh. She bit her lip and took the picture, but before she sent it, she zoomed in as far as her phone would let her to make sure nothing truly private was showing. The lamp light cast a bronze glow over her skin and somehow made her look...sexier. At least sexier than she felt on a daily basis. Or sexier than she'd felt since before meeting Connor.

I'm stroking myself, imagining coming on that thigh of yours. And it's hard to type with one thumb. He'd added a crying laughing emoji.

Emerson opened her drawer and pulled out her vibrator. She snapped a photograph of it. *I've got a stand-in for you.*

Rolling onto her back, she turned it on, and placed it on the spot she knew would get her off quickest.

Connor responded. *Fuck, I wish I could see that in real life sometime. The idea of you using it right now is such a fucking turn-on.*

Too far past the point of responding, she rocked against it, tightening her abs as she thought of Connor in his bed masturbating to a photograph of her and the mental image of exactly what she was doing right now.

It was enough to send her over the edge, sensations coursing through her, that immediate moment of almost blacking out from the pleasure of it all. It took her breath away.

A moment later, her phone buzzed. *That was the next best thing to being buried deep inside you, Em.*

Funny, she'd just thought the exact same thing. *Yeah, battery-operated boyfriends don't cuddle.*

Just debated getting in the car to come see you for that very reason.

She liked that he held her after they'd made love. It affirmed that she was really something more than convenient sex.

Is it weird that you mean so much after such a short time? she asked.

There was a pause of a few minutes, and just as her doubts began to crash in, he replied.

More than dry chocolate brownie with melty ice cream?

Emerson grinned. He'd remembered their conversation in San Francisco. *Perhaps a bit more than that.*

More than the Chinese food in that Cleveland mall?

She thought for a moment and then typed. *That might be stretching it.*

He sent her a grinning emoji.

Then a heart.

No, Emerson. It's not weird. This is like chicken stuffed with lemons and butter and herbs. We had to experience everything else to realize just how special this is. Good night, sweetheart.

Her heart soared as she hugged her phone to her chest. She wasn't weird.

She was falling in love.

T*hank you for the flowers. They smell glorious.*

Connor wasn't certain what had inspired him to arrange the delivery of white roses to Emerson, but somewhere between getting home to his condo the previous evening and messaging with Emerson, he realized she had become the difference in his day. And it hadn't been the fact she'd been willing to shock the hell out of him with some fucking sexy pics and an orgasm. It was knowing it was her. Emerson. She was likely in the distillery, building something with her family, fighting valiantly to find out what the hell kind of mess her father had left her in. Yet she still had the capacity to be balanced, sweet, and caring.

"Connor," his father called as Connor passed by his office on his way to the supply chain department, interrupting his thoughts.

"What can I help you with?" he asked, curtly.

His father sighed. "It's been nearly two weeks, Connor. Is this…atmosphere…really necessary?"

Connor took a deep breath before answering. "I'm being professional. I'm surpassing my targets. And my team is assisting every other department in the business with the exception of finance. Do you have any *genuine* concerns?"

Sweat dotted his father's forehead. "That wasn't what I meant, Connor. You're being…"

Connor stood silently and let his father flounder.

"You know what I mean," Donovan blustered.

"No, Dad. I don't. As I explained to you *ten* days ago, when I came to see you, I find it unacceptable that you made the decision you did. I find it abhorrent that you did it without the decency to speak with me first. That decision stalls my career aspirations for the next five years. And I'm not prepared to let that happen."

A meeting broke out across the hallway, and Connor watched as the participants headed toward the elevator. Men in suits. Another distribution deal. Finch Liquor Distribution was the riverbed through which all liquor flowed, but there was nothing to hold on to. And while he worked hard and did a great job, Connor suddenly realized he wasn't in love with what he did. It wasn't passion that got him out of bed in the morning; it was routine. He didn't show up every day because he loved liquor distribution, he showed up because it was expected, because it had been drilled into him every day since he could remember that Finch would be his one day. Suddenly, not only did he question if that was what he wanted, but worse, the idea that this was all he had going for the rest of his life left him dumbstruck.

While Connor floundered with the feeling of a man

lost at sea without a compass or life vest, his father pressed on.

"Step into my office for a moment. I have something I want to discuss," his father said gruffly.

"Can't it wait, Dad?" Connor asked. "I have something I need to do real quick."

His father shook his head. "This is important, and I'm sure it's something you'll want to hear."

The sudden seismic shift in Connor's belief system left him feeling as though he were wide open. He wasn't certain how to process what had just happened and felt unusually vulnerable. But he took a seat.

"I know you're mad at me." His father sat down behind his desk. "I promised you my job when I turned sixty. And one day, you'll turn sixty and still feel the bite of ambition and goals left undone like I do. Perhaps then, you'll understand why I made the choice I did."

Usually, he knew how to respond to his father, but right now, his head was full of questions about his own ambitions and goals, so he remained silent.

"I don't want you to leave," his father said. "Cameron says you'll wait, but I'm not so sure. You mentioned your career stalling. As a result, I'm creating a new C-level position. Chief Strategy and Marketing Officer. It will put you on the same level as Cameron. The head of Marketing will now report to you instead of me."

The idea should have quelled Connor's growing unrest, but it didn't. If anything, it fueled it.

"I'm giving you a pay raise, starting immediately. One that would bridge the gap between what you get paid now and what you'll get paid when you take this job. It will be an extra seventy-five thousand a year. And I've arranged for a retention bonus to be given to you. An additional one-hundred-thousand-dollar one-time, no-strings payment in the hope you'll stay on."

So many thoughts raced around Connor's head. It was certainly a lot of money. A one-third increase in his salary. And the bonus would lower his mortgage. But the idea that Cameron was continuing to interfere with the way his father treated him and the business concerned him.

"Cameron doesn't know shit, Dad. He's a mediocre CFO who knows which side his bread is buttered because he knows you'll never fire him."

Donovan tapped his fingers on the table. "That's your uncle and my brother who's given me decades of great service without complaint—you'll show him the respect he's due."

Connor coughed. "Due? He's not *due* anything. You've paid him way beyond his market value for all that time."

"You need to take care of him when I leave, Connor. You need to leave him in place."

Connor's anger rose, a burning tide in his gut. "Given that's five years from now, we don't need to worry about it. A lot can happen in five years."

"Son," Donovan warned. "Five years is the blink of an eye. Trust me. This will be yours then. I hadn't realized it was such a fucking imposition on you for me to keep control of the business I built until then."

Connor shook his head. "That isn't the point and you know it."

Silence settled on the room, a heavy mantle that Connor could feel on his shoulders.

"Anyway," his father said, his tone now lighter, as if the words they'd exchanged no longer mattered. "I've given our conversation some thought. The one about the next five years. And the downturn you suggest will happen has me concerned."

There were too many U-turns and zigzags for Connor to keep up with. "In what way?"

"I'm fully aware I've built a business on solidly drinkable mass-market liquor. That I've gone for volume consumption rather than highbrow lines. And you might be right. In the longer term, that won't be enough."

Connor studied his father carefully. "And?"

"And I want you to draw up a list of artisan producers with the capacity to increase production to midlevel volumes. Don't bring me places that can make a thousand cases here and there. I want someone who can make it to at least half a million bottles within a year of us buying them."

Connor's pulse began to increase. Was his father giving him the go-ahead to start putting his long-range plans in place now? "You want me to look at acquisition targets?" he clarified.

"I do. Stick with white spirits only. Look at those which could possibly gear up to diversify. Bring me a vodka distiller who, with the right investment, could be tooled up to make tequila, you get the idea. And when we build this business, it can all report to you."

Connor's mind churned with everything his father told him. It must have been kismet that he'd realized the business wasn't what he wanted. That a title change and a lot more money were never at the crux of his ambition. The *challenge* was. That was what he needed more than the other two. This was the universe giving him what he'd wanted to manifest. A pivot into something he cared deeply about.

"I'll get my team on it," he said. "We'd already made a start, kicked the tires on a number of firms. I'll get that list of distilleries, clear out any non-white spirits, review the list against the criteria you laid out. I'll add and subtract potential targets based on that."

He mentally flicked through his presentation, recalling what had been included. "When did you want it by?"

Donovan stood. "I think you should make it a priority.

Think a five-year plan, starting at somewhere in the region of twenty million for the first year, forty million in the next, and so on, going up in twenties over the five years, to a hundred million in year five."

Three hundred million across five years in total…and to think that at the party he was convinced all hope was lost. "You won't regret this," he replied.

Donovan huffed. "Maybe. Maybe not. And listen. About Cameron…he's not fully on board with the plan. I'll talk him round."

Connor debated his next comment mentally before he spoke. "Cameron doesn't have your business acumen. He'd never have the lifestyle he has now if it weren't for you. Make sure his counsel to you isn't heavily influenced by that."

"I'll do that." Donovan walked toward the door. "Your retention bonus will be in your bank account by the end of the week. And one final thing…in the review of potential assets…include Dyer's."

It felt as though his father had sucked all the air out of the room.

Include Dyer's.

His father had resolutely rejected the idea of procuring Dyer's. He'd wanted no part in buying something he felt he should have owned. No matter what tactic Connor had tried, he hadn't budged from his position.

But *now* he wanted it. Now, after Connor had let go of the idea of acquiring it himself. Now, after he'd confessed his growing feelings to Emerson.

The idea of his father getting his hands on Emerson's company was against everything Emerson stood for. Quality over quantity. She'd told him enough times.

What would it do to their fledgling relationship if Emerson understood it was a possibility? He'd asked her so many questions about the business in their conversations, she'd assume he'd been plying her for information.

Which he had.

At the start.

Before he'd realized how much the business meant to her, before he'd realized what a wonderfully caring woman she was, the way she put her family first. Before he had seen her in her element in the distillery, before he'd seen her raw and naked and vulnerable in his bed.

Before his father had made it clear he was never going to purchase it.

Fuck. His father had played the one move he hadn't seen coming.

He couldn't include her distillery without risking their relationship, and he had to do everything in his power to make sure that didn't happen.

Chapter Eight

"We are so ridiculous," Emerson said, looking at Ali who sat opposite her, tucking into a stack of pancakes.

Ali's cheeks were stuffed with food, but she pointed her fork in Emerson's direction, chewing until she could swallow. "Yes, but this is way better than suffering through another workout."

Instead of going to their class as planned, they'd left their cars in the gym lot and walked until they'd found a spot to eat breakfast. Emerson looked down at her own plate. Waffles, strawberries, and a side of whipped cream. Oh, and syrup. Lots of syrup.

"We're stuffing our faces while wearing active wear." Emerson sighed as she took another gooey mouthful.

Ali laughed. "This is true. But tell me this. Would you rather be here or doing burpees?"

Emerson shook her head. "Is that even a real question?"

"What can I get you?" she heard the server ask behind her.

"Could I get a Greek yogurt, plain. Blueberries on the side. Two egg white burritos, and no salsa."

Emerson knew that voice and turned to see Connor checking his phone, his brow furrowed. He was dressed in a black suit, his hair still wet. She knew he'd been to the pool. Her body lit up at the sight of him. God, he was so delicious.

"That sounds like a disgustingly healthy breakfast," she said.

Connor looked up and flashed a smile that showed his dimples. He checked out her plate as he walked to her table. "And that looks like something we should eat on the weekend...in bed. Oh, sorry," he said, glancing over at Ali. "Didn't realize you had company."

Emerson laughed. "Connor, this is my best friend, Ali. Ali, this is Connor."

They shook hands as Emerson scooched over in their booth. Connor sat down next to her, placing a gentle kiss on her lips.

"Would you like some while you wait for your order?" she asked.

His hand slid along her leg beneath the table. "Don't tempt me. I love waffles."

In response, she dipped a piece of her waffle in the cream, added a strawberry, and ate it in one bite, over-exaggerating her moan as she chewed.

Connor raised his eyebrow as Ali laughed. "So, did you two just finish up at the gym?" he asked.

Emerson shook her head and grimaced. "We *parked* at the gym. Does that count?"

"And we walked lots of steps here. Like *all* the steps," Ali added.

Connor grinned. "It's all about balance, right?"

"Two egg white burritos and Greek yogurt," the server called.

"I gotta go. Have a meeting in half an hour." He kissed her cheek. "Nice meeting you, Ali." He stole a strawberry from her plate and dipped it in the cream before popping it into his mouth. "Mmm. You are such a bad influence. Call you later."

She watched as he grabbed his food and disappeared onto the street.

"Okay. You did not tell me he was *that* cute," Ali said, waving her fork accusingly. "Like, holy shoulders, Batman."

"It's ridiculous how good looking he is. Clothed and naked. And he's a good human being, too."

"This sounds like more than a casual thing."

Emerson took another bite of her waffle, thinking she might make them for him on the weekend. "I think it is. It's just a struggle to find the time I want to spend with him."

Ali reached for her hand. "Em. I love you. With my whole heart. Your dad put so much responsibility on you, it's almost not fair. But if something is really important to you, you'll find time for it. Even if it means eating breakfast at stupid o'clock. Right?"

Emerson knew Ali had a point. She just didn't know how to reprioritize.

She was still thinking about Ali's words later that afternoon as she discussed pricing with Jake.

"We can only make what we make," Jake said with a shrug of the shoulders. "That's the volume we can sell. If we can't afford to refurb right now, we'll deal. If we can't buy a new still, we'll deal. Have you considered increasing the retail price for Dyer's Medallion?"

They'd market reviewed and tested that price a million times. "You know why we settled on it."

Jake nodded. "I do, but that was before we knew it was going to win a medal for us in San Francisco. And now we have a supply and demand problem. Because of its popularity, it's more in demand. So let's test if people are willing to pay more for it. I'm only talking about a couple of bucks a bottle."

Pricing elasticity was something she'd studied. It was more work, but as Ali had said, if something was truly important, she'd find time. "That's not a bad idea, Jake. I'll look into it."

Her phone rang, and she looked down at it. It was the bank, hopefully it was Dawson. "Sorry, I have to take this," she said.

She headed for the exit at the rear of the warehouse as she answered. "This is Emerson."

"Emerson. It's Dawson. I have that information for you. Sorry it took so long to gather the checks."

She sat down on the step by the door to the warehouse. It was the only sunny spot, evading the shade thrown by the main distillery building. "No worries. Who were they to?"

"They weren't paid to companies. They were sent to personal accounts. That doesn't mean they weren't for services. Do you have a pen?"

Emerson flipped the productions schedule over. "Hit me," she said.

"Forty thousand was to a Robert Harding. Twenty thousand to a Kim Lee. Fifteen thousand to a Henry Haverstock."

She began to write them down, but as soon as she heard the surnames, her heart dropped to her stomach.

Holy shit.

Emerson kept writing the names and amounts, trying to fight back the tears.

Anderson Laurence.

Thomas Dunn.

She wrote down about fifteen more names.

"So, that's the list, Emerson. I hate to do this, but we're going to need an explanation within fourteen days as to what these payments are for. You'll get copies of all this in writing to assist you in your investigation."

Fighting down the wave of nausea, she swallowed deeply. "That's a great help, Dawson," she said, her voice too bright, too sharp. "I'll be in touch."

She hung up the call and placed her head on her knees.

What did you do, Dad?

Robert Harding had hounded Olivia, in and out of work, to the point of her breakdown. Disappointed groom or not, he'd shown her sister no care. Kim Lee, the sweet mother of Laura Lee, who had wanted the perfect wedding for her daughter and had threatened them with a lawsuit. Henry Haverstock had unsuccessfully reported them to the city council to see if he could get the distillery's permits revoked.

Goddamn it.

It made no sense, yet it made all the sense in the world. The checks had been made out to the brides and grooms of weddings that were cancelled. Had her father taken out the loan in the guise of renovations to quiet the outrage aimed at the distillery and her sister?

Tears filled her eyes. It was just the kind of thing her father would do to protect them. And he'd probably had a plan for how to get them out of the mess it created.

Why didn't you tell me what you were doing, Dad?

"Hey, Em, I was thinking about that pricing thing?" Jake said, striding toward her. "Wait, what's wrong?" He sat down next to her on the step, and as soon as his arm went around her, she cried into his shoulder.

"Look at this." She handed Jake the list of names and explained to him what their father had done.

"He did it for Liv, didn't he?"

Emerson nodded. "I think so. He was too good a man to be a businessman. We all knew that."

Silence fell between the two of them, each of them churning through their thoughts.

"So, you think the bank is going to recall this loan?" Jake said.

"I do. I talked to Connor about it, and he said—"

"Stop a sec. Connor? The Mercedes parked outside your house?" Confusion reigned in Jake's eyes as he whipped his arm from around her shoulder, making Emerson feel even worse. "And how long have you known?"

Crap. Just crap.

"I'm sorry, Jake. I found out last week there was a loan, and I only found out today what it was for. That was the call I just took. I figured if Dad had paid for new stills, or a deposit on the renovation or something, it would have been a nonissue. I didn't want to worry you, or especially Liv, with it if it was a false alarm."

"Okay, I get the timeline. But how did you think it was okay to discuss it with some guy none of us know before you talked to us?" Jake's hurt tone only served to increase the anxiety and guilt she felt.

She sighed, lifting her face to the sun for a moment. "I'm sorry. Connor is…special. We met a month ago. He's in the liquor distribution business. I needed someone to talk to who wasn't…vested…someone who wasn't going to be hurt by all of this, who could be impartial."

Silence descended again, and Emerson, exhausted, let it. They sat there so long that the sun had shifted, and they were sitting in the shade.

"What happens if they recall it?" Jake asked, quietly.

"Then we have to pay them back. I had a thought last night, which I'm still not sure how I feel about, but we could use funds from the sale of the house to invest in the business, then use those funds to pay back the loan. I don't think that is what Dad would have wanted, but I don't know how he intended to make this right, either."

"Take my share. I'll manage just fine," Jake said.

"We can use mine, too," Emerson said. "It'll be enough without stopping Olivia from buying a place of her own. It's just that I thought…naively probably…that when we took over, it would go a whole lot smoother than this."

Jake threw his arm around her neck. "Yeah. I just created a Best in Class-medal gin, so my side of the business is going fine."

Emerson snorted. "You are an asshole."

"Yup. We'll get through this, Em, I promise."

She just hoped Jake was right.

———

As Connor pulled up in front of Emerson's, he wondered if he shouldn't actually arrange another date for the two of them. The kind where they got dressed up and he took her out. It had been nice to meet one of Emerson's friends. He wondered if Ali had a boyfriend and if they could all go out together. Maybe he could organize something with Blake and Talia. Or do something simpler, maybe. Just the two of them. Like take a hike nearby. Take in the leaves changing color. He could hardly believe it was nearly November. Thanksgiving was just around the corner, and for a moment, he allowed himself to envision them spending it together.

She'd told him she'd be in the garden, so he took the path down the side of the house, through the gate that was kept open with a large gray stone, and to the backyard. Emerson was on her knees, reaching into one of the vegetable beds, digging up the remains of plants that had offered their last vegetables.

"Hey, Emerson," he said loudly to avoid scaring her.

Emerson turned and smiled. "Hey." She tugged off her gardening gloves as she stood up. "How was your day?"

How was your day? His first thought was how that sounded so fucking good. To have someone care enough to ask and genuinely want to listen.

"Good. It got even better when I walked around the corner and saw you on your knees."

At the sweet sound of her laughter, he pulled her into his arms, letting his hands slide down to rest on her butt. When she stepped up on her toes, he kissed her more deeply than he'd anticipated. He couldn't help it.

"I should be offended," she said.

"Only if you don't like the idea of getting on your knees for me at some point. You have a fantastic ass, and I like the view. I call that a win-win."

Emerson screwed up her face. "I don't see how I win. You missed something there."

"You get me, of course," he said, holding his arms out to the side, twisting slightly from left to right.

She shrugged. "I suppose you'll do."

"How was your day?" he asked. "You look tired."

"I have a white wine in the fridge and a black bean chili with cheese dumplings in the oven. I'll tell you over dinner."

Over food and drink, Emerson explained the call from the bank and the conversation with her brother. Once they'd cleaned up and poured out the last of the wine, they moved to the living room.

"I'm happy to meet them," Connor said as they sat down. "Jake and Olivia. Just tell me when and where. I don't want to end up on the wrong side of them because we were private with this. It's not intentional. I was just thinking earlier how it was nice to meet Ali. And I really think you'd get along with Talia, my friend Blake's partner."

"I'd like that. We're starting the process of going through Dad's things tomorrow." Emerson shifted to face him. "Could you pop over before you head back into town?"

"That sounds good. Or I could go work out and then pick up lunch and drive it over for you all. Something social instead of something so personal to your family. That said, I'm also totally willing to help if you want."

Emerson nodded. "Even better. I'd be happy to meet your family, too, you know, if you want me to…or no rush, if you're not ready for that."

Connor took her hand in his. *"'Tis a fucking tangled web we weave when we practice to deceive." Or whatever that Walter Scott quote was.* "I'd like you to meet them, too. It would reassure my mom to see I'm capable of dating." *My dad, on the other hand, might run us both out of the fucking house.*

"You've not had too many girlfriends, then?" Emerson asked with a smile that reassured him she wasn't being irrationally jealous.

He shook his head. "I have a past, for sure, just like everyone does. But I've always been—"

"Discrete? Chivalrous?"

"Yes, at least I hope the women in my past would think so. Loyal, honorable, perhaps too protective at times…I'm only human. What about you, Emerson?"

She tilted her head, her lips pursed as if trying to calculate something. "Probably only three relationships that meant something. High school first love, college, which became long-distance and petered out, and something here a couple of years ago. There were others in between but nothing worth a mention."

For some reason, it reassured him to know something of her past. If they were building what he was hoping, and if at some point he was going to have to tackle his father, it gave him confidence that their relationship would be worth the difficulty he'd face.

"What are you going to do about the bank?" he asked.

"Wait until the letter comes in the mail with the details. I'm sure that will tell us. Worst case, we sell my dad's place and Jake and I both put in one hundred twenty-five thousand each of our shares."

"You seem pretty pragmatic."

Emerson nodded. "You didn't see me crying in the fucking warehouse parking lot."

"Nobody said leaders needed to be strong all the time, Emerson." He reached for her hand, stroking the back of it with his thumb. "You care so deeply about your family, the distillery, the people who work there, this code of quality. These are all great traits."

"Even though I'm also a wishy-washy ISFJ on the Myers-Briggs? I did the test once and it confirmed what I already knew. *Ready to sacrifice* and *happiest behind the scenes*. I have difficulty saying no and quietly take on details others neglect just because they need to get done. I hate the telephone. I'm pushing against my type."

Connor laughed. "You didn't have any problem saying no when I asked you to get out of my seat."

"That's because you were rude and I don't like inconsiderate people."

He pulled her across his lap, happy to see her smile. She'd worried him earlier when she seemed so down. "Have I changed your mind?"

"The jury's still out," she said, kissing him so quickly he almost missed it.

Connor wrapped his arms loosely around her and looked straight into her eyes. They crinkled with mirth as she tried to remain composed. God, she was lovely. How wrong his father was to hate her family so irrationally.

At least he hoped it was irrational. Even if it wasn't, the sins of Paul Dyer should not have to be paid for by his daughter.

"How was the distillery established?" Connor said. "I just realized I don't know anything about its history."

Emerson settled herself against his shoulder. "The short version is that my great-grandfather used to brew what is essentially moonshine, and he and Dad spent their weekends making it. He had this old column still that he'd make this almost deadly high-proof white liquor in. When he passed away, my then-eighteen-year-old Dad asked if he could have it. He played around with it in my grandfather's garage, and eventually bought a pot still made of copper, so he could start to infuse flavors into a neutral ethanol base. He really studied the science of it, but it was the artistry of infusing flavors that he loved the most."

Connor struggled to imagine the man his father had resented so much being a curious young man who cared about his grandfather. And he realized, as he looked at Emerson, that Paul Dyer had passed his love and knowledge on to Emerson without demanding she learn it. For a moment, he wondered how different his relationship with his father could have been if his father had taken the same approach.

"So, how did he turn his hobby into a business?"

"That's the cool part," Emerson said, and he wondered if she realized just how much her face lit up when she talked about her family. "My great-grandfather was a smart man. He set up a trust so that my father could access it when he was twenty-five as long as he'd gone to college. So, Dad graduated, returned to Denver, and waited for the fund so he could set up his distillery. It wasn't a huge fund because my great-grandfather wasn't wealthy by any means, but it was enough to make a start…to put deposits on things, make down payments."

"Did he take a partner or a loan or anything?"

Emerson grinned. "Both. Of a fashion."

"Are they still part of the business? What happened to them?" he asked, aware that his questions were becoming more personal. There had never been a rumor of a silent partner, so she must be talking about his father.

"He married her. My mom's father was a neutral alcohol manufacturer, a supplier my father was thinking of using. Instead, he ended up marrying my mother, and her father gave them the rest of the money they needed as a wedding present. I was born shortly after."

He married her.

Not the explanation he was expecting. "So, there was never anybody else involved?"

"Why are you so interested in whether there were other people?" Emerson's expression turned puzzled. "It's been a family business since the beginning. From the stills in the garage, to me and Jake and Liv there today."

"Sorry," he said, trying to think of a plausible reason she'd believe why he was pushing. "Sometimes I slip back into business mode. It's a hard habit to shake. These are just questions I'd ask people who were going to distribute through us."

Emerson's expression eased. "I totally understand that. I have some pictures from the start of the distillery, if you are interested."

"I'd love to see them," Connor said.

Emerson left the room to get them.

Fuck. He needed answers. For him to be able to speak with his father about Emerson, about their relationship, he needed to know to what extent his father had been involved from the Dyers' perspective. But from what Emerson had told him, his father had no involvement at all. It made no sense.

"Here," Emerson said, coming back to the room. She

handed him a set of photographs. "Don't worry, these are duplicates. There's Mom and Dad on the day the distillery opened."

"You look a lot like her," Connor said. "It's the eyes, I think. And the hair."

Emerson ran her finger along the edge of the photograph wistfully. "I looked like her but acted like my dad… they always said I was the perfect blend of both of them. Jake is more like Dad, Liv is all Mom, and I'm in the middle."

Connor turned to the next photograph. Men were lifting barrels into place in the warehouse. "That's Stan," she said. "He grew up with Dad and was one of the first hires. He still works with us today. Over thirty years of service and barely misses a day."

They skipped through a handful more, Emerson explaining the story behind each one. Some with humor, some etched with nostalgia or a hint of sadness. Connor turned to the final photograph.

"Group shot," she said, holding the last photograph. About fifteen people stood outside the front of the building. "Dad couldn't remember why everyone was assembled outside; he thought it was a celebration of being ready to open or something."

And there, standing at the edge of the photograph, arms crossed in a style Connor recognized, was his father.

Chapter Nine

Emerson tried to move but couldn't. She was delightfully held in place, her back pressed up against Connor's chest. His arm was wrapped around her, his calf over hers.

The warmth of his breath tickled the back of her neck.

If there was a better way to wake up, she couldn't think of it.

Their evening had ended quietly. Connor had suggested a walk, and even though it had gotten dark, it had been nice to be out in the fresh air. When they'd arrived back home, it was late, and so they'd climbed into her bed and fallen asleep together.

But now, with him pressed against her, she hoped she could convince him to make love before she got up to make waffles for breakfast. Not only did she crave the intimacy between the two of them, but deep down, she needed something to ground her, to even out the keel of sadness at what the day held.

Emerson turned in his arms.

"What's got you so squirmy this early?" he mumbled, barely opening his eyes before closing them again.

"You," she whispered. She reached down between them and gently stroked the tip of her finger along his heavy length. "This."

This time Connor opened his eyes, and despite having to blink several times, finally got them to stay open. "You have my attention."

She loved the way his voice sounded like gravel.

Connor wrapped his arm over her and pulled her closer as his erection grew harder and firmer. "Kiss me," he commanded.

Nothing in the world was better than Connor's lips on hers. The way he teased, the way he used his tongue against her, the way he bit her lip gently before releasing it. She loved every playful minute.

His hand squeezed her hip before reaching for her breast. He held it in his hand, his thumb brushing the tip of her nipple, causing her to gasp.

"I love that sound, Emerson. When I do something you like."

"I love the way you make me feel. It's like I have no inhibitions with you."

Connor moved down the bed a little. When he licked her nipple, she gasped again, when he sucked it into his mouth, teasing it with his tongue and teeth, she cried out.

He lifted his head and grinned at her, his blue eyes looking lighter in the hazy morning sunlight. "I like you this way. Uninhibited."

Emerson turned in his arms, arching her back against his chest. It was too early to get on her knees, but the idea that he might slowly ease into her from behind, sliding in inch by delicious inch, caused a flood of tension in her muscles.

Connor placed a line of kisses along her spine, moving upward until he reached her neck. His hand moved between her legs, circling her clit but never applying enough pressure for it to do anything other than tease her.

Pressing back against him, she felt the hard lines of his erection pressing against her butt. She smiled when he slowly ground against her. Slow and steady.

In time to his own action, he slid his finger inside her. Moving back and forth at the same pace.

"Fuck, I could come just doing this," he muttered into her hair.

She understood his meaning. Flutterings of a pending orgasm gathered deep in Emerson. She reached into the drawer of the bedside table and pulled out a condom. "This is good," she murmured, "but this will be better."

Connor ripped the packet and slid it on. Positioning himself behind her, he lifted her thigh slightly, and she placed her hand between her legs to help ease him in. As he inched into her, the delicious burn of being stretched filled her, creating wetness that eased the journey.

When he withdrew, she braced herself, and as she'd envisioned, he entered her more firmly in one smooth thrust.

"So tight," he groaned. "You feel so perfect."

Emerson placed her hand behind her and gripped his hip, encouraging him to take her hard. "Please, Connor."

Needing no further encouragement, Connor spared her nothing. His hand returned to her clit, applying pressure just the way she liked, spreading her wetness until it was a frictionless spiral of pleasure.

"Just like that," she gasped.

Thrusting vigorously, she could feel his muscles clench and release as he pushed in and out, driving deeper until she could no sooner figure out where she ended and he began.

Stars began to circle her vision.

"I'm gonna come any second," he grunted. "It feels too fucking good."

As he began to jerk against her, forcing himself as deep as he could go, she came around him, gasping for air at the intensity.

"Ah, ah," she cried, shuddering.

Connor wrapped his arms around her, pulling her flush with his body, occasionally pushing against her, eking out the last sparks of pleasure.

"Holy shit, Em. I think I just had an out-of-body experience."

The thought that it had been as intense for him as it had been for her made her smile. "It just keeps getting better," she said. "As we get to know each other's bodies."

Connor kissed her cheek and slid out of her. "And I look forward to exploring more of you later. I don't know that I have any energy left after that to work out with. I wish every workout ended quite so spectacularly."

He disappeared into the bathroom, and she shame-lessly watched his ass until the door closed.

"Should I run and get us some breakfast while you get cleaned up?" he asked when he came out again.

Emerson stretched lazily, then dragged her butt out of bed. "I have a surprise for you for breakfast."

Before she could put her robe on, he pulled her in for a hug, nipping playfully at her ear. "Is it you? Do I get to eat you for breakfast?"

Emerson giggled. "No, but I got you the next best thing. Waffles and all the trimmings."

Connor grinned. "Morning sex and waffles. You might be the perfect woman, Emerson."

"I wondered if it fit with your….thing." She waved her hand in the direction of his chest down to his abs.

Connor laughed loudly. He reached for her hand and

kissed her fingers. "It's so cute the way talking about my body flusters you. Plus, I brought my trail bike with me. Three waffles with cream and syrup is about seven hundred calories. I'll burn that in a little over an hour. So, all good."

He took the robe from her hand and helped her put it on, then playfully tapped her ass, sending her in the direction of the kitchen. "Go feed me, woman. Sex with you has me dying of starvation."

Ninety minutes later, she let herself into her father's house with her key. He'd insisted they all keep one and had encouraged them to visit anytime.

This will always be your home, even if you live somewhere else, he'd said.

"Jake, Liv?" she shouted.

"I'm in the living room," Olivia yelled in reply.

Emerson walked into the room to find all the doors to the media center that ran along one wall open. "How had I never noticed that Dad held on to so much junk?"

Olivia, dressed in leggings and a long-sleeved T-shirt, hugged her. "I don't know, but I'm already getting jitters about clearing this stuff out. It's foolish to expect this to all be a mistake and for him to walk back in through the door, right?"

Emerson shook her head. "It's not foolish. I think it's human. If this is too soon, we don't—"

"No," Olivia said firmly. "I want to start this process. I'm just being silly."

Emerson reached for her sister's hand. "Not silly, either. I'm sure we're going to find all kinds of stuff that make us pause today. He was a sentimental man. I'm sure there are going to be all kinds of mementos."

Olivia nodded. "I guess so. Jake is out in the garage and toolshed; he's got four tarps in the backyard. Keep. Sell. Donate. Toss. We figured we'd each take an area and give it a go. Then go through the piles together and divide up what we want to keep or sell."

"Sounds good to me," Emerson said. There wasn't a ton of room in her own home. She had all the furniture she needed and was happy for Liv to take it all to set up her own place. There were some personal items she'd love, like their grandfather's fountain pen that had become her father's. After their mother's death, most of her things had been divided by the three of them, but her father had been reluctant to part with her engagement and wedding rings. Perhaps the engagement ring should pass to Jake, but she'd love her mother's wedding ring if Olivia was okay with it. "I'll make a start on the office," she said.

"Urgh, you are welcome to it," Olivia said. "I went in there to clean and walked straight out again. It's a disaster."

Emerson walked down the hallway, running her fingers along the wood paneling below the rail. It was something they'd all done so many times, she swore she could feel the ridges. She pulled the door open and immediately understood Olivia's point.

Books on steam engines, Victorian architects, and water wheels. The walls were covered with sepia photographs and line drawings in graying ink of antique equipment and machinery. Her mother had always said stepping back to his office was like stepping back a hundred years in history. Emerson always felt there was something magical in the technical drawings rolled up in cardboard tubes, like hidden treasure to be discovered.

The rest of the house had been decorated by their mother, but this was all him.

Emerson began by opening the window to let some air into the musty space. She took down the yellowing net curtains and could see Jake carrying a large and obviously heavy box from the toolshed.

The bookshelves were likely the easiest place to start, and she began to pull books off and place them in piles in the hallway.

Keep. Sell. Donate. Toss. She'd follow Jake's designations.

It was tempting to run her fingers over every book's cover, to take a quick flick through the contents. But she knew that as soon as she did, she would end up taking days. Dust left an outline on the shelves of where the books had been, a clear marker of the past and present.

Everything seemed suddenly temporary in the big scheme of things. Even this house.

Her father's legacy was the distillery, and he'd trusted her to ensure it stayed in the family, no matter what it took. She couldn't let him down, no matter the personal cost.

Papers, crammed between books and within their pages, fluttered to the ground. Notes and doodles of designs for stills, ratios, and combinations of flavors. They were everywhere. Emerson began a pile on her father's desk. All of it should belong to Jake.

There was a personal laptop on his desk, and Emerson placed it in a pile of things to take home with her. She already had his business laptop at home, but there may be family photographs and other things they'd want to keep on there.

On top of the bookshelf sat two large banker boxes. Emerson pulled the stool over to the shelf. Balanced precariously, she reached for the large box and slid it toward the edge of the shelf. The weight of it threw off her balance when she took the full brunt of it.

"Shit," she gasped as she wobbled with it in her hands. Emerson placed the box on one of the lower shelves before she climbed off the stool. As she transferred it to her father's desk, she noticed her mother's handwriting on the lid. It must be her things.

Emerson opened the box and was immediately hit by the faintest trace of her mother's perfume, forcing her to bite down on her tongue to prevent tears from forming. Everything still felt so very raw. Even though her mother had been gone for fifteen years, her father's death had opened up old wounds.

There were envelopes of letters and plastic wallets of documents. Today was probably *not* the day to go through them.

She was just about to reach for the first wallet when she heard the doorbell ring and then the front door open.

"Hey, you must be Olivia. I'm Connor."

Shit. Emerson glanced down at her watch. It was lunch already. And he was here as promised. She slammed the lid back on the box. The keepsakes would definitely be better to tackle on a different day.

She clambered over the piles that had begun to grow near the door and down the hallway. "Hey," she said, as Olivia and Connor shook hands. "Liv, Connor. Connor, Liv," she said.

Both of them looked at her and laughed. "I think we figured that out, Em," Olivia said drolly. "Pleased to meet you, Connor."

Connor carried a couple of bags in one hand, and he held them out to Olivia. "Emerson said to bring lunch."

"Emerson?" Olivia said, curiously. "Thank you. I'll take the lunch *Emerson* thoughtfully asked you to pick up into the kitchen."

Emerson tried to bite back a grin at the confusion on Connor's face. "You don't go by Emerson, do you?"

Then she laughed. "Not around people who know me well, but as I said, you were being an asshole when I told you not to shorten it."

Connor pulled her playfully toward him and kissed her. "Are you ever going to let me live that down?"

With pursed lips, she shook her head. "Probably not. In case you hadn't noticed, I kind of like the way you say Emerson."

He moved his lips to her ear. "In case you hadn't noticed, I occasionally slip and call you Em when I'm deep inside you."

"Now, *that's* a win-win."

He smudged his thumb along her cheek. "You had a little dust," he said, his voice rough at the edges like frayed rope.

"Is he here?" The voice of her brother boomed from the kitchen. There was a moment's pause and then peals of laughter.

"Ready to meet Jake?" she asked.

"For you, anything."

For the first time in his life, Connor deliberately and carefully got his numbers wrong.

He sat back and looked at the report for his father on possible acquisitions. Everything in it was meticulously researched, conservatively estimated, and hit all of his father's objectives.

Except Dyer's Gin Distillery. There was no way he was going to let his father get his hands on Emerson's distillery.

No one number was hugely inaccurate. But the sum of every positive number being rounded down, and every negative one being rounded up was just enough to put Dyer's in the middle of the pack with at least three other distilleries looking better. If he could put his father off the scent, it would solve all his problems.

With Dyer's out of the picture as a possible asset for acquisition, there would be no conflict of interest with regards to him dating Emerson. And he was deliberately tuning out the irony that the entire exercise to make it look that way was a giant conflict of interest.

He flipped to his Excel spreadsheet and looked at the real numbers, which told a very different story. They had space to expand, capacity, a loyal and capable leadership team with Emerson, Liv, and Jake. They had the combined skills to run the place well and create new products.

The lunch he'd had with Jake and Olivia had proved that.

Jake had been thrilled to see old drawings and papers of his father's that Emerson had found in the office. He talked excitedly about some of the formulas and how he could combine them with flavor profiles he was already working on.

And learning so much more about Olivia, he could see why Paul Dyer had been so protective of her. She was a whip-smart sweetheart. She mentioned plans and campaigns she'd thought of. Bright, innovative approaches. He found out she was responsible for the Medallion branding he'd admired.

They'd talked about future plans, such as a canning line for Dyer's on-the-go mixer products and a range of spin-off items for the distillery store.

As a businessman, he would have invested in them in a heartbeat.

But as a man halfway to falling head over heels…

Perhaps he was being a fool.

Perhaps the years of holding out on a serious relationship had been for a reason. Perhaps Emerson had clouded his vision.

But he knew that wasn't true, could feel the truth down to his bones. He knew full well what Dyer's was worth…he just felt Emerson was worth so much more than all of it. The fact that he didn't understand why his father was in the goddamn photograph when there was no record of him in the distillery's history bothered him, but not as much as it maybe should have.

They'd juggled the weekend. After helping her work through more of her father's things on Saturday, he'd helped her decorate her home for Halloween. They'd hung small ghosts from the tree in the front garden, set gravestones around its base, and laid cobwebs and black plastic spiders over the bushes beneath the windows. Later that afternoon, he'd driven the two of them back downtown to his condo, where they'd showered, together, and went out for dinner. On Sunday morning, he'd dropped her off at the distillery while he'd gone to work out and collected her when she was done. They'd spent the afternoon hiking before returning to the condo, where she'd helped him prep his meals for the week ahead and had even eaten one for dinner.

How is it? he'd asked.

She'd shrugged. *Nothing a bottle of sriracha can't fix.*

After they'd eaten, they'd made love on his sofa as the sun went down. And all he wanted to do was watch the sun go down over Emerson's naked body for the rest of his life.

He adjusted himself, suit trousers not being the best material for hiding the makings of a hard-on.

Once the documents were printed and he'd gathered his wits, Connor made his way up to his father's office on the floor above his. Cameron was in the office next door, with his chair facing away from Connor. He appeared to be in the middle of a phone call, with the hand gesturing he was doing, which was perfect. The last thing he needed was Cameron trying to force his way into the meeting.

"Dad," he said, tapping on the door as he pushed it open.

His father motioned for him to take a seat as he said goodbye to whomever he was speaking to on the phone.

Connor could hear the faint strains of Cameron in the

office next door. Why had he never noticed that before? He wondered how easily his own voice carried into Cameron's office.

His father slapped the phone down on the desk. "What have you got for me?" he asked, holding out his hand for the report.

Connor handed it to him. "This is the updated report on potential acquisition targets. Do you have time for me to take you through it?"

"CliffsNotes version, please."

"Flip it open, and we can dive in. We looked at thirteen assets. Seven from our original list, five new adds, and Dyer's, as requested."

Donovan mumbled in agreement. "Good, good."

"Page three has the list of criteria and scoring process. Read through it and tell me if it makes sense."

Connor leaned back in the chair. His father always did better with guided reading rather than Connor explaining it verbally to him.

"What's this?" Donovan asked, pointing to one of the columns.

"Estimated bottle production. We don't know for sure beyond publicly available sources from news interviews, company websites, et cetera, what the exact production volumes are for the privately owned distilleries...such as Dyer's, for example."

His father sniffed at the mention of the name. "And Paul Dyer is bound to have inflated the numbers on their site."

Connor didn't correct him that he'd gotten the number from Emerson when she'd been reviewing the production schedule while eating breakfast on Sunday. He'd knocked ten percent off the production volumes in the report. Let his father think the number was actually inflated when it was understated, he'd only think even worse of the company.

"This is good, Connor. Where are the recommendations?"

Connor flicked through his own copy of the document. "Page thirteen. All the backup is in the appendix."

Donovan flicked to the page, studied it for a moment, then closed it and slapped it down on the table. "Dyer's goes to the top of the list," he said, suddenly.

"Sorry, what?" he asked, his skull feeling like a giant rock had landed on it.

"Dyer's. I want it. And word on the street is we could get a great fucking deal for it."

Emerson. Shit. Whatever his father knew had put a glint in his eye.

Play the fucking game, Connor.

"What's the word you heard?" Did his voice sound tinny? Jesus Christ. He'd walked up those stairs ten minutes ago convinced he'd done a good enough job at hiding Dyer's success, and without even reading the presentation thoroughly, his father wanted the company anyway. He needed to find his poker face. "I know I was pushing to acquire Dyer's earlier, but it doesn't make sense looking at these numbers."

"They're about to owe the bank. Loan gone wrong. Misappropriated funds. Who knows? Paul Dyer always was a crook. He stole from me, who knows who else he'd steal from."

What the fuck. Dad knows already.

"Cameron caught wind of it through a friend at the bank," he continued. "Apparently, Dyer borrowed some money to renovate and then siphoned it away somewhere."

Man. Emerson was going to lose her shit when she found out his father knew. Wait, what was he saying? Emerson would never know because he couldn't tell her about any of this. Fuck, how could he explain all this to her?

"I don't want to move yet," Donovan continued. "I want to wait until the deadline for the repayment has passed. Those Dyer kids will be either short of cash or screwed completely. Either way, I'll get a better price than if we go in now. Knowing that, can you rework these figures on the company value and risk? I want the lowest of lowballs."

Connor stood. "Got it," he said as he walked toward the door. The sooner he was out of there, the less chance his father had of realizing something was wrong. "I'll get it back to you as soon as possible."

He had no intention of stealing Emerson's company from beneath her, but he had to think through what he could do to distract his father.

"Oh, and Connor, Cameron is going to need to see this."

"Well, I'll let you take him through it," he said without turning around. He needed a plan, time for him to think through the options. There had to be a way to get his father off the fucking topic.

He pulled the door open wide and let it close loudly behind him. Not exactly a slam, nothing deliberate, but satisfying all the same.

He jogged the stairs down to his office, and when he stepped inside, he did something he never did. He locked the door.

Perching on the edge of his desk with his back to the door, he took in the sun going down over the city and thought of Emerson again.

How far was he prepared to go to keep Dyer's Gin Distillery in Emerson's hands?

All the way.

The answer came unbidden.

His emotional response was way ahead of any intellectual considerations. But even thinking it through, he still came to the same conclusion. It didn't really matter what the sacrifice was. If Finch Liquor Distribution only bought the second most attractive asset, it was still a fucking good deal. The greater concern was if his father approached Emerson directly for a deal. She'd never look at Connor the same way again. It would ruin what the two of them were building.

Perhaps he could do some more digging on the second best company instead, blow them up, ever so slightly inflate the numbers to get his father's interest. And Cameron would never go into the depth of research Connor did to find him out.

Or perhaps he should come clean to his father, tell him about Emerson, and quit before he got fired.

Quit?

Could he really walk away from everything he'd worked for, everything he'd been promised? He could get another job...but what if it weren't in Denver? He'd never be able to pull Emerson away from the distillery.

So that was the question he needed to answer.

If it came down to it, was he really prepared to risk it all for Emerson?

Chapter Ten

"What are you up to?" Connor asked as he placed a glass of wine next to her elbow.

Emerson looked up from the laptop she'd just switched on. The sun was setting over the Denver skyline in a breathtaking display of deep purple and orange, but the view couldn't match Connor. He was dressed in shorts and a sleeveless T-shirt, a towel thrown casually around his neck.

Emerson couldn't resist a study of his arms…they were just so…capable.

"You keep looking at me like that, and I might just have to get a workout in some other way," Connor said, humor dancing through his words. "Want to burn six hundred calories with me?"

Emerson laughed. "I don't want to know how much work six hundred calories would be."

Connor moved her hair over her shoulder and kissed the side of her neck. "I think it's sex twice on the kitchen counter and a blow job in the shower…give or take a few calories."

She leaned back in the chair and looked up at him. "I

feel like *I'd* burn more of the calories during the blow job. All you'd have to do is stand there."

"Are you negotiating with me again?"

Emerson shrugged. "Just stating the facts as I see them."

"Fine. A sixty-nine on the rug. Equal calories."

"Go. Go to the gym," Emerson said, shooing him away. "Put in some work and you might be in half-decent shape by Christmas."

He lifted his top to reveal his perfectly crafted abs. "You think these need work?"

"Oh my god. Stop," she said, reaching for the hem to pull it down. "You are insufferable."

Connor laughed. "Okay. I'll stop. What are you up to?"

"It's Dad's personal laptop. I'm going through it to see if there's anything we need to keep on here."

"You want me to stick around? If you need me to, I can skip the gym," he said, placing a hand on her shoulder.

Emerson shook her head. "I'll be fine. You go ahead. I'll start dinner if it becomes too much."

From her seat in the armchair by Connor's living room window, she could see the bag of groceries they'd picked up from the store down the street. Steak, sweet potatoes to make wedges, and the fixings for a salad.

"Okay, I'll be back in an hour." He kissed the top of her head before heading to the building's gym.

She opened the laptop to be greeted by a password screen. Despite warnings to her father, he'd stuck to the same old passwords, arguing that he'd forget if he had too many. The first, a combination of their mother's date of birth and the name of the restaurant they'd gone to on their first date, didn't work. The second time was the charm.

1son2ake3via

The last three letters of his children's names in the order they'd been born.

The desktop was intimidating, folder after folder with names that really only made sense to her father. Unease shivered down her spine. This was her father's private property. For a moment, she wondered if she should simply close the laptop and put it away forever. It felt more personal than the books on the shelf in his office.

She sat back in her chair and picked up the glass of wine Connor had left her, a robust Shiraz from Australia's Barossa Valley. She held it to the light, taking a moment to appreciate the ruby hue. It was thick, syrupy, and when she put her nose to the glass, she could smell the jammy, plum aromas. It tasted as good as it smelled, and it was tempting to simply retreat to the sofa with a good book.

She placed the glass back on the table and decided to start with his email. There were messages from old friends, random emails from stores he liked to shop at, and newsletters from industry organizations he'd been a part of.

Some she typed out brief responses for, others she unsubscribed to and then wondered why she'd bothered. It felt as though they were loose ends of her father's life that needed sewing up.

The next email was from the insurance company, and Emerson wondered why it hadn't been sent to his business email address. She opened it.

Mr. Dyer, I repeat my apologies that we are unable to help you further. We have read all of the information you have provided, and while we are saddened to hear about your daughter, we are unable to act. This issue is now closed.

Emerson's heart began to race, and she took a gulp of wine.

She opened the thread of emails. Twenty, maybe thirty of them. The urge to just get to the punchline nudged her on.

The first few were her father making the claim. He'd asked for some clarity on the claims form, some other questions about timeline and process…the usual.

But the fifth took her breath away.

Please find attached the papers emailed to us by Olivia Dyer, on your behalf, for the purposes of the assessment of the policy three years ago. As outlined, the distillery, warehouse, and other buildings are included. The events hall was not and is, as such, not considered insured by this office.

Emerson slumped back in her chair.

Oh, God. Dad. Liv.

She opened the file, already fearful that she knew the answer. When Olivia had sent the documents required, they were all there…except the events hall.

They had no insurance. There was no coverage for the weddings they'd had to cancel. There was no damage cover to repair the building.

Her breathing shallowed as she fought to push the panic that was rising back down. She checked the date of the final email, the first one she had seen. Her father had received the email thirty-six hours before he'd gone to the bank to take out the loan. Five days after Liv's breakdown.

So that's why you didn't tell us what was going on.

Liv had been causing them all so much worry with her erratic behavior and deep depression. Their father hadn't told them because Liv would have felt it was her fault for sending the papers in incorrectly, no matter how much they would have reassured her.

Her heart ached for her father working through it all alone. The desperation he must have felt. Tears burned her eyes.

Those last few days before his heart attack, her father had looked more tired than usual. Dark circles had ringed his eyes. When Emerson had asked him what was wrong, he'd told her he thought he was coming down with something. She'd tried to encourage him to go home, to take a few days off and get some rest.

But he'd seemed more committed to his work than ever.

They'd argued about the production schedule, him trying to push for more production, her pleading for the investment they'd needed so badly.

Oh, God. Their argument.

She'd piled on when she should have been trying to lighten his load.

He'd been carrying the burden alone, trying to figure out how to fix things. And the stress of it had killed him.

Oh, Daddy.

She let the tears come. There was no point fighting them. She cried for Liv. She cried for her dad. And out of self-pity, she cried for herself. How on earth could they move forward? She couldn't lie to Jake and Olivia about a non-existent insurance payout.

She'd have to tell them both.

Perhaps together was better.

It isn't the end of the business. It isn't the end of the business. It isn't the end of the business.

She repeated it over and over.

They had the means to pay back the loan from the sale of the house. It wouldn't go under. And if she had to sell her house, the business could have whatever equity was left in it. They'd stay afloat, and if Olivia altered her plans slightly, they might have enough for a fourth still. They could make it work.

There were also emails to the brides and grooms whose weddings had been cancelled. Deeply personal emails from her father, begging them to stop, offering them cash. Some of them had been kind in their acceptance. Others had argued and bargained to get more.

The shock left her cold, and she wandered to the

bedroom to grab her sweater. A pile of Connor's laundry sat on a chair, waiting to be put away. There was a hoodie, one he wore to go to the gym. She pulled it on, and it smelled of his laundry detergent.

It smelled of comfort.

The sleeves were too long, so she pushed them over her wrists. Suddenly tired, she sat down on the bed. The month felt as though it were a hundred days long. Tomorrow was Halloween, but the excitement she'd felt for her favorite holiday, second only to Christmas, was gone.

She slipped beneath the covers and closed her eyes, thinking of her father until sleep claimed her.

"Em, sweetheart…are you okay?" Connor's voice sounded as if it were down a deep well. "Emerson?"

Groggily, she opened her eyes. "What time is it?" she muttered.

"A little after eight. I just got back. Have you been crying? Come here." Connor pulled her to him, and she put her arms around him. "What happened?"

Emerson told him the whole story. No tears this time because she had none left. When she was done, he looked as shocked as she felt.

"I'm so sorry, Em. For what it's worth, I have huge respect for your father, trying to do what was best for Olivia."

"Me too. It didn't need to kill him, though. And he could have told me." She looked at Connor. "Why *didn't* he tell? Did he not think I would have supported him? Helped him?"

"From what I know about your family, your dad remained your father first and the owner of a company second. He took care of you before he took care of business. He's the complete opposite of my dad. Believe me, I think I'd have preferred the way your dad did it, Emerson."

Deep down, she understood what Connor was trying to say, but pain rose to the surface faster than understanding. "If he didn't think I was ready or able to help him with this, how on earth did he think I was ready to run this distillery? He wants me to be the glue, but I don't know how. I'm so tired right now."

Connor pulled her in even tighter, and she realized his skin was damp from his workout. "These are wobbles, Em. You know how to run the distillery, you know how to organize people, products, logistics. You know how to get the best out of people. You know this industry. All of that you know."

He gripped her chin and tilted her head to look at him. "What you are dealing with right now is a lot. In the last three months, your father passed away, you inherited a business with some baseline issues. You've had to deal with probate and changing everything to do with the business into your name. You've dealt with wills, his house, your grief. Olivia. Your father's request to be the glue. It's no wonder you're fucking tired."

Emerson shrugged. "Maybe. As I was falling to sleep, I was wondering if we shouldn't find someone with more experience...someone who could navigate all this with a little more grace than I seem to be able to."

Connor shook his head. "No. That's just exhaustion talking. Dyer's is yours. But if I can point out one thing, in the spirit of being open with you. You're doing exactly what your dad did. You are carrying it all alone. Don't you think Jake and Olivia will feel the same way you do now if you don't involve them, talk to them? They're smart, Em. And I know Olivia has had some issues. But I don't think she's as fragile as you and Jake currently treat her."

His words struck her heart. God, she'd been so stupid. She was mad at her father for doing exactly what she was doing.

"I hadn't thought of it that way," Emerson said.

"That's because you aren't as clever as me," Connor said with a smile.

"I don't smell as bad as you, either."

Connor laughed and nuzzled the side of her neck. "Nothing smells as good as you, Em. Want to shower with me?" He stood and offered her his hand.

"Sure," she said, letting him lead her into the bathroom, knowing full well he'd take care of her.

———

"Perhaps when we're out of the shower you can put this back on," Connor said, tugging at the hem of his hoodie. "Like, just this. No underwear."

His comment brought a smile to her face, just as he'd intended.

When he'd returned from the gym, he'd called her name. He hadn't been immediately worried when she hadn't answered. But when he walked into the bedroom and found her on his side of the bed, tucked up as if to protect herself, tear tracks on her face, and his hoodie keeping her warm, his heart had skipped a beat.

Intuition told him that the reason for the upset must have been something on her father's laptop. And when she'd woken, Emerson had confirmed his fears. She'd also confirmed something else he'd already started to believe. Paul Dyer had been a good man. Everything he'd done, his every action, had been to protect Olivia and to look out for those who had been affected by the wedding venue damage.

Once in the bathroom, he helped Emerson undress. He pulled his hoodie gently over her head before laying it on the counter. The care continued as he stripped her of the rest of her clothing until she was naked before him.

But his first thought wasn't anything remotely sexual. It was to look after her, to bring color back to her cheeks.

Connor turned on the shower, putting his hand under the spray to make sure it was the right temperature. He moved two towels within reach before stepping out of his own clothes.

Connor opened the door to the shower wide, but Emerson didn't move. "Are you okay, Em?"

Somehow, she'd become his everything, and he wasn't quite sure how. It had happened quickly, like a thunderbolt. And she'd chosen him as her rock during what was probably the most stressful period of her life. She'd become his lover, his friend, and she trusted him as her confidant.

"I love you," Emerson said suddenly.

It was as if she'd read his mind. They were both naked, as vulnerable as human beings could get, as the shower softly steamed up the bathroom.

"More than dry chocolate brownie with melty ice cream?" He took her hands in his, kissing each knuckle in turn.

"It looks like it."

"More than General Tso's Chicken from the Cleveland mall?"

"That *still* might be pushing it," she said. "But you're definitely a solid second."

Connor slid his hands to her cheeks, holding her gently because she was the most precious thing in his life. "I'll take melty ice cream because I love you, too, Em."

Their mouths lingered against each other for a moment, and Connor knew they were at a tipping point. While he loved the feel of her body as it moved against his, he wanted to care for her more.

"Come on, shower," he said, leading her under the steamy spray.

Emerson tilted her head back and let the water sluice through her hair.

Connor reached for his shampoo and poured a generous amount in his hand. At some point, they should probably get around to leaving things at each other's homes for convenience instead of always having to carry things like a toothbrush with them.

"Step out of the spray a little," he said, and she followed his instruction.

He ran the shampoo through the lengths of her hair before returning to her scalp to lather it. In all honesty, he had no idea if he was doing it right; he'd never washed anyone else's hair before. But from hearing Emerson's soft moan as he used his fingertips against her scalp, he figured he was probably doing okay.

When he was satisfied it was soapy enough, he nudged her back under the spray. His dick didn't get the whole "caring" message as it sprung to life as he watched rivers of soap bubbles run down her breasts.

Emerson lifted her arms to help rinse the soap from her hair, making her nipples stand to fucking attention.

Connor turned away for a moment and busied himself with quickly washing his own hair. As he stepped beneath the water to rinse it, Emerson glanced down at his dick and bit her lip.

"Stop," he warned. He leaned forward and stole a gentle kiss. "I'm trying to be a gentleman."

He repeated the steps he'd taken with the shampoo but using conditioner this time, and as she rinsed, he grabbed his body wash. She was going to smell like him, he realized as he poured a generous dollop into his palm.

"You don't need to do this, Connor," Emerson said, turning to face him.

Connor applied the soap to her shoulders and arms. "I may not need to, but I want to. I really do love you. I want to take care of you. I can't describe it any simpler than that. This is way more than simply sex. It always has been."

He soaped her breasts, trying his damnedest to ignore her perfectly pert and erect nipples and the appearance of goosebumps on her skin as he gently washed between her legs.

"Connor," she gasped, moving gently against him.

Unable to resist, he placed his lips against hers, capturing her sigh. "Not yet," he murmured.

Quickly, he finished his own ablutions, and once they were both rinsed, he wrapped Emerson in a large, soft white towel. It swamped her frame, and he took the time to dry her thoroughly.

While he dried himself, Emerson reached for the hand towel next to the sink and pressed it against her hair.

"If you want to slip my hoodie back on, I'll cook—"

"Make love to me, Connor," Emerson said, dropping the towel that covered her body.

Fuck, she was set to test his resolve. "As much as that would be my absolute pleasure, you've had a fucking huge shock tonight. It's going to take a lot to process, I'm sure. Let's get some food in you and—"

"What if it's not your food I want in me?" She stepped up to him, placing her hands on his chest. "What if I just want your warmth and comfort?"

Connor cricked his neck before looking at her. He should stand firm. Her emotions had been running high, and she was likely exhausted.

But then she moved her hands to his shoulders and stepped into his space, until her naked breasts were pressed up against his chest.

"Fuck, Em. I wanted to care for you."

Emerson took his hand in hers and led it between her

legs where she was already soaked for him. "Then care for me," she whispered.

Unable to resist any longer, Connor lifted her into his arms and perched her on the edge of the bathroom counter, her legs open to him. His knees landed on her towel as he dropped to the floor. With his eyes on hers, he licked her gently, once, then again. Teasing her with his tongue.

"Harder," Emerson cried.

Connor stopped immediately. "Oh, no, babe. You don't get to drive. You asked me to take care of you like this. I'm going to decide what that involves."

Emerson bit down on her bottom lip and watched his mouth as he placed it on her very center. "Connor," she gasped.

Running his tongue down the length of her, he tasted more of her sweet flavor. His dick throbbed beneath his own towel, and he grabbed it in a firm fist for a moment to ease the ache.

He placed one hand on her thigh, holding her open, and slid one finger inside her. Fuck, she was so wet for him. It was a wonder. He increased the pace of his thrust, increased the friction of his tongue on her clit.

Emerson grabbed his hair, and he didn't fucking care. Let her ride his face into oblivion. If that's what she needed to get over the day she'd had, he was totally here for it.

"Oh, Connor, I'm…"

Her words petered out, but he could feel her as her channel fluttered around his finger, as her body shuddered.

Connor stood and placed her legs around his waist before he picked her up and carried her to the bedroom. When he slid into her, he wanted to be in the bed he was coming to think of as theirs.

He laid her down gently, her head on his pillow. She fit

perfectly…in his bed and his life. Her skin was soft beneath his fingertips as he ran them along the side of her face. "You okay?" he asked. If an orgasm was all she needed from him tonight, he'd be happy with that. "Do you want more or rest?"

"More," she whispered.

Once sheathed in a condom, he climbed between her legs, letting his weight rest on her. "I love you," he said, sliding her hair back from her face, letting the words dance around his tongue.

Emotions filled him at the knowledge she felt the same way about him, too. It was like the warmth of the bright summer sun on his skin…comforting and nurturing.

Their lips met, and Connor kissed Emerson deeply until they were both breathless and Emerson squirmed beneath him. He reached between them for his dick, edging it into her fractionally and slowly.

The tension he felt in his balls was almost unbearable, but he wanted to possess Emerson's very being. He wanted her desperate and begging for release.

"Connor, please," Emerson cried out, arching her hips in a bid to receive more of him.

"Slowly, babe," he grunted, aware of how deep his voice sounded.

He inched back and then slid forward until his dick throbbed, a pulsing sensation, like he was coming without ejaculating. He held still for a moment.

Emerson wrapped her arms around him, pulling on him to go deeper, but she was no match for his strength. He simply held his position over her and pinned her hip to the bed with one arm.

"Argh," she cried in frustration. Her eyes were filled with fire, a definite change from the glassy look she'd had when he'd returned from the gym.

Connor edged back and slid in a little deeper, knowing

his own willpower was going to give soon. She was so warm and wet and welcoming, and he was so on edge.

"I love you," he repeated.

"Then make love to me," Emerson said, exasperation filling her words.

Connor kissed her again. "In good time, Em."

He began to move in a steady rhythm, back and forth. Emerson was so wet there was barely any friction, just the delicious pressure of her as she clenched around him.

He slipped his hand behind her knee and opened her wider, allowing his hips to sink farther until he was so fucking deep inside her. Bottoming out on every stroke, hitting Em in the place she loved most, the spot guaranteed to get her off.

She was close to coming again. He could feel it.

His own orgasm was building, hurtling down his spine to the finish line.

"The way you grip me," he gasped as it started to become more sensation than he could bear. "How wet you get. Fuck."

"I'm so close," Emerson cried.

"Me too. Let go, Em, I've got you."

As Emerson came around him, he gave up all attempts at slow. He plunged inside her, filling her fully, pounding deep. Fuck, the feeling was intense. He'd never felt anything like it.

His orgasm hit him, thrust after thrust of near-painful spasms as he emptied so completely inside her.

And as he finally came down, with his head in the crook of Emerson's neck, their limbs wrapped tightly around each other, he realized that not only did he have her, but she had him.

Chapter Eleven

Connor pulled up outside his mom's place and killed the engine. As expected, Derek's car wasn't in the driveway. He wanted to catch his mom alone.

He jogged up the steps and knocked on the door. Alyssa answered a few moments later, wearing a paint-smudged apron and a streak of white paint across her cheek.

"Connor, what a pleasant surprise. What are you doing out of work so early?"

He kissed her cheek as he stepped inside the hallway, cluttered with coats and shoes. "I wanted to see you...well, I wanted to talk to you."

She closed the door. "Of course, head on into the kitchen. I just brewed some coffee. Help yourself and pour me one while I go deal with my painting stuff."

Connor wandered into the kitchen. The mottled marble counter was spotless, a complete contrast to the hallway. The cups were still in the cupboard above the toaster, and he grabbed them before pouring two mugs of steaming hot coffee. They took it the same. Black and strong.

Alyssa wandered into the kitchen wearing a pair of slim jeans and a bright yellow sweater. "You don't look old enough to be my mom," he said, and Alyssa blushed.

"Okay, what did you do that you need to kick it off with compliments? Do you need bail?"

Connor laughed. "If I needed bail, I wouldn't be here asking you in person. And can't a son compliment his mother once in a while?"

She fluffed her hair. "Fine, yes, I don't age. I'm Denver's very own Dorian Gray." She took the cup he offered and sat on the stool on the opposite side of the kitchen counter. "What's up?"

Man, where to start. He'd tackle the easiest part first. "I met someone," he blurted.

His mom reached across the counter and grabbed his hand. "You did? Tell me about her." Excitement lit up her face, and he decided to let her have her moment of enjoyment before he told her the bad news.

"Her name's Emerson. She's brunette, but it has hints of red and gold if it catches the light right. And pretty brown eyes that crinkle when she smiles. She hates my meal prep food but doesn't mind when I disappear to swim or bike or run or whatever."

"I'm not going to swoon over the way you noticed the colors in her hair even though that's the cutest thing ever. Do you have pictures?"

Connor pulled out his phone. He'd taken some pictures of them, of her, when they'd been hiking. "Here." He pushed the phone toward his mom.

"Oh, Connor, she looks lovely. But more than that, the way you look at her…" She put her hand over her mouth, and he couldn't decide if she was in shock or about to cry.

"Okay, Mom…it's not that big a deal."

"It's a big deal, Connor. Does she make you happy?"

He rolled his eyes at that. "Do you think I'd be telling you about her if she didn't?"

His mom grinned. "Right. Yes. Of course. How did the two of you meet?"

He told her about the flight, about ending up in the same seat.

"Kismet," she declared. "I always thought you'd find the woman you were meant to marry when you weren't looking."

"I'm going to pretend you didn't just leap straight to the M-word."

Alyssa gestured with her hand as if brushing him away. "Oh, shush. What does she do?"

Connor paused, and momentarily the joy he'd felt at telling his mom slipped. "Her name's Emerson Dyer."

"Oh, what a lovely name, and she does what for…oh. Oh. Like *the* Dyers?"

He nodded. "Yeah. And after Paul Dyer's death, she's *the* Dyer."

Alyssa cupped her mug and took a large gulp. "I'm taking it that your father has no idea about this yet?"

"That would be correct."

For a moment, they were both silent.

"Do you love her?" his mother asked.

"That's the easiest part in all of this. Yes. Yes, I do." After her bathroom declaration forty-eight hours earlier, he'd never been more certain of anything. His feelings for her had been growing at such a strong and sudden pace, he'd struggled to articulate it. But when he'd come home from the gym to find her in bed, in his hoodie, her tear-stained face on his pillow, he'd realized he'd do just about anything to fix whatever had upset her.

And watching her rally to hand out candy the previous evening had solidified the idea that he loved her. He could see the two of them, handing out candy to children together for the next fifty years.

"And what's her take on this feud between your fathers?"

Connor shook his head. "That's the weirdest part of all this. She knows nothing about it. We've talked at length about the beginnings of the distillery, and she has all these photographs and information about the start. I saw Dad in one photograph, otherwise there's no mention of him. Emerson is completely unaware that Dad has hated them all these years."

Her mother frowned. "That is the oddest thing."

Connor walked around the kitchen counter and pulled out the other stool. "Now, I don't know how to tell her that I knew about her family before we met. And I made this proposal to Dad that we divest from mass liquor into more artisanal products. Dad got on board with the idea, but now he actually wants to buy Dyer's because he heard they are in financial difficulty."

His mother placed her hand on his knee. "Oh, Connor. And are they in trouble?"

He took a sip of his coffee. It was bitter, acrid even, as it went down his throat. "Nothing that will take them out of business, but they've taken some knocks, not least that Paul died."

"That must be a lot for Emerson," his mother said.

Connor nodded. "It is. And you know the craziest thing?"

"What's that?"

"From what I've learned about him, I actually really like Paul Dyer. Did you ever meet him?"

Alyssa stood and wandered to look out of the kitchen

window. "I didn't. I met your father four months after Paul had stolen the company from him. Two or three months later, I was pregnant. I was still twenty-one, and Donovan swept me off my feet. I didn't see then just how bitter he was." She turned around. "I've often thought of Paul as the other person in our marriage. I think that's the reason we didn't last."

"In what way?"

His mom pursed her lips. "I don't know, Connor. Your father grieved the loss of the company something fierce and was consumed with working every hour God sent to *beat* Paul." She put air quotes around *beat*. "He'd spend so much time talking about how different his life would be if Paul hadn't taken everything that mattered to him."

"I can only imagine how bad it was back then, that it still bothers him right now."

Alyssa nodded. "I always felt like I was second fiddle. I sometimes think he married me on the rebound from that darn distillery. And the way he threw himself into his work at that time left him with no time or energy for me, or us. He was a husband and father in name only."

Connor looked over to Derek's kitchen table that he used to hide under as a child and pretend he was sailing a pirate ship to Derek's old, battered leather lounger that Connor was allowed to sleep in when he was sick, snuggled under thick blankets. And beyond that, to the garden where Derek had taught him how to throw a ball and to the patio chairs where Derek had set him straight on the facts of life.

Derek had been the present father that Donovan had never been, and Connor had a realization he was putting all of his efforts into impressing a man who had never really thought of him as a son...more as a talented heir apparent...another feather in his crown.

"Are you okay, Connor?" His mom walked toward him.

"Sorry, I was just thinking how good Derek has been to me. To us."

Alyssa smiled broadly. "He has, hasn't he? He made so many sacrifices, worked two jobs at times, to look after us."

"I should do something to pay him back for that," Connor said. "I don't know why it hasn't occurred to me before now."

His mother ruffled his hair, something she'd done for as long as he could remember. "Oh, Connor. He doesn't want paying back. You don't owe him or me anything. You, the wonderful, if not slightly anal, man you are is enough."

Connor laughed. "Thanks, Mom," he said sarcastically. "Did I mention Emerson changes the time she wakes up every morning and hates my food prep? And she makes me waffles I can't resist."

Alyssa laughed. "I like her already. But Derek doesn't expect anything from you. He always said it was our job to raise you to be a fine, honest, young man. On the way home from your father's birthday party, he said to me that we'd done a great job. He loves you. And all those sacrifices you make for someone you love don't feel like sacrifices. You do what you have to do to keep them safe, to help them grow, to show them the possibilities of joy and happiness."

Connor felt his heart expand. Who knew a grown man still needed parental acceptance? And why was he chasing it from his father, who only cared about what Connor represented as a part of his personal legacy?

The ground beneath his feet suddenly felt unstable as everything he thought he'd been chasing had begun to unravel.

What if the path he'd been on since he was old enough to remember wasn't the path he wanted to take anymore?

E merson saw the lights of the distillery floor go off in her peripheral vision as she heard Jake shout farewell to some of their employees.

Yippee-Fri-Yay. She'd woken up that morning with a panicked feeling that it was Monday and she hadn't written the production schedule. The calendar on her phone that she'd reached for groggily had confirmed it was indeed Friday, and she still had the day to write it.

She looked at the round table in her father's office. The old kitchen table from her mom and dad's first apartment was lovingly referred to as *the boardroom table*, and it was here she intended to tell Jake and Olivia everything.

Connor had been right. She'd been wobbling. He was also right that she'd been trying to be the stoic one and carry the weight of it alone. Jake and Olivia were smart, pragmatic, and as committed to the distillery as she was. It was time to stop thinking about all the plans she'd felt slip away and write a new one.

It was time to build Dyer's Gin Distillery Part II.

"Hey," Olivia said, walking in with a box of doughnuts, which she placed on the table. "I figured if this meeting was to happen in here, we'd need sugar. I like what you've done with the office."

Emerson looked around, seeing it from Olivia's point of view. Everything was filed, the surfaces clear, and Emerson had brought in some plants from home. Lavender, her favorite, and lots of green foliage.

"Up until you said that, I was still thinking about it as Dad's office. But you're right. It does look different."

Olivia threw her hand over her sister's shoulder. "It's yours now. And it looks more like it. When we renovate, we should get some better paper storage solutions than these ugly green filing cabinets, though. Or even better, perhaps scan everything so we can go digital."

When we renovate…

"I'm ready," Jake said, bounding into the office. "Oh, you brought doughnuts. I always said you were my favorite sister."

Emerson shook her head as Jake opened the box and pulled out a Boston cream.

"Alright," Emerson said. "Let's take a seat and get started."

Once everyone was seated, doughnuts in hand, she began.

"Before I get into the meat of this, if at any point this becomes more than you can deal with, Liv, you tell me to stop, and we'll figure out how to take it from there, okay?"

"Okay." Olivia placed her doughnut on the table. "I said a version of this the other day at Dad's, and I'll say it again. It's time we moved on from you all acting as though I'm going to fall apart. Just let me get on with it. I know my limits, and I have a plan for if I feel like I'm regressing. I'll let you know if I need you."

"That's fair. I'm sorry if we've been smothering you." Emerson reached for her hand to give it a quick squeeze.

Olivia squeezed her hand back, but then let go. "You have, but I get why. Now it's time to stop. So, what do you need to talk to us about?"

"The distillery is not in the shape we thought it was in. And to fix it, the actions taken by Dad might have made it worse."

Emerson explained from the beginning, the sequence of events from the storm, to the insurance, to the loan being recalled.

When she was done, Jake and Olivia sat in silence.

"I really screwed up, didn't I…all those years ago when I thought I was helping out?" Olivia said, finally.

Emerson shook her head. "Do you remember the first time Jake nearly blew up Patience, and she was off-line for a month? And we thought Dad was going to throw a fit?"

Jake groaned. "Do we have to bring that up again?"

"Yes, we do," said Emerson. "Because Dad screwed up by not talking to us about the financial problems. I screwed up trying to do this on my own. My point is, we've all screwed up. And we are going to screw up again while running this place, I'm sure. The proof in this pudding will be what we do next."

"Do you have a plan?" Olivia asked. Jake turned her way, too. It suddenly hit her that she'd chosen the seat their father had always sat in, instead of the one next to Jake she usually took.

"I do. It's ugly, and it will take work on all our parts, including you, Liv."

Olivia smiled. "I'm ready."

"Me too," said Jake.

Emerson was boosted by the unmitigated support. "You guys don't even know what it is yet."

"Fair enough," said Jake. "Me too, as long as I get whatever botanicals I want for the next iteration of the Dyer's Medallion."

Emerson shook her head. "I'll set a cost per bottle, and you can have whatever botanicals you want within it."

Jake laid his head down on the table theatrically. "This is going to be worse than negotiating with Dad." He lifted his head. "Fine. I agree."

Olivia laughed. "Go ahead, Em."

"First, we sell Dad's house. Jake and I are willing to put our shares back into the distillery to ensure the loan gets repaid and the bank doesn't come after us. We'll need a quick sale, so the sooner we can get the house ready, the better."

"I want to put my share in," Olivia said.

"No," said Jake. "You are the least financially secure of all of us. Em and I own our own places, and we can cover the mortgage and bills. You're twenty-six and—"

"I'm twenty-six, and I can save for a frigging deposit like you two did," Olivia said firmly. "Getting a roommate in a rental for a couple of years is not going to kill me. Next item."

Olivia's sass reassured Emerson that she really was back on track. "If that's the case, the plan just got better. We pay back the loan and use the rest to renovate the actual distillery. It's not enough to do everything we want, but we can change the layout of the main floor and buy a new efficient still. We hire a second distiller to work with Jake. We could even split production into two shifts. Earlies and lates, so the stills run for sixteen hours a day with breaks in between. The second distiller takes on our old lines, Dad's recipes."

"We could call them Dyer's Vintage. New packaging with new promotion behind them," Liv said. "See if we can breathe some new life into them. The London dry style never goes out of fashion, but perhaps Jake could just tweak them a little…different juniper source or something."

Jake nodded thoughtfully. "I agree with the plan, I'm a little concerned with the execution. Check on the Dyer's Vintage, we can definitely spruce that up, and it's a great idea."

"Medallion is exceptional, Jake, and we need you to take it forward. Expand the range," Emerson said.

"I'll give it some thought. I'm killing myself trying to get production out, but I'm loathe to hand it over to anyone else just now because quality is our superpower. I see what you're trying to do, but let me think of a different way to do it. Perhaps promote someone and separate the preparation from production; have them start earlier. I don't know. But I'll get you the improvement you need."

"Liv, Jake will also need your help on Medallion, too. Let's find a way to ride the momentum. Let's issue press releases, let's update our social media, let's revisit how we use our tasting rooms."

Liv tapped her pen on her notebook. "One of the things I'd been thinking about was renting it out during the day for corporate events. We've focused on big events…like weddings. But there are lots of smaller conferences we could cash in on."

The idea felt solid to Emerson. "Whatever you've got. I'm going to tackle the costs, overheads, and pricing. Jake made a point that we should review our price positioning, given the success of the product, which I'll do. I'm going to renegotiate everything from our utilities to the blessed seaweed you use that will cost us a fortune, Jake. Literally line item by line item."

Jake leaned forward. "We can't compromise quality, Em. It's why we won the Best in Class."

Emerson nodded. "Agreed. I wasn't so much thinking about changing sources but renegotiating on the grounds that we need a higher quantity thanks to the extra volume the still will give us, and therefore deserve a better bulk price."

Olivia grinned. "I like it, Em. We'll make more, sell more at a possibly higher price, and it will cost less to make."

"It means we'll have to wait on the events hall. But with the increased production, we should be able to afford it before next year, or perhaps be in much better standing with the bank to take out a loan."

Emerson sat back in her chair and took a bite of her doughnut.

"One hell of a plan, Em," Jake said.

It was.

And she had Connor's pep talk to thank for giving her the confidence to come talk to Jake and Liv. When they were done, she was going to go to Connor's to update him and say thank you.

And perhaps work out some of her excitement on him.

Chapter Twelve

Connor fiddled with his cuff link, then straightened the knot of his black tie that matched his black suit and black shirt. He caught sight of his reflection in the window of his apartment and sighed. Goddamn, he was actually nervous.

Forcing himself to relax, he shook out his shoulders and arms.

It's just dinner.

It had been his idea to celebrate the conversation she'd had with her siblings. To celebrate that no matter what the world threw at them, the Dyers were going to be just fine. What had possessed him to suggest they hit Maison Noir and dress the part, he wasn't sure.

Except he remembered how Emerson had looked when they'd met in the garden at the awards in San Francisco, and he wanted to give them both the opportunity to dress up and enjoy life a little.

It had been her suggestion that they get ready separately when she had disappeared into the second bedroom two hours ago. Since then, he'd heard her listen to a country compilation, a food podcast discussing the history of pasta, and a meditation app. In the meantime, he'd swum, worked out, gotten a haircut, caught up on the news, and showered. And it had been nice doing all those things wondering what exactly she was doing in the bedroom.

Just as he was about to pour himself a drink, he heard the clip of heels on the wooden hallway. "Connor?"

"I'm in the living room," he said.

When she stepped around the corner, he gaped. For sure, his jaw hit the floor.

Emerson stood tall in a deep red dress that set off her tanned, smooth skin and dark hair. The fitted bodice accentuated her breasts as it did her waist. The wide skirt ended just below her knees.

And she wore heels that matched the dress.

Her hair was up in a messy updo that framed her face perfectly. And dear God, those red lips would be the end of him.

"You're perfect," he said.

Emerson laughed shyly and bobbed a little curtsy. "It's all new. And I still suck at walking in heels."

Connor crossed the room and took her hand. "Heels. No heels. I love you just the way you are." He pulled her close, as if they were dancing to some imaginary music.

"You look incredibly handsome in this suit," she said, running her fingertips along the ends of his hair. "I like your hair."

"Funny, I was just thinking how much I like yours. Up like it is now, or down when my fist is curled in it while we—"

"Connor," she said, cutting him off playfully. "If you behave, I might let you try that again later."

Connor laughed. "If I kiss you right now, am I going to ruin your lipstick?"

Emerson shook her head. "Twenty-four-hour inde-structible lipstick. At least, that's what the label says."

He leaned forward, savoring the feel of her soft lips as they met his. Damn, he wanted to stay in and make out instead. He wrapped his hands around her, only to feel skin. Her back was totally exposed.

"I like this dress even more," he murmured, running his fingertips along her spine. "Are you sure I can't convince you to stay in and order pizza?" Connor pulled her closer, hoping that she could feel exactly what she was doing to him. His dick was aching for her. "I can think of at least ten things I'd like to do with you while you're wearing this dress."

Emerson grinned, slowly looked down at the growing tent in his pants, and then back up, pinning him with those eyes of hers that positively sparkled with excitement. "I'm certain pizza in bed with you would be incredible, as would be the ten things. But tonight, you promised me a wonderful dinner, so perhaps you can tell me about them en route. Let's go."

Connor lifted Emerson's hand to his lips. "Your wish is my command. Do you need a coat?"

"My purse and wrap are by the door. And if I get too cold, you'll give me your jacket, right?"

As she turned to grab them, and he caught sight of the exceptionally low dip of her dress and the bow at the base of her back, he figured he'd give her just about anything she asked for.

"Can one of the things I do to you in this dress start in the car?" Connor asked as he opened the door to their ride. "My tongue somewhere it shouldn't be in public."

Emerson blushed. "Save it for later," she said, looking around to see if they'd been overheard.

Once at Maison Noir, the host seated them in one of the round booths and left them with their menus. The deep burgundy leather sofa, dark wood, and low lighting was perfect.

Emerson groaned when she looked at the menu. "Don't you just love it when you open a menu and immediately see so many dishes you'd like to try?"

Connor leaned toward her. "Kind of like when I look at you and think about ten things *I'd* like to try?"

Her eyes met his. "Tell me another," she dared him.

For a moment, he debated whether she meant it or not, but the way she looked at him, the way her lips were ever so slightly open, told him she did. He moved closer in the booth and whispered into her ear. "When we get home, I'd like for you to kneel on the edge of the bed in this dress while I take you from behind. I might even take a fistful of this glorious hair of yours...hold you in place while you come." He ran his fingers gently down her spine.

"Is that before or after I wrap my lips around your—"

"Welcome to Maison Noir," a female voice said. "Can I get you an aperitif while you look at the menu?"

Emerson blushed, while Connor moved slightly away from her, but threw an arm around the leather seat behind her. He'd never been less happy to get service, no matter how crisp the woman's black uniform and attitude were.

He wanted Emerson to finish that sentence more than anything else in the world.

"Could I get a French 75, please?" she asked, without glancing down at the cocktail menu.

Connor grinned. "I'll take a gin and tonic. Dyer's Medallion if you have it."

"We do. It's my current favorite," the woman said.

"I like the taste of Dyer's, too," he said, winking in Emerson's direction.

When the server disappeared, Emerson turned to him. "Oh my god, do you think she heard?"

Connor tipped her chin and pressed a brief but intimate kiss to her lips. "I doubt it, but honestly, I don't care. She probably doesn't give a rat's ass that we were flirting. She's probably thinking about how many of the specials there are left and whether she gets next Tuesday off on the staff rotation. Anyway, I want to hear what of mine you were considering wrapping your lips around."

Emerson grinned as she shook her head. "You are incorrigible."

"Only when I'm aroused," Connor replied.

She lifted the menu to hide her face from his. "I'm thinking oysters," she said.

He pressed down on the top of the menu with two fingers so he could just see her eyes. "Nature's aphrodisiac? I approve."

Their drinks came, and they placed their orders. Oysters and the seared snapper for Emerson and the Wagyu beef tartare and the short rib for him. With a light Beaujolais cru to dance between the lightness of Emerson's seafood and his own meat choices.

"I'm glad things went well with Jake and Liv," he said over their appetizers. "I'm glad they were reasonable."

Emerson nodded. "Me too. I'd never really thought about what Dad would leave us, beyond the distillery. And so, the fact we get to use his estate to keep the distillery is a bonus."

In between courses, Connor resumed his teasing of Emerson, offering her more suggestions on the ten things he wanted to do to her. By her reaction to number six—in his arms up against the wall—and number eight—seated on one of the stools in the kitchen with him standing in front of her—they already had an outline of how exactly their return to the condo was going to go.

By the time he hit suggestion ten, they were just waiting for the bill.

"I don't know if it was your plan all along," Emerson

said, quietly, her voice husky. "But I'm so turned on right now that I might spontaneously combust."

She bit her lip as she looked at him, and he'd seen the look in her eyes before. The look that told him that she was on the edge before she lost control. It left her looking just a little wild and reckless.

Connor reached out and placed his palm against her cheek. "I've been hard as a rock since you appeared in the condo wearing that dress and lipstick. When I race, it's important to not go out too early. You have to know your pace. Steady, letting it build. And you need to save some energy for that final burst at the end, savoring the anticipation of crossing the line rather than just hurtling toward it. Savoring the anticipation of you tonight has been fucking glorious."

When the bill arrived, he paid, refusing Emerson's offer to split it. He used the time to cool his thoughts. Jumping into borderline frozen rivers, running at five in the morning in the snow. Anything to ensure he could do all the things he wanted to with Emerson when they got home.

———

I t felt as though the oxygen had been sucked out of the car. Connor's hand edged its way along her leg from her knee. His fingertips trailed her inner thigh, her skirt bunching up as he moved higher.

Emerson glanced in the direction of the driver, half expecting his eyes to be glued to the rearview mirror, watching as Connor began to undo her, to make good on the promises he'd whispered in her ear over dinner. Relieved, she found his eyes focused on the road in front of them.

Connor leaned his elbow on the window, hand in his

hair as he studied her, his gaze intense. It was a wonder there weren't physical sparks flickering between the two of them, igniting the seat.

Neither of them said a word.

Emerson answered the question of how far she'd let him go almost as soon as she'd thought it.

As far as he wanted to.

The tip of his finger brushed against her red lace underwear, making her gasp and her stomach muscles clench. She wanted more immediately, but his hand never ventured quite far enough to allow him to apply any pressure.

The side of Connor's mouth tilted in a smirk. He knew exactly what he was doing to her, or in this case, what he wasn't doing to her.

She squinted in a mock frown.

Soon, he mouthed.

Emerson let her head fall back on the headrest as she heard Connor chuckle. He moved his hand, the loss of connection immediate. Once he'd straightened her skirt back down, he lifted her hand and brought her knuckles to his lips. He kissed them gently and then lowered her hand to his hard erection where he flattened her palm against it. He laid his hand over hers to ensure she didn't grip it, rocking once, then twice against her.

Okay, so she was doing to him what he was doing to her.

Fair was fair.

This time, she smiled and prayed the driver stepped on the gas.

When they pulled up outside Connor's apartment building, she reached for the door.

"Wait," Connor said, pulling a twenty out of his wallet before telling the driver to keep the change. He stepped out of the cab, and Emerson bit her lip as he discretely adjusted himself before walking to her door.

He opened it and offered her his hand.

"Thank you," she said, stepping out of the cab and walking in front of him into the building. She looked over her shoulder and found him running his tongue along his lower lip as he watched her hips sway.

"Are you checking me out?" she asked.

"Too fucking right I'm checking you out. Walk ahead of me," he encouraged.

Knowing he was watching caused goosebumps to ripple across her skin. It felt voyeuristic of him, yet she felt safe under his heavy gaze.

When she reached the elevator, she pressed the button as his hand slid around her waist. Connor pressed his lips against her skin. "When we get into the apartment," he murmured. "All bets are off. You asked me what I wanted to do, and I told you. The fact that your panties are wet tells me you want what I'm offering. You change your mind, let me know. Otherwise, this goes how I want it."

A shiver trickled down her spine at his words. It was perhaps the most erotic warning she'd ever been given, and she couldn't wait.

"Connor," she breathed.

The elevator doors opened, and she caught sight of the two of them in the mirrored walls. Connor dressed in all black behind her, the blood red of her dress. As she stepped inside, Connor pressed the button for his floor and then spun her around. Her back hit the mirror as he slammed his lips against hers. She could feel every muscle, every part of him pressed up against her body...so close it felt as though they were one person.

Their teeth hit, their tongues dueled. Connor thrust his fingers into her hair, holding her exactly where he wanted her. She couldn't move, pinned in place by every part of him.

The elevator slowed, the characteristic gentle bounce before it came to a stop, and Connor moved to stand alongside her. She bit her lip, holding back the grin of excitement as he reached for her wrist, slipping his fingers around it instead of holding her hand.

It felt like an ownership of sorts, the sort that shouldn't be so much of a damn turn-on.

"When we get into the apartment, I'm going to slide those panties down your legs in the hallway, and then you have the sum total of five seconds to hop on the stool in the kitchen. Do not remove your heels," Connor said.

"Can I say one thing?" she asked.

Connor stopped in front of the apartment door. "Always," he said, his voice sounding as though it were loaded with gravel and whiskey.

"I really like this side of you, Connor. I feel safe pushing boundaries with you."

He looked off down the hallway for a second, but he wasn't fast enough for her to miss the grin that crept onto his face. When he looked back at her, the grin was gone, replaced with a need and urgency that was hard to miss. He ran a finger along her cheek.

"Nothing between the two of us is wrong as long as we agree we want to try it. You'll tell me if something isn't right?"

Emerson nodded.

The door unlocked with a click, and Connor pushed it open, leaving her no option but to walk beneath his arm to step inside. He turned the lights on as the door shut behind them.

As good as his word, Connor silently inched her skirt up her thighs until he reached the lace waistband of her thong. Slowly, he slid it down her legs.

"Step out," he said.

Without being reminded, Emerson walked to the leather stool in the kitchen and hopped onto the seat. She crossed one leg over the other and leaned her arms back on the counter.

With her red underwear still in his hand, Connor stalked toward her. He loosened his tie, sliding it from around his neck before he placed it on the table. Stalked was such a perfect word. Every step had purpose, his eyes never leaving hers. And it was she that he was coming for.

"You and this dress," he muttered as he got close to her. He reached for her knees, his fingers tickling the soft spot behind them, and she uncrossed them at this gentle pressure. His palms pressed her thighs open.

Emerson watched as he rolled the hem of her dress higher and higher until she was exposed to him. The temptation to close her knees, to pull her dress down, was great. The vulnerability she felt was overwhelming her. But the look of adoration on Connor's face kept her pinned in place.

"Beautiful," was all he said.

His hands skimmed along her thighs until his thumbs reached her clit. She gasped as one thumb pressed against her wetness, before sliding up to her clit, then his other thumb repeated the action. A steady drumbeat of pressure and release.

Pressure and release.

Emerson allowed her head to drop back, and Connor wasted no time in pressing kisses along her collarbone, nibbling, biting, and leaving a trail of sensitized skin.

When his finger slid inside her, she reached for him, grasping his bicep as he worked his way deep inside her.

"Connor," she gasped.

He slid his finger out of her and placed it in his mouth. "You taste so good," he said, before sliding back inside her.

More firmly this time. Two fingers stretching her wide. He curled them upward, reaching the place within her that caused her muscles to tighten and the telltale signs of a pending orgasm to rush down on her.

Emerson began to move against him, but Connor grabbed her hip, holding her exactly where he wanted her.

She groaned in frustration.

"Patience, Em."

Connor pulled a condom from the inside pocket of his suit jacket before unzipping his trousers. Freeing his length, he rolled it on. He reached behind her, grabbing her ass and pulling her toward the edge of the seat, lining them up at the perfect height.

"Watch," he instructed, his own eyes focused on the place where his cock rubbed against her.

With a single firm push, he slid all the way inside her.

"Ah, god. Connor."

He pressed his forehead to hers. "So good every time."

With his thumb circling her clit, he proceeded to withdraw and slide back home.

Home.

She'd never been more certain that with Connor she'd found it.

Ignited sensations started to flame to life. A loud roar that overtook her ability to think straight.

The sight of him, the sound of their bodies meeting. The fact she couldn't move given the grip he had on her hip. It kept her focused on the one place she felt everything.

"Connor," she cried, feeling her orgasm bear down on her. "Please."

"Look at me, Em," he growled.

When her eyes met his, the look she saw in them sent her over the edge.

Fuck.

Nothing had ever felt better than Emerson coming around his dick, but once she'd caught her breath, he slid out anyway because if he didn't, he was going to come...and he didn't want to. Not yet. Not while they were both in the mood to explore each other without any kind of barrier between them.

"Connor," she sighed.

He ran his thumb along her cheek. Yeah, he definitely didn't want to come yet because he wanted to keep that look on her face for as long as he could. The look that told him she was right there with him. The one that said she was fuck-drunk on him and wanted more.

Her lips were soft, pliable. And it was tempting to slide back inside her and finish. "You good, Em?" he asked.

"I'm better than good by quite a large margin."

He took her hand, helped her down from the stool, and spun her so she faced away from him. He slid the straps of the dress from her shoulders, taking a moment to cool his heels. It was a snug fit over her hips, and he appreciated the way she wiggled to help him drop it to the floor.

And then she was naked apart from the heels. Her back to him, he could see the curve of her hip, the roundness of her ass, the length of her tanned legs looking as sexy as all hell in her deep red heels.

When she widened her stance slightly and glanced over her shoulder to look at him, he realized he was well and truly sunk for her.

"You look fucking perfect, Em," he said.

She smiled. Smiled at him like the sun rose and set with him.

He slid his jacket off and placed it on the back of the stool. All the while, her eyes were on him. Slowly, he removed the cuff links and reached alongside her to place them on the counter. The shirt buttons were next.

"Can I help?" Emerson asked.

Connor shook his head. "You touch me now and I'm going to bend you over that counter and take you until you can't stand."

Even as he said the words, the vision of her, face down on the poured concrete surface, his hand in her hair, filled his mind.

He slipped out of his shirt and made fast work of the rest of his clothes until he stood naked behind her.

As exposed as he'd ever felt.

His dick ached to be inside her, but he allowed it to slide between the cheeks of her ass, savoring the softness of her naked skin against his.

Emerson sighed and let her head drop back against his chest.

Her neck called to him, and he pressed a train of gentle kisses and soft bites along it. Connor spanned her waist, sliding his hands until he cupped her breasts. Pert nipples teased him, and he suddenly wanted them in his mouth.

"Hold on," he said, lifting her into his arms.

"Wait, what?" she said and then squealed. "Oh." She wrapped her arms around his neck and pressed her lips to his chest...and suddenly the bedroom seemed too far away.

Instead, he laid her down on the blue rug in the living room. "I can't wait," he gasped as he raised her feet to his shoulders and slid back inside her.

Still so wet from her earlier orgasm, she offered little resistance, but the position made everything feel so tight. He'd had sex before. Plenty of it. But this, with Emerson, was different.

"Em," he gasped.

Her hands were over her head. Her breasts bounced as he thrust into her. She was so uninhibited, so…in sync with him, he felt almost delirious.

Gently, he lowered her legs to either side of his hips and slipped off her shoes. As he lay down over her, he pushed himself deep inside. "Tell me you feel this, Em," he said gruffly. "Tell me you feel the connection between us."

Emerson placed her hands either side of his face, and while his friends would probably call him a pussy, he felt so cherished. "I feel it. I've felt it for a while."

He rolled them onto their sides, remaining deep inside her, and kissed her tenderly. Softly. With his hand twisted up in her hair, he held her to him. His body wanted to move, to continue whatever this was until he was completely spent.

But his heart needed a minute. Sixty seconds to process just how much she meant to him. He should probably say something. Perhaps explain why he suddenly felt like he'd just been poleaxed. Instead, he kissed her again. Passionately. Messily. And they began to move. He withdrew from her mouth and drove himself home. Emerson tilted her hips towards him, meeting him.

She was so wet and warm and ready for him. They fit together in every conceivable way.

"Em," he said, rolling them so she was on her back again, so he could pin her to the rug and thrust into her.

Sweat rolled between her breasts, between their stomachs. "I'm going to need you to come soon," he gasped. Taking his weight on one arm, he slid his hand between them, circling her clit, applying the pressure he knew she loved.

"Yes, Connor," she cried, one hand around his neck, the other holding on to his arm.

His orgasm built, the tightening of his balls, the juggernaut currently steaming down his spine. His head spun, but he kept his eyes on Emerson. Watching as her mouth opened in shock, as she held her breath and then gasped as she tightened around his dick.

It was all he needed to let go and join her, pulse after pulse in glorious agony.

His whole body shook as he sucked in gulps of air. Unable to maintain his own weight, he slumped over her, his nose pressed against her neck. Her skin damp and salty against his lips.

Their hands linked above her head as he regained his breath.

Feeling his dick slide out of her, he reached to make sure the condom came out, too. With a groan, he rolled onto his back feeling totally spent. Gathering Emerson close, he tucked her under his arm, and she laid her head on his shoulder.

Neither of them said a word.

It felt like the moment after he'd finished a race, in the few minutes that followed the celebration. The mental silence and clarity that followed was something he'd always sought. Peace to a brain that always worked on overdrive.

"I feel like I should have said grace," Emerson said.

Connor ran his hand through her hair, getting his fingers caught in the completely disheveled updo. "Grace?"

"You know, to be thankful for all the things I was about to receive."

Connor laughed, the action jostling his now-aching body. He could do an Ironman, but sex on the condo floor seemed to have fucked with his posture.

"Are you really okay?" he asked, glancing down at her.

"I'll probably be sore tomorrow in places I didn't know about. But, yes. I loved every minute of what we just did."

He pulled her tight. "I loved that it was you. You surprised me and turned me on more than I thought was possible. The image of you standing by the kitchen counter in just those fucking heels is likely going to haunt me at the most inappropriate moments for the rest of my life."

"Knowing it was you gave me the confidence to do that."

Connor's heart squeezed at the thought of it. "We never really talked about preferences before tonight. About what you like sexually. And what I like. Perhaps we should do that."

Emerson circled her fingers on his chest, then raised herself on one elbow. She probably wouldn't appreciate him telling her that the lipstick she'd believed to be indestructible wasn't. He thought it was cute.

"I don't ever want to get hurt. Emotionally or physically. Name calling or pain. But this…you taking the lead the way you did tonight. I enjoyed this."

He took her fingers in his hand and kissed them. "We're on the same page there. I can't imagine doing either of those things. I'm not big into role-play, like pretending I'm your patient and you're my nurse…but I guess that's fine because your idea of that is dressing like a Wookiee."

Emerson snatched her fingers away and laughed. "I was a child."

"A child with dubious tastes."

Quiet blanketed the two of them again, and Emerson placed her head back on his shoulder. The feel of her body pressed up alongside his was more comforting than sexual now.

"I liked the way you spoke to me. It was hot. Not going to lie," Emerson said, softly.

Connor smiled and pressed a kiss to the top of her head. "Glad I could be of service. I liked the heels. Well, you in the heels with nothing else. Surprise me like that every now and then and I'll be a happy man."

"Noted. I'll set a reminder in my calendar."

She said it so primly he couldn't help but laugh. He freed his arm from beneath her and stood. "We should go to bed before we pass out down here." He offered Emerson his hand and helped her to her feet.

"I might have friction burns in places I probably shouldn't, but I wouldn't change it." She blushed as she spoke. "Not sure I'll be able to look at the rug in quite the same way again. Or the stools."

They looked in the direction of the kitchen, where their clothes lay strewn around the island. "I don't know," Connor said with a laugh. "I think we should christen every piece of furniture that'll take our weight."

Emerson grinned and then yawned.

"Let's get you into bed," he said, leading her to his room. Once they were curled up under the sheets, her back pressed up against his chest, he kissed her softly. "I love you."

"I love you, too," she mumbled, telling him exactly what he'd hoped to hear.

Chapter Thirteen

"How are you doing now that you're back?" Emerson asked Olivia as they walked to the benches outside of the distillery for a bracing mid-afternoon cup of coffee. The leaves had fallen and crunched beneath their feet. Connor was right, November had come in with a roar. It was like they'd skipped fall and gone straight from summer to winter.

"I'm tired in a good way," Olivia replied. "But I've only begun to scratch the surface of what we need. I queued some social media posts to share over the next couple of weeks. But most of my time so far has been spent building the mother of all to-do lists."

Emerson took a seat on the bench. "I'm going to find it hard to not remind you to take it easy. I know you said you don't want mothering, but..."

Olivia dropped down onto the bench, pulling her light jacket closed. "I know you are. Since Mom died, you've been a mom to Jake and me as much as you've been a sister, and Dad let you. It wasn't fair of him to let you take that on."

It wasn't fair of her to criticize their father, either. "He was busy. He needed someone to—"

"Yes, but it didn't need to be you. You need to have a life outside of this. To see friends. To spend time with Connor. We're old enough to handle our share, Em."

The words hit Emerson in her chest. "When did you get so wise?"

"I've had time to think things through. And it's always easier when it's someone else's problems. I get it. As for me, I'm only doing afternoons. And I know my own limits. I promise I'll tell you if anything gets hard. The truth is, I'm enjoying being here. I wasn't worried about coming back *because* I know you and Jake are looking out for me."

"Fair enough," Emerson replied. "It's pretty great having you back and seeing you around the place."

"It's nice to be back in the office. And it will be great to get the events side of the business off the ground again in the tasting rooms, beyond those that were carried on while I was gone."

They sipped their coffee in silence, watching Stan, the warehouse manager, ensure the latest delivery got packed up and shipped off. The idea that it was headed to people who would love it warmed her insides.

She thought of Connor, the way he'd enjoyed her gin on Friday night, the way it had loosened his reserve. She remembered the words he'd spoken to her and grinned.

"You've been smiling like that all day," Olivia said. "What's got you in such a great mood?"

Connor.

They'd spent the most amazing weekend together, but Friday night, after they'd returned from dinner… Gah, just thinking about it now made her want to clench her thighs together. He'd taken her just the way he'd promised. He'd been ruthless, pounding into her.

And it hadn't been enough. In the morning, they'd had

sex in his shower with her back against the wall and her legs wrapped around him. On Sunday morning, she'd been as sore as if she'd played six straight sets of tennis. Sex had become her new exercise.

And their relationship had evolved almost overnight. They had been closer, more tactile, more open and honest.

"Em," Liv called out. "Earth to Emerson."

"Sorry," Emerson said, taking a sip of coffee to clear her head. "It's Connor. He's the reason I'm in a good mood."

Olivia squealed. "Yay. I'm so glad. He's a really nice guy. And seems to get what you do. You complement each other."

"Which is why somebody needs to pinch me. I've fallen for a guy in, like, five seconds."

"Sometimes when you know, you just know. And perhaps it's genetics. Mom and Dad always said they fell in love with each other on the day they met."

Emerson remembered the way her mother had once explained it. "She said it was like a thunderbolt." The word suited her own situation perfectly.

"I'm happy for you, Em. Honestly. You needed something good after the last little while. You deserve it."

Emerson patted her sister's leg. "Thanks."

"So, is it serious?" Olivia asked.

"Certainly on my part, and I'm pretty sure it is on his." She *knew* it was. In the early hours of Sunday morning, he'd told her so. As she'd hovered on the edge of waking. He'd told her how he saw what they had as something long-term, not just for now.

Em, it's hard to believe that only two months ago you weren't in my life, but now I can't imagine you out of it.

"Well, I'm glad he can see just how special you are… like the rest of us do." Olivia checked her watch. "Should we head back in?"

When they arrived back at the mezzanine, Olivia disappeared into her office.

Liv's words boosted Emerson as she sat down at the round table in her office and began to tackle the mail from the weekend. She separated it into piles. Bills to be paid, things to do, circulars to be tossed. A large brown manila envelope caught her eye. Her name and address were printed on a label. Emerson ripped it open.

A copy of a presentation dropped out. It had notes scribbled on it in what looked like Connor's writing. *Finch Liquor Distribution Potential Acquisitions.*

It seemed odd that Connor would send her something in the mail, seeing as they'd woken with each other that morning. He'd not even mentioned he would be sending her anything. But she began to flick through it anyway.

The first few pages were interesting. Details of how the marketplace was changing in favor of higher-end, artisanal products. Perhaps that's why he'd wanted her to see it. It was certainly reassuring to know that her segment continued to grow. What had once been called *mother's ruin* was now a highly profitable product.

There was a doodle in the corner, a circle that had been repeatedly drawn over and over, and the thought of Connor sitting bored in a boardroom somewhere made her smile. From what she knew of the man, he much preferred to be outside.

The next few pages were the criteria for an acquisition strategy. The type of company that would be a good fit for Finch, what the parameters for success would be, what the anticipated costs would be…before and post-acquisition. Connor had built quite the framework and she wondered how he'd gotten some of the information.

After that were pages that looked to be describing potential acquisition targets all over the country. Perhaps *that* was why he'd sent it to her, to review the list. She'd heard of the first few companies.

Wow, some of her peers were worth a considerable fortune.

She turned the page, and there, in the title, was DYER'S GIN DISTILLERY.

Loan foreclosed.

Minimum deal. Wait until after loan foreclosure.

The words began to blur. Emerson's head began to spin. She felt sick.

She reached for the envelope and peered inside to see if there was a note of any kind. But there was nothing. Just the presentation.

The next page continued under the heading ASSESSMENT OF ASSETS.

Jake Dyer is behind Medallion's success…

Emerson Dyer, new but competent CEO. Lacks experience…

She did. She couldn't deny it. Never in a million years had she thought she'd be put in charge. And she'd rather her father still be here than be holding any important title. But to see it in 12-point Helvetica font was like a slap to the face. Harsh and instant.

Old assets in need of renovation…

Turn events hall into expanded distillery. Move into other white spirits? Tequila?

Tears stung as her anger began to boil.

Had he been using her to get information? She studied some of the numbers. A couple were wrong. More than a couple. They all looked low.

She reached for her phone and dialed Connor's number. Wherever he was, he better have an answer as to why she'd been sent this. Or, more importantly, why he'd even written it in the first place.

She dialed his number, only for it to ring and go to voicemail.

She'd been a fool to trust him. Perhaps she should have done more due diligence about him before diving headfirst into a relationship with a man that she barely knew.

No.

Before she jumped to conclusions, she owed it to Connor to let him attempt to explain.

And she did know him…she knew him as intimately as a woman could. He couldn't have been pretending to have a relationship with her for information, could he? Friday night couldn't have been faked, could it?

She dialed the phone again and got his voicemail for a second time. His phone was never out of his reach.

What if he were ignoring her?

She turned to the third page. A simple pros and cons.

Under pros: *Was initially a Finch asset before being taken over by Dyer.*

She placed her phone down on the table and picked up the presentation.

…initially a Finch asset?

What? It had never belonged to anyone other than her father and mother. Why on Earth would Connor think it had ever been anything other than her family's?

Oh my god. That night. When he'd come over, he'd picked her brain about the distillery. She'd told him everything she knew. She'd even shown him photographs. And he'd pushed back then, asking if there had ever been another partner. He'd wanted to get her to admit to something she couldn't, that there had once been another partner. Had he been trying to catch her out or garner a confession of sorts?

But which Finch thought they had owned it? His father?

Yes, she'd definitely been a fool.

Emerson picked up the phone again, letting it ring again. This time when she got voicemail, she was ready.

"I don't know what game you're playing, Connor. But finding out I'm an acquisition target for you by mail is a shitty way to draw a line under things. And to think I let myself fall in love with you."

When she was done, she steeled herself. For the first time in months, she was going home early. Somewhere she didn't need to explain how the bottom had just fallen out of her world. She felt like the tail of the gin. Lost, unfocused.

She just needed to get home before she fell apart.

"You heard me, Connor. Is it true that you're in a relationship with that Dyer woman?"

Donovan Finch stood behind his desk, his face flushed and sweating, a sure sign his father had moved beyond anger into rage.

When his father's assistant had called to ask him to come upstairs urgently, he'd assumed there was a business emergency. A supply chain screwup, an unexplainable profit and loss gap, perhaps a negative press complaint. Emerson's number had popped up on his phone as he'd jogged up the stairs, but he'd sent it to voicemail, knowing she'd understand that he had work to attend to.

When he walked into his father's office two minutes later, his father had greeted him with a simple statement. *What is your relationship with the Dyer woman?*

His father wouldn't be this incendiary about a rumor.

Connor wrestled with what to say next.

His phone rang again. Emerson. If his father saw who it was, he might just have a heart attack.

"What is it you think you know, Dad?" he asked as calmly as he could muster.

"I have it on good authority that you're in an intimate

relationship with the Dyer woman, and I want to know why my son would do that?" His father slammed the desk as he spoke.

Connor looked to the vent system that he knew filtered through to Cameron's office. "Unless you want the whole office to hear this conversation, I suggest you take the volume down a notch."

His father's eyes narrowed, and Connor could feel the invisible daggers. Perhaps antagonizing his father wasn't the best idea.

"Do you think if I actually gave a shit what the people here thought, I'd still be doing this job long after I said I'd retire? Wait, is that why you did this? To get back at me because I didn't retire?"

Connor huffed. "Of course not. I'm not a fucking twelve-year-old pissed that his allowance got cut. Am I mad you dropped your decision on me in front of people who work for us? Yes, I am. But did I go and build a relationship with a woman just to piss you off? No."

His father sat down. "So, you are admitting that you're in a relationship with the Dyer woman."

"Her name is Emerson. Stop calling her *the Dyer woman* just because you had a beef with her father a million years ago."

"A beef? A *beef*? Need I remind you, Connor, that he took everything that was important to me?" His father stood again and began to pace back and forth in front of the window. "You have no idea how hard it was to come back from that. Everything I did after was five times harder."

Connor took a deep breath. He was so done having this conversation over and over with his dad. "I do, Dad," he said calmly. "You've told me repeatedly. I know it's been your goal to smash him to the ground, to beat him using some metric you've never shared, but the man is dead. It's time to let go."

"How dare you—"

"How did you find out?" Connor's temper simmered beneath his cool veneer. He had no idea where the conversation was going to end up, but now he was fully in it and determined to walk away with all his questions answered.

His father pivoted suddenly, his pacing coming to an abrupt halt. "Why does it matter how I found out? It's true, so why should you care?"

Connor shrugged. "Fair point. The truth is, now that you know, I don't care. But it would be good for you to confirm it's the snake I think it is who came running to you to wipe his nose for him like a five-year-old, kind of like he's been doing for years."

His father glanced briefly towards Cameron's office. "Discussing that would get us nowhere."

"You know what, Dad? It would actually get us *somewhere*. The fact you looked straight toward Cameron's office tells me everything I need to know. He's desperate to discredit me, to position himself as your only reliable replacement." The only question remaining was how did Cameron find out?

This time his father studied the adjoining wall between their offices. "At least Cameron knows what it means to be loyal after all these years."

Connor huffed and shook his head. "You've always confused his self-serving actions with loyalty because he's always been able to spin them in a way that appealed to you. He knows I would fire him in a heartbeat and replace him with a capable CFO. And he would do anything to make sure his paycheck was safe."

"And I come back to the point you're just pissed off that I decided to stay on for another five years."

Connor stood. "Am I pissed that yet again, Cameron

influenced you to make a move that protects him? Yes. Am I pissed off that he talked you into staying on for another five years? Yes. We've had this conversation already. This is old news."

Donovan walked toward him. "And what have you done, Connor?"

"Done?" Connor asked. "I studied hard to meet your expectations of me. I went to the school you wanted me to go to, even though you reminded me a million times a semester that the tuition was so high. When I told you I'd pay, you balked at what your friends might say. I came to work for you because that was what *you* expected as repayment, and thanks to my input, there's been a meaningful change on every single business metric."

"And yet still you found the time to fuck the daughter of an enemy whose company we wanted to purchase at a knockdown price. Were you screwing her or screwing me? Or was it both?"

Connor's fists clenched, his jaw flexed. He was a heartbeat away from laying out his old man on company property. "Don't," he hissed. "Don't ever talk about Emerson like that. Like she means nothing."

"SHE *IS* NOTHING!" Donovan yelled. "Any which way I look at this, you acted unscrupulously at best, unprofessionally at worst. Did you start this relationship to get information for us? Or did you start the relationship to spite me? Neither shows you in a good light."

He thought back to his first meetings with Emerson. He'd been curious about the Dyer family and the woman, about why they held such sway over his father. And yes, there had been a time, a small window when he'd considered owning the distillery as much as he'd been interested in Emerson. But something shifted the night he'd visited her at the distillery, and suddenly she was the only thing that really mattered.

Connor shook his head. "I need to get out of here before I say something unrecoverable. I'm going to work from home tomorrow, and I'll be back on Wednesday. We'll talk then when we've both had time to calm down."

"I need your pass," his father said, holding out his hand.

"Are you firing me?" Connor said, aghast his father would take it that far.

"Not firing…reviewing. I'm putting you on notice that your behavior is unacceptable to the business, putting our longer-term strategy at risk, and we'll both need a period to review. In the short term, you need to break things off with the Dyer woman."

The years he'd put in waiting for the chance to lead this company, to sit at the very desk his father was now leaning against flashed before his eyes.

Was Emerson worth giving up everything he'd worked for?

Fuck.

It was the easiest *yes* in the world. Connor unclipped his pass from his suit trousers. He'd need to go back to his office to collect his jacket, laptop, and car keys, but he could exit the building without it.

"I can't believe it's come to this, Connor."

"I can't believe you're going to let a decades-long grudge against a dead man come between you and me. And for the record, Dyer's is never going to sell to you, whether I'm here or not. I've gotten to know a thing or two about them, and I'll tell you this, I envy them. I envy their relationship with each other. They're builders, not buyers, and that distillery brings the three Dyer siblings together in a way that I couldn't imagine until I met them."

Regret seemed to flood his father's features, and for a moment, there was a waver of doubt. Whether it was for him or the loss of a potential asset, Connor wasn't sure.

The door swung open, and Cameron popped his head inside. "We're ready to take you through the projected year-end performance and Christmas sales expectations," he said.

Connor bit down on his tongue. Hard. There was so much he wanted to say, but with his father already against him, adding Cameron to the fire would be like adding accelerant.

"Will you be joining us, Connor?" Cameron said, his voice thick with disdain.

"I'm pretty certain you already know the answer to that." Connor headed toward the door.

"I'll get Cameron to send you a copy," his father said. "You can look at the numbers at home and let me know—"

Connor brushed past Cameron. "Don't bother. Seeing as you trust Cameron's advice so much, let him make the decisions."

He jogged back down to his office, and while he wanted to slam his laptop shut and leave, there were several people waiting on things from him and his team. And if he'd learned one thing from Emerson, it was that the people who worked for him deserved better than the treatment his father handed out.

His father and Cameron would be in the financial performance review for hours, so he had time to finish what he needed before they were out of there. He called each of his team leads to inform them he was taking a couple of days of personal leave, ensuring they were okay with taking on some actions in his stead. And he took the time to respond to some time-sensitive emails that needed moving along.

Two hours later, he collected his things and took the stairs out of the building, savoring the burn in his legs and thankful his car was parked out front.

Once inside, he remembered that Emerson had been trying to call him earlier. As he pulled away from the curb, he checked his voicemail.

I don't know what game you're playing, Connor. But finding out I'm an acquisition target for you by mail is a shitty way to draw a line under things. And to think I let myself fall in love with you.

Connor pressed replay, his heart pounding. He couldn't have understood that right.

And to think I let myself fall in love with you.

Fuck...What had Cameron done?

Chapter Fourteen

Emerson pulled into the driveway of her father's home. If there was anywhere she would be able to find out what had happened when Dyer's Gin Distillery was built, it was in her father's office.

Olivia was at work. She'd been concerned when Emerson had told her about the massive headache she had, which wasn't wholly untrue. Emerson felt as though she'd been processed through one of the stills and spat out the other end. When Liv had offered to drive her home, she'd declined.

She let herself into the house, stopped in the kitchen to get a glass of water, and then walked to the office.

It felt as though the fabric of her relationship with Connor had just unraveled, but instead of being able to form a cohesive thought or emotion, she was adrift, unable to latch on to any thread long enough to process it. In any event, she chose action. Sitting wouldn't answer the questions she had.

Her first thought was to go through the filing cabinets that still hadn't been sorted. The first drawer she opened was simply household bills. Twelve months of cable, gas, credit card, and bank statements. Her father had been meticulous in some ways and messy in others.

The second drawer contained old correspondence. Personal letters, old Christmas cards, and tchotchkes from weddings, birthdays, and funerals. As she flicked through them, her father began to take on a different shape in her mind. People cared deeply about him, about their mother. There were in memoriam cards from her funeral.

Emerson felt tears rise. She couldn't deal with the painful trip down memory lane when her heart was already in such turmoil.

Her phone rang, and she dug it out of her purse.

Connor.

With a sickness she felt down to her toes, she sent him to voicemail. When she'd called him from the distillery, she'd been operating on pure anger. But now she needed to pull herself together before talking to him. She couldn't go from reading how her mother's loss had affected so many to talking to him. She turned her phone off.

She'd call Connor when she was good and ready.

Emerson worked her way through each drawer, putting the papers that could be shredded into a large cardboard box.

The fifth drawer she opened in the second cabinet promised more relevant information. She found the original floorplans for the distillery. The old building had once been a machine shop. Emerson ran her fingers over the old photographs. It was barely recognizable, except for the roof, and the windows that ran along one wall. Dirt and grime covered ancient machinery, the floor was rough concrete with fine ridges in it to stop slipping, so unlike the smooth grip of the distillery's floor.

There were folders from the architect, from the builders, from the electricians. Drawings, invoices, letters, copies of emails.

But nothing that pointed to there being any other partner involved in the business. Her father or mother's name was on everything. There were no suppliers named Finch.

Emerson slammed the drawer shut.

Drawer six was equally a dud. Old employment files with lists of names revealed nobody by the name of Finch. She had no idea why the acquisition document would suggest the distillery had originally been a Finch asset.

Holding on to her father's desk, she pulled herself up from the floor. A wave of panic swept through her. Were she and Connor really done? The thought left her breathless. She held on to a sliver of hope that all wasn't lost. That there was some possible, feasible explanation as to why this all had happened.

Her mother's boxes were still on the desk.

Perhaps there could be something in there that would be of use, since her father had always been clear that they had been equal partners in the distillery.

The first box was a different kind of memory lane. The family christening gown that she and her siblings, along with her mother, and grandmother, had all been baptized in. A little pair of Nike shoes in the tiniest size. Baptism and confirmation cards for all three of her children. Sonogram images which, given the date, were of Olivia.

Every item had been placed in the box with tremendous care. Heirlooms that her mother would no doubt want her and Jake and Liv to pass along to their children.

The second box was papers, much like her father's filing cabinet drawers.

Many of the letters appeared to be from her mother's teen years, referencing camps her mother had obviously attended.

At the bottom of the large box was a smaller, brown

one. It was unadorned; no writing marred the surface or hinted at what was inside.

Emerson opened it carefully, and inside was a pile of letters. She pulled the first one out of the box.

Dear Rebecca,

You know I'm not a particularly dramatic man, nor am I a natural romantic. But I can't imagine my world without you in it. I'm begging you to reconsider your decision. I love you with all my heart. Please, call me so we can talk.

D

There was no date on the letter. Just words scribbled in ink. Curious, she opened the next letter.

Dear Rebecca,

I'm sorry I've not been around the distillery much the last few days. I need to talk to you, alone.

D

Emerson looked at the envelopes…there was no address on them. Just her mother's name. Whoever had sent them had either handed them to her or popped them in her mailbox. Perhaps they were from a first love.

How she wished her mom was with her now, so she could ask her how to handle her heart, which felt as though it had been macerated.

She pulled another envelope. When she opened the letter inside, small pieces of paper fluttered to the ground like confetti from within.

Rebecca,

I need to go away. I can't imagine being here every day and seeing you as I have for the past few months. I can't sit here and watch you and Paul go on about your lives as if I meant nothing to you. And I hate that you thought so little of me that you felt the need to share this with Paul.

If you had given me time, if you had given me the opportunity, I would have willingly shown you how good we could have been together. The kind of life we could have had. I would have given you the world, because I love you.

How can you say we wouldn't have been good together? You never gave us a chance. If we had met before you saw Paul, who is to say what might have happened? And how can you be so sure of a man you have known mere months?

I have torn up the check you sent me. Do you really think this was about the money? I invested that money in the distillery for us. For you and me. Do you think I want it back if I can't have you? You insult both of us by returning it. Keep it, burn it, pay for your goddamn wedding with it. I don't want it back.

Paul will never be the man for you. He lacks ambition. He lacks the drive to turn the business into anything other than a petty enterprise. So, keep the money. It will not do anything for Paul, just like he won't do anything for you.

It was never about the money. It was always about you.

D

So, there had been another investor.

Emerson began to gather the torn pieces of paper together on the desk. Like a good jigsaw puzzle, she looked for the corners, for the straight edges. She gathered anything with writing on it…the bank logo, the lines of the check, her mother's handwriting.

The light was fading outside the window, and Emerson clicked on the desk lamp. The amount came together quickly: ten thousand dollars. The date came next, mere days before the official opening of the distillery.

Days.

She put her mother's signature together and the amount written in words.

And finally, the name.

Donovan Finch.

Emerson reached blindly behind her for her father's chair and slumped into it. For whatever reason, Donovan Finch had been there at the beginning. She had no idea how her father and Donovan knew each other, but they had. And from the check, they had all gone into the distillery together.

She wondered if it were possible to go back to the very first bank records for the business. Ten thousand dollars, while a lot of money, was not enough to renovate an entire building. Even allowing for inflation, it would only be worth a little over twenty-five thousand dollars. Perhaps he'd wanted a minor share.

Perhaps her father had invited a friend along on his venture.

Emerson pressed against her temples with her fingertips. Her brain was going to explode.

Connor had been right about one thing in that document. His father *had* been involved. And if that was what was fueling the consideration to acquire the distillery, she had a modicum of sympathy for Donovan.

But to continue a grudge over thirty years was messed up.

Either way, she had it in writing from Donovan that the distillery was to keep the money.

And she had no intention of handing over any part of the distillery in return.

———

Connor peered one last time through Emerson's living room window before climbing back into his car.

Two stupid hours he'd spent, trying to do the right thing before he left work, only to find a bigger mess waiting for him outside. Whatever Emerson had seen, whatever she thought she knew, needed discussing. He needed to apologize and come clean. And he needed for her to see things as they were.

That he was madly in love with her.

Whatever had happened in the past was the past.

He'd driven home after his altercation with his father, deciding to check there first. He'd given Emerson his spare key to let herself in before they went out to dinner on Saturday, on the off chance he was out, and she hadn't returned it. Given his condo was on his way out of town, it made sense to check there first.

He'd debated where to look next. He'd tried her phone a couple more times and messaged.

When she hadn't gotten back to him, he'd driven over to the distillery. Olivia had told him that Emerson had left for home due to a headache. From the cheery greeting, Emerson hadn't told Olivia anything about her message to him. And he didn't want to borrow trouble by asking.

Instead, he'd driven over to her house. And here he was now, like a fucking peeping Tom, peering in through her windows even though her car wasn't in the driveway and there wasn't a single light on inside the place.

Although, if she had a headache, perhaps she'd taken a car service home, or perhaps Jake had dropped her off. The lights would be off if she had a headache, right?

He tried her cellphone one more time, not surprised when it went into voicemail again. What if she were really sick? What if she were asleep? Either way, he should be with her, taking care of her, with or without the bomb that had exploded between them.

Wait.

It came to him where she was. He started the car and began the short drive to her father's house.

Liv said Emerson had "gone home." She referred to both her own house and her father's place that way.

Home.

A place he'd never really understood until he'd met Emerson.

As he pulled onto her father's street, he saw Emerson's car on the driveway and the lights burning in the house.

Relief flooded through him—at least she was safe and hadn't driven off the road or any of the other horrible things he'd imagined.

Connor parked the car and jogged up to the steps, knocking twice before he opened the door and stepped inside.

"Em?" he shouted. "It's Connor. Where are you?"

There was a moment before Emerson stepped out of her father's office. Her eyes looked puffy. She'd been crying.

"Are you okay?" He took a step towards her, to pull her into his arms, but she put her hands up to stop him.

"We need to talk," she said bluntly before turning to walk into the kitchen.

He heard the faucet, and when he followed her, he saw her sipping a glass of water. "I'm sorry I didn't answer your call straight away," he said. "I can explain later, but I want to know what you saw."

Emerson placed her glass on the counter and reached into her purse. She pulled out a document, and he immediately realized what she had in her hand.

Fuck.

Not only was it the proposal document, it was *his* copy of the document. With his writing on the cover.

Cameron had done this. He was going to fucking hang him out to dry when he was done. He'd see to it that no one would hire him. It was still killing Connor that he didn't know how Cameron knew.

Then he looked up and, seeing the hurt in Emerson's eyes, made a promise to himself. When this was over, Cameron would be ruined.

"Em," he said softly. "I'm sorry. I can explain. Shit,

that sounds so lame. Please, let's go sit down, and I'll tell you everything."

"You can tell your father he's never going to get his hands on my distillery," Emerson said, her voice laced with anger.

"I already did. That's what I was doing when you called me. It's the reason I couldn't answer the phone. Please, this will all make so much more sense when you know all the details, I promise."

Emerson eyed him cautiously. "Fine. You have ten minutes."

Ten minutes he could work with. His negotiation skills had never let him down. Surely, they wouldn't fail him now. He reached out to take her hand, but she brushed by him as she made her way to the living room. As he followed her, he admired her response, even more so when she sat on the chair, rather than the sofa.

"Yes, my father wants to buy the distillery, but his interest in *acquiring* it is a recent thing. This all goes back a really long time, and for reasons I've never been able to find even a modicum of evidence for, he believes Dyer's was his and was taken away from him. He's always thought your father took everything that was important away from him. I've grown up on stories about how your father screwed him over."

Emerson leaned forward in her chair. For a moment, she looked as though she were about to say something. Instead, she sighed and leaned back again.

He ran his palms down his jeans. For some reason, he felt as though he were about to give the pitch of his life. The consequences of not sealing this deal with Emerson were greater than he could allow himself to consider. "Anyway, literally the week we met on the plane, I'd been pushing my father to acquire distilleries. The industry is changing to artisanal, to quote you, 'quality over quantity.'

I felt it would be best for our business if we vertically integrated to own and develop some artisanal distillers of our own."

"Was Dyer's in contention then?" Emerson asked.

Connor ran his hand along his jaw. "Here's the thing… it was, because of me. I wanted it. You make great products and need investment. But I knew there was no point in pushing it because Dad would never agree to it. He said he didn't want to put another penny in Paul Dyer's pocket."

Emerson squinted slightly, something she did when she was thinking, he'd noticed. "So, when did we end up as the main target? After you got to know me? When you'd found out about what was going on with the loan, you thought we'd be willing to sell out at some rock-bottom price?"

"No," he said, quickly. "Look, I know this looks bad, but that isn't it at all. Not on my end, anyway. I got on that plane, and there you were. And you were so right. I was being obnoxious. I didn't know who you were until the flight attendant mentioned your name. My head was in my ass, and you saw that. I was intrigued, Em. By this woman who ran the company that seemed to have so much sway over my father."

"Curiosity killed the cat," she said with a huff.

"Touché. But then I got to sit next to you that night. And I got to learn more about you. More than that, I liked you. This woman who should, by all accounts, be my mortal enemy. And yes, to be transparent, I was still on the fence as to whether acquiring you would be a good move. I left the ballroom because my father was furious that you'd won a medal."

Emerson tapped her fingers on the chair. "So, how does he go from not wanting to hear anything about Dyer's to us appearing in this?" she said, waving the document at him.

Connor took a deep breath. If he were honest with

Emerson, she could use the information to cause trouble at the bank. But if he weren't, then she'd never have reason to trust him ever again. "It was a couple of days after you'd first stayed over at my place. I thought I could talk him out of it. Look. Look at the numbers, Em. They are all lowballed. I thought I could distract him. Smoke and mirrors. Make other candidates look better. But then a week later, he wouldn't let it go because someone at the bank told my uncle that they were about to call in the loan."

Emerson stood. "Isn't that illegal? What the hell, Connor. Why didn't you tell me?"

Connor rubbed his face with both hands. "I've screwed up plenty in this. I thought I could figure this out, make it go away. You had so much to worry about already. I didn't want to burden you."

"Burden me? Connor…I…I had a right to know."

Connor stood and walked in front of her. "I see that. But you were better than all of us. You've found a way out of the mess started by the storm. You've figured out a plan to solve it without any external investors. You aren't at risk from my father."

"Is that why I haven't met them? Your family?" Her voice was quiet, the anger replaced with hurt.

"Fuck, Emerson. The easy answer is yes, but it's much more than that. My father had promised to retire, the company was meant to be mine. But my uncle convinced him to stay on for another five years, and that left me in the wings again."

Emerson stepped away. "So, starting a relationship with me was to spite him?"

"No." His chest started tightening. The conversation was getting away from him, and he needed to find his footing. "Em. No. Was getting to know you fueled by a curiosity I've had since I was old enough to recognize the name Dyer? Sure…but, damn… *You* were the reason I fell in love with you."

"Don't say that right now," Em said, wrapping her arms across her chest.

"But it's the truth. Don't you think it would have been a whole lot easier if I hadn't fallen in love with you? After that announcement that my father wasn't going to retire… I've been adrift. The only solid part of my life since his big announcement is you and what we were building."

As soon as the words had left his mouth, he felt the strength in them. In that moment, the only thing he wanted to walk away from this mess with was Emerson. If he lost his job, his company, even the tenuous relationship he had with his father, so be it. What was it his mother had said? *All those sacrifices you make for someone you love don't feel like sacrifices.* He finally understood what she meant.

He placed his hand on her cheek, breathing a sigh of relief when, for a moment, she leaned into it before pulling away.

Emerson inhaled deeply. "There's something you should know. Your father wasn't mad about losing the distillery…"

What?

"What do you mean?"

She tilted her head in the direction of the office. "Come look at this."

Connor followed her, and once in there, she handed him a letter. He recognized his father's handwriting immediately.

Rebecca,

I need to go away…

I can't sit here and watch you and Paul go on about your lives as if I meant nothing to you…

You never gave us a chance…

I have torn up the check you sent me. Do you really think this was about the money?

It was never about the money. It was about you.

"It was about your mother?" Connor asked, shock muddling his brain.

Emerson nodded. "It appears so. There's the check."

Connor looked at the fragments that had carefully been put back together on Paul Dyer's desk.

"I checked our personnel file, everything. I have no record of him on the books. Nothing."

"There is one place," Connor said, his mouth still dry from the revelation. "He's in the photograph taken the day before the distillery opened."

"You're sure?" She reached for an envelope on top of one of the filing cabinets. As she rifled through the files inside, Connor could see they were the photos from the evening she'd shown him.

"That one," he said quickly, stopping her. "Right there." He pointed to his father, and for a moment, they were both silent.

"Em, I know this is all a lot to process for both of us, but I—"

"I'm tired, Connor. And I need some time to think about this." Emerson placed her hand to her forehead.

"That's okay. I've got some gym clothes in the back, and I can go get us some food. We can talk some more."

Emerson put her hand on his arm. "No, Connor. I need some *time*. Time on my own to think this through. To process what you said. I can't do that with you here. I need some breathing room. I need you to go."

As his heart raced, he searched her face for clues. A part of him wanted to stay, to convince her that they could work through this together...but one thing he respected was her absolute right to process this however she needed to.

"I'll go. But know two things, Em. I love you. More than any of this. More than my job, my company, my dad. And second, I have faith in you as the CEO of Dyer's. It doesn't matter what my father wants to do, even if he comes to you directly without me, don't sell. You'll do more with Dyer's than he ever could. Act like the owner you are."

With his heart breaking for her, and for them, Connor turned and left Emerson's father's home, making sure he locked the door behind him.

Chapter Fifteen

As the sun peaked above the horizon, Emerson knew that today was the day she was going to act like the kind of boss she'd always intended to be. If there was a silver lining to the goddamn awful cloud, it should be that.

She set the coffee to brew and walked to the fridge to get the carton of milk. As she opened the door, she glanced at the funeral order of service she'd left pinned to it. Her father's face greeted her, as it always did. The sight of his name in the simple gold script that usually made her heart squeeze and stomach churn, for once, brought a sad smile to her face.

"Oh, Dad," she said, wishing he were still here to whisper guidance.

You can do this, Em.

The voice in her head blended with tones of her father's, such that she didn't know whether the words of motivation were her own or a message from him. Sleep had been tenuous. She'd spent most of the night trying to make sense of everything Connor had told her, and everything she had learned about the one-sided love affair between her mother and Connor's father. Love affair was the wrong word. It was neither love, nor an affair from her mother's perspective. Just one man's attempt at owning a woman who didn't feel the same way.

But Connor shouldn't be blamed for the sins of his father, just like she shouldn't be held responsible for the sins of hers, right? After all, hadn't he tried to deflect his father to protect her?

She finished making the coffee, extra strong, and took one last glance at her face in the mirror. What was the saying about how you're braver than you believe and stronger than you seem? A. A. Milne, she remembered. With a sip of her coffee, she sincerely hoped that was true today.

Concealer covered the bags under her eyes, blush added a pink, fresh hue to her cheeks. And her resilience muscles were firing on all cylinders.

Ali had offered to come over with ice cream, but she'd needed to be on her own. It had mattered to her that she figure out her thoughts without letting anyone else influence her.

Connor had been right about one thing.

You'll do more with Dyer's than he ever could. Act like the owner you are.

She put on her usual jeans and blouse, but partnered it with a jacket instead of a sweater, and low-heeled boots.

Her phone pinged as she walked toward her car. A message. From Connor.

I woke up thinking about you and then I remembered what had happened yesterday. It was like the most fucking awful dream that you realize is actually real. Please, don't give up on us...on me. Don't give up on me.

There was no way she could reply yet, so instead, she climbed into her car and drove to the distillery.

When she arrived twenty minutes later, she headed

straight to her office and made a list of things that were on her mind, starting with the organizational structure. By ten o'clock, she was done.

She sat back in her father's old chair, the leather creaking. While it was a comfort, it wasn't practical, so she made a note to buy herself a proper office chair with her own money. Unable to resist the notifications on her phone, she opened them. There was another message from Connor.

Okay. Here's the thing. I love you. And up until yesterday, we were building something fucking special. Let me make this right. Let me show you how much you mean to me. Where are you? I have something I need to tell you.

Emerson placed her phone back down on the desk, her heart like a yo-yo between her throat and stomach.

At ten thirty, Olivia and Jake walked into her office as she'd requested.

"Finch Liquor Distribution felt like we were an at-risk distillery that they would be able to purchase at a rock-bottom price. We are not going to let that happen," she said.

"Wow," Jake replied. "That's quite the opening to this meeting."

"Connor did what?" Olivia said at the same time.

Both looked shocked.

"This is going to take a lot of explaining, but there's something you need to know about how the distillery got off the ground, to make sense of everything."

She pulled Donovan's letters out of her purse and explained everything she now knew about his role in the start of the distillery, ending with his final letter to their mother.

"From the letters, I don't think Mom was ever unfaithful to Dad. I think Donovan wanted Mom to be his and was crushed when she didn't respond to his advances, which appeared to include investing in the distillery to win her over."

Olivia shook her head and reached for the final letter. "I wonder why Mom and Dad never mentioned it?"

"Why would they?" Jake said. "It's not exactly relevant. Old acquaintances. Old memories. He didn't mean anywhere near as much to them as they obviously did to him. Donovan Finch carried a grudge for a fuck-ton of years because he lost a business, a woman, and a possible friend in Dad. I don't condone what he did, but that had to hurt. And assuming the guy wasn't wealthy, it was a lot of money back then. Like, twenty to thirty thousand or something."

Emerson nodded her agreement. "Doesn't make it right, but it certainly adds perspective."

Olivia took her hand. "So, how does Connor fit in to all this?"

Emerson rolled her head from side to side, loosening the stiffness in her neck and shoulders. "That's where it gets complicated."

She explained the series of events, how Connor was intrigued by this story that caused such anger in his father, and how Finch Liquor Distribution needed to change strategy before he and Emerson even met. And how there was an overlap of his feelings for her and his responsibilities to the company.

"So you kicked him to the curb, right?" Jake said.

Olivia shook her head. "That must be awful for you both. Him caught between you and his father. You caught between him and the distillery."

Jake looked at Olivia. "Are you shitting me? The guy pulled a dick move on Em."

Olivia shrugged. "Yeah. He did. But some of the best meet-cutes are enemies to lovers."

Jake did a double take. "Meet-what?"

"When two people meet for the first time before they fall in love." Olivia rolled her eyes as if it were obvious.

Emerson smiled for the first time since the previous morning. "I appreciate the support, both of you. But I didn't call this meeting to discuss me and Connor. That, I've got to figure out on my own. But what I did want to know is how far you both got with the plans we discussed a week ago."

Olivia looked at her. "What you need is an afternoon of self-care. You should go home and—"

"Thanks, Liv." She didn't mean to cut her off quite so abruptly, and she knew her sister had her own history of developing the skills to look after herself. "I know you're concerned, but I'm okay. I did plenty of self-care last night. Well, at least, I did enough to get some clarity. And someone reminded me that I've got the skills and the smarts to navigate this company. So, from now on, that's what I'm going to do. Jake, do you want to go first?"

Jake studied her carefully. "I just need to say this. I don't like it—what Connor did. You might be older than me, but I'm still your brother and the only guy left standing in this family. Whatever you and he decide, I'll be having words with him."

Emerson sighed. "I really wish you wouldn't, even though I appreciate your need to defend me. But I think this family has gone too long with too much left unsaid. I don't need you to fix this for me, and I certainly don't want you to ruin it for me, whichever way I decide."

Jake nodded and, for a moment, she remembered the petulant child she'd had to coax to crawl. His solemn facial expression reminded her of his early efforts.

"Understood," Jake said. "Right, so I had some thoughts about the different labels we currently produce, and here's what I was thinking."

Emerson listened to the plans, making notes, offering

suggestions, challenging assumptions. He'd taken her suggestions and made them his own. When Liv took over, Emerson was thrilled to see that not only had Liv done the same, but she'd met with Jake outside the distillery to work on branding ideas together.

"One big component is to restart events in December," Liv said. "Christmas means peak times for gathering. A wedding planner called to ask about availability on Christmas Eve for a discrete celebrity wedding and is bringing the couple over next week. I'm going to start the campaign from there. Parties, small weddings. We'll need to rehire some staff because we let everyone go when it became clear the events hall wasn't going to reopen. We can start light. Easy-to-make-ahead foods…charcuterie, pizzas, desserts. Let us organize your work event, that kind of thing. See if we can't get some movement. I figured full staff Thursday through Saturday, part-time for the rest of the week. It's still the first week in November; not every-body has made New Year's plans yet. The tasting rooms can hold eighty people max, but for a black-tie event, we could sell the tickets for a hundred bucks. Minus costs, we'd still make a decent profit."

"I love it," Emerson said. "I love the plans. Let's see what we can pull off before Christmas. Olivia, what about you when it comes to moving out?"

"I don't want to rush looking or hold up the sale. I'm hoping I can crash at one of yours if the closing date ends up being before I have found a place."

Emerson and Jake both nodded their heads. "Of course."

"I gotta go," Jake said, heading for the door. "I left a batch running, and I need to go check it to see if I need to cut the tail yet."

"And what about you and Connor?" Liv asked, once Jake was gone.

Emerson blew out a breath. "I'll keep you posted."

Olivia stood and gathered her things. As she passed Emerson, Liv placed her hand on her shoulder. "You two are so good together. I'm probably being some kind of naive Pollyanna, and I understand you're hurt. But in some ways, it just proves how similar you are."

Emerson looked up at her sister. "How so?"

"Because you were both trying to handle everything on your own, when what you should have done is allow others to help."

The words struck her like a blow. Had they really been that similar in their approaches? She had been trying to protect her siblings, Connor had tried to protect her. At the end of the day, when it mattered, he'd tried to dissuade his father.

But what future did they have if his father hated her on sight?

Connor knew he was supposed to stay away from the building, but it was no use.

He'd swum, he'd worked out, and he'd ran. He'd drunk whiskey with Charles because the idea of drinking gin or drinking alone was just too much. Charles had listened, called him a *fucking bell-end*, then had lent his ear and wisdom.

As a result, Connor knew he had to sort himself out before he could fix things with Emerson.

And now that he knew the truth of what was in his own heart, he needed to speak to his father. Without his pass, he couldn't just walk inside. But thankfully, the security guards knew him, and, because his father hadn't taken any action beyond retaining Connor's card, they manually let him through the barriers to the elevators.

On the way to his father's office, he ran through all the things he needed to say. His father wasn't going to be pleased to see him but that was the very least of his problems. He needed to make sure that his uncle wasn't there because he had some home truths to deliver.

That was the reason he was there so early. His uncle never hit the office before nine.

Connor shook his hands, something he did routinely before he dove into the water. He visualized the nerves he carried flying from his fingertips like water droplets, allowing his fingers to fill instead with adrenaline that would power him through the race.

Somehow, this meeting felt more important, more vital.

As he rounded the corner, he saw his father, coat still on, disappear into his office. Connor's footsteps hastened as he hurried to catch him before he started making calls.

"Dad," he said as he stepped through the door, closing it behind him. "We need to talk."

His father turned. "I thought I'd taken your pass away. You shouldn't be here."

"You did. But I learned some really important information last night that I think you should be made aware of."

His father glared at him. "Go home, Connor. I'm too mad to talk to you rationally."

Connor walked toward the desk, where his father was currently getting comfortable. He put his palms on the ornate desk he'd once thought he'd end up sitting behind.

"How did he find out?" he demanded.

"Connor, this won't get us—"

"How did he know?"

"He saw you leaving Maison Noir together."

Connor sighed. Given their charged mood when they'd left the restaurant, there would have been no misconstruing their relationship. "Cameron provided Emerson with a

245

copy of the strategy document. She knows all about your intentions."

His father's eyes suddenly met his. "That is a bold insinuation, Connor."

"To deliberately cause trouble, Cameron sent my copy of the strategy deck to Emerson. He knew she would read it, and she was rightfully furious. Cameron broke every single company rule when he sent it to her."

Lines furrowed his father's forehead. "Don't be ridiculous, Connor. She probably found it while snooping around your apartment. Or perhaps you left it at her place deliberately."

Connor shook his head. "Nope. It was sent to the distillery for her attention. And I left that document locked in my office on Friday. Cameron saw us in the restaurant on Friday, and suddenly this document is in her hand Monday morning?"

His father's fingertips drummed the edge of the table. "Still don't buy it, Connor. You're just mad because of what happened yesterday. And as you said, it was locked in your office."

"Our passes all open each other's doors, remember? Yours, Cameron's, and mine. And it will take you two seconds to call security and find out whether Cameron let himself into the office over the weekend, something he normally never does."

Donovan looked toward Cameron's office. "I have to admit, this all feels a little pathetic."

Connor's rage spilled over. "Pathetic? I'll tell you what's pathetic. Cameron's games. He's played you, and now he's attempting to play me. It's never going to work, the two of us in this company. I've outgrown all of this."

It was true. If he'd wanted backstabbing and intrigue, he'd have gone to Wall Street and made a killing. Instead, he'd followed the path expected of him, and had found the same behavior; he just didn't get paid enough to tolerate it.

"So, what? You are going to quit and walk away from all this over a woman?" his father spat, suddenly standing. "No son of mine would be that foolish."

Connor scoffed. "Are you kidding me? This whole *thing*...this whole stupid issue is because you quit and walked away from Dyer's Gin Distillery over Rebecca Dyer."

His father stopped in his tracks. "What did you say?"

There was nothing left to lose. "I know, Dad. How you were in love with Rebecca Dyer, but she was never in love with you."

"I don't...that's not..." His father's face burned red as he blustered.

"There's no point arguing. I've seen the proof. I know you invested ten thousand dollars because you hoped it would help buy her affection. And I know that you ripped up the check when she tried to pay you back and returned it to her."

All the life seemed to leave his father's body, and he slumped to the chair. "I should have cashed that check," he muttered.

Connor's anger slipped away, and he sat down, too. "It was never about the money," Connor said. "Was it?"

His father waved away the question. "It was a long time ago, Connor. The details fail me."

Of course they didn't. The man wouldn't have held on to the grudge for so long if they had. "No. They don't, Dad. And I get it. I really do. To answer your question, yes, I would walk away from all this for *Emerson*. Not just *a* woman, but *the* woman for me."

"So, now the Dyers will take my son as well as my money." It was a statement, not a question.

Connor remained calm and took a breath. He'd fought

his father many times, and he knew that his father's natural response was to deflect. "No, Dad. Emerson isn't taking anything away. You made the ultimatum, Dad. You took my pass away to make a point that you could take all of this away from me if I didn't end it with Emerson. And overnight, I realized two things. I don't care, and it's actually the right thing for me."

His father lifted his head. "What do you mean, it's the right thing for you?"

"Taking that chair you're sitting in right now was all I've ever let myself focus on. You pushed me, steered me, and somewhere along the line, I bought into the lie that it was what I wanted. I was wrong. It was what you wanted for me...no, it was what you wanted for yourself. But I realized that I need to try something else. Something new. I want to build something."

"You can build businesses here," his father said, panic in his voice. "We talked about this. The acquisitions." It was clear, in spite of everything, that his father had never intended for Connor to leave the business for the long-term. This had all been a petty attempt to keep him in line. To remind Connor how much he owed.

Connor shook his head. "Not as long as you're still here. We don't have the same vision or set of ethics on how to treat family and employees. And even if we could somehow get past that, I wouldn't come back as long as Cameron is still here. He crossed a line this weekend, and I'll never be able to trust him. I won't work in a situation where my every move is questioned. To be honest, even if you told me that you would retire today with no provisions for my uncle, it still wouldn't be enough. This isn't what I want to do."

"So, you're *really* going to quit and walk away from all this over a woman?" Incredulity etched his father's face.

"No, I'm going to resign because I want something

more for myself. This whole thing with the distillery, with Cameron, and you staying on…it just made me realize that it isn't what I want."

"And what do you want, son?"

Connor's chest squeezed at the affectionate term that had come too late to be of any value. "The truth is, I don't know. Something smaller, I think."

"And the Dyer girl? Do you want her, too?"

Connor grinned. He knew the answer to that question. "Please. Call her Emerson. And I do, more than anything. The jury is still out on if we'll be able to get past this. Cameron's trick may have done irreparable damage."

His father paused. A long, deep sigh escaped his lips. "I'll find out who broke into your office and mailed that to the Dyer—to Emerson."

"Thanks, Dad. Look, I'm sorry to leave you in the lurch. I'll make sure I do a proper handoff. And if you decide to act on replacing Cameron, I'll help find a replacement."

Donovan looked crestfallen. Losing his son, and potentially his brother, wouldn't be an easy burden to bear. "Was she happy?"

"Emerson? No, she was pissed and tore me a new one."

His father smiled sadly. "I meant Rebecca. Did Paul give her a good life?"

Connor's heart ached for his father for a moment. In the early hours that very morning, he'd felt a sense of panic that he'd not be able to make things right with Emerson. To feel that way for the rest of his life would be horrific. "Yeah, Dad. He did. They were good together. Loved each other. Loved their kids. And Paul never attempted to find another woman after Rebecca died. Emerson told me he once said that he'd had his one chance at true love with Rebecca and that he'd never been able to get his head around replacing her."

Donovan swallowed deeply. "Good," he said gruffly. "That's good."

A realization hit Connor. What was it his mother had said when he'd spoken with her about their divorce?

I always felt like I was second fiddle. I sometimes think he married me on the rebound from that darn distillery. And the way he threw himself into his work at that time left him with no time or energy for me, or for us. He was a husband and father in name only.

It wasn't the business he'd rebounded from. It was Rebecca Dyer. His mother would never need to know.

"I'm sorry, Dad. About Rebecca. I get it. I worry Emerson isn't going to get over this."

Silence settled over the room. He wondered what Emerson was doing right now. She was his next stop, but he knew he couldn't go see her until he'd righted this part of his life, this part of his story, first. He needed her to know that she had nothing to worry about from his motivations.

All he wanted was to love her.

"I suppose I should meet her at some point," Donovan said eventually.

Connor stood. "I'd like that, Dad. You'll really like her. From what I've heard, she's very much like her mother."

His father stood and walked over to him, reaching for his hand. "In that case, I wish you luck in fixing things. I hope she listens to you."

"Me too," Connor said, shaking and then releasing his father's hand.

Because he couldn't imagine another hour without her in his life.

Chapter Sixteen

Emerson pulled up outside Connor's building and stared upward in the direction of his apartment. She'd sat alone with her thoughts in her office for a little while after her meeting with Jake and Liv.

Words hadn't come when she opened her phone to find messages from Connor about wanting to meet up with her. He'd thoughtfully stayed away from the distillery but had offered to meet her wherever she wanted.

His place was close by. It was private. No more spying from Connor's dubious uncle.

While she'd be safer in her home, she needed somewhere to retreat to if the meeting didn't go as she hoped.

She stepped out of her car and locked it, straightened her jacket, and walked into the building. As she entered the elevator, she thought of the night they'd spent together just last weekend, of the way he'd kissed her in the very spot she now stood. She'd never look at the mirrored walls the same way again.

Nerves fluttered in her stomach like trapped butterflies trying to escape, and goddamn if her palms weren't a little bit sweaty.

The door to his apartment loomed down the corridor, and the walk down the gray carpet felt like the length of a mile. As she approached, she took a deep breath to steady herself, then knocked firmly.

Footsteps grew louder as he walked toward the door, and Emerson's butterflies grew proportionately with the sound.

"Hey," Connor said, pulling the door wide open so she could pass by. He reached for her but then pulled back. "Sorry. Habit. We should talk first."

He looked as unhappy as she felt, and her first thought was how wonderful it would have felt to be wrapped in those strong arms of his, to rest her face against his chest while he held her.

"I agree." She placed her purse on a hook by the door as she had gotten into the habit of doing.

Emerson walked to the living room and sat down on the leather sofa.

"Can I get you a drink? Wine or coffee or something?" Connor asked, rubbing his palms down the front of his jeans. Perhaps he was as nervous as she felt.

"No, I'm good, thanks."

Connor joined her on the sofa, sitting close enough that she could feel the warmth that always emanated from him, but not close enough that they touched. The vibration was still there. The one she always felt when they were in each other's orbit, the thing that had made everything feel so goddamn magical.

"How are you?" Connor asked earnestly. He studied her eyes and bit his lip as if concerned.

It wasn't glib small talk; Emerson could tell the difference. "Not the greatest twenty-four hours of my life, not the absolute worst, but close."

Connor put his arm along the back of the sofa. If she leaned into the cushion, his fingertips would be able to reach the ends of her hair. She loved when he played with it while they watched TV together.

"I'm sorry. For all of it. I confronted my dad this morning."

While she hadn't had any expectations of how their conversation would go, she hadn't expected that. "What did he say?"

"He confirmed what you found out. It was never really about the distillery, it was always about your mom. He loved her, even though it was unrequited. More than he loved my mom. I think that's why their marriage failed. My mom is an incredible woman, but she wasn't the person my dad wanted to be with. My father was desperately unhappy."

Emerson's stomach flipped. "That's so sad, for everyone involved."

Connor shrugged. "Perhaps. Your mom married who she was meant to. Mom's happy with Derek, and he's the right guy for her. It's just Dad."

He reached for her hand, laid his fingers on hers, and the buzz of connection was just as strong as ever. "Fuck, I'm sorry." He pulled his fingers away again. "It's just... you're here, which I am so fucking relieved about. And the last time you were here, it was the night we went to dinner, and we came back here, and...well. It's like memory and habit and...I just want to hold you, and I want you to hold me back. And I wish I could go back to the beginning, to the airplane, and start this all off differently." Connor leaned forward and placed his head in his hands before running his fingers through his hair. "I resigned today."

Emerson, still reeling from his emotional outburst, couldn't hold in her surprise. "What? Why would you do that? I hope you didn't do it for me?"

Connor shook his head. "No, I did it for me, Em. Well, mostly for me. And some for us. Spending time with you, getting to know you, and Jake and Liv, and what you do at the distillery, I realized I'd never really gotten to build something from the ground up. I'd been programmed since birth that I was going to take over the family business, but unlike you and Jake and Liv, I'd never been asked if I actually wanted to. It had always been assumed."

Connor got up and paced along the blue rug he'd made love to her on so thoroughly only days before.

"And then my father decided he was going to stay on for another five years, and my uncle showed his true colors because it was him who sent you that document. And I could have stood and fought for the company to be better, but I couldn't find the energy. I'd lost respect for my dad, and even if I got what was mine, then what? I'd be running a company I wasn't passionate about. Not like you are when you talk about your work."

Emerson huffed. "Hardly. I've been bouncing from one catastrophe to the next since we met."

Connor came back to the sofa, sitting so close their knees and thighs touched. This time he did grab her hands, holding them firmly in his. "But don't you see, Em? You held on with Liv and Jake. You found a way. You picked yourselves up. And together, you're working on a way out. Because you care. Because you're damn good at what you do. I fucking admire that."

His words hit her firmly in the chest.

Had his actions been reckless? Yes.

But had they really done any harm? No. Not to her *or* to the distillery.

And he cared for her, passionately. He respected her. He recognized her need to rebuild Dyer's. To protect Liv and Jake. *She* inspired *him*. He accepted her fully, as she was, slightly flawed, still learning, still a work-in-progress.

Before she could stop herself, Emerson leaned into him and their lips met furiously. Connor's hands slid to her face, into her hair, holding her in place as his tongued explored hers.

"Fuck, Em," he gasped, before kissing her again. "I'm so sorry."

How had she thought she could live without this in her life? How had she considered that she could let a man who held her in such high regard go?

"Wait," Connor said, his voice straining as he placed his hands on her shoulders and gently pushed her away. "As much as I want to fucking devour you, I can't until I know this is all squared away. Make-up sex and break-up sex are two decidedly different things, and I need to know which it is we're about to have."

Emerson bit down the smile that threatened. "It's make-up sex, Connor. But you're right. There are still things we need to discuss."

Connor ran a hand through his hair. "Thank fuck for that, Em." He took hold of her hand and pressed a kiss to the back of it.

All of her insides were churned up. And she banked the need to slide her fingers beneath the waistband of his jeans. "You said you quit. What do you intend to do now?"

Connor's eyes were hooded as he looked at her, his chest inflating and deflating at a rate far faster than normal. She was glad he was as breathless as she was. "I'm fortunate to have time to figure that out," he said, finally. "I have savings, a decent network, some active investments that pay monthly. It's not enough for the long-term, but it means I can be selective. I think I need to take my time and decide."

"And your father knows there's no way on this green earth that I'll sell the distillery to him?"

Connor nodded. "That's a definite yes."

There was one last thing that was bothering her. Perhaps it was too soon in their relationship for it to be an issue, but she needed to know. "Does he know about me? About us?"

Now it was Connor's turn to smile. "He does. I told him this morning how much you mean to me. He suggested it might be time for the two of you to meet."

"And your mom?"

Now, Connor laughed. "I told her about you the day after Halloween. I said I'd set something up for this week but then time kind of got away from me. Is there anything else you need to know, or is now when I get to lay you down on that rug and finish what we started because I'm really fucking ready to do that again?"

Emerson stood and slipped off her jacket as she backed away from the sofa in the direction of the bedroom. "The rug got painful after a while, and I don't intend for this to be over quickly. Make-up sex should take a while."

Connor stood and ran a hand along his jaw. "See, I disagree there. Make-up sex requires fire. Passion. Urgency."

She slid her fingers to the buttons of her blouse and began to pop them open slowly. "Everything comes to those who wait."

Connor stepped in her direction, a slow and steady prowl. "What if I'm not a patient man?"

The way he looked at her made her want to melt, to strip her clothes off and to hell with the burns of the stupid blue rug.

Emerson slid her blouse down her shoulders and let it drop to the floor. "Who says we only get to do it once? We could do fast, then do it slow."

"Are you negotiating with me again, Dyer?" He reached for his belt, sliding it through the belt loops before dropping it on the sofa.

"I intend to make negotiating with you a permanent habit," she said. "Just putting you on notice."

Connor grinned, then suddenly leaped for her, pinning her against the wall, his hard erection pressed up against her. "I just remembered something," he said, placing a row of kisses behind her ear.

The sensation made her knees weak, and she was grateful for Connor's weight keeping her pressed to the wall. "What is it?" she gasped, aware of just how breathless her words sounded. He did that to her. Caused her to lose control.

"This. You and me. It's a permanent thing, right?" Connor stopped kissing her and stepped back a little, giving her breathing space. He placed his hand to her cheek. "I'm serious, Em. This. Us. It's going all the way, right? Not today. Not right now. But we'll get a place together. We'll get married, someday. Kids, if we decide we want them. I want more than make-up sex. I want a commitment that you feel the same way I do. That from the moment I lay you down on my bed, we're building a future."

He held her gaze as he spoke, and she felt every single word.

"I want that, too," she whispered. "All of it. I was worried it was too soon to say it."

Connor leaned forward and kissed her. Slow, deep, drugging kisses. The kind that turned her to mush. "From the moment we met, you've never had a problem saying what was on your mind to me. Don't start now."

Emerson smiled. "You are never going to let it go that I sat in your seat, are you?"

Connor bent forward and swept her into his arms.

"Never."

Epilogue

S now was beginning to fall hard as the last truck pulled out of the distillery on Christmas Eve. Deliveries that would make their way around the country in time for New Year's. Emerson ticked the last order off the list and sighed with relief. Stan had left half an hour earlier. She'd sent him home because there was no point in both of them waiting for the truck to leave.

She checked the clock on the wall. Noon exactly. They were closing early after a hellishly frantic push for volume. With the new shift pattern Jake had established, production had increased by twenty-three percent. And the supply cost negotiations Emerson had conducted, along with the dollar increase in retail price, had generated seven points more margin. Things were moving in the right direction.

"Did it get off okay?" Connor asked as he strolled into the warehouse. He wore a thick black hoodie and a beanie, dark blue jeans, and a thick-soled pair of boots. Some days he still wore his suits. Like the days when he went to Finch Liquor Distribution to help his father as Connor transitioned out of the business, or to help him find and interview a new CFO to replace Cameron. The security footage had proven what Connor suspected. That Cameron had gone into his office and taken his document.

He wrapped his arms around her, pulled her close, and kissed her soundly.

Somewhere between the two of them making up and standing here now, he'd become the de facto Sales and Marketing Director for Dyer's Gin Distillery, a job she had sucked at and was glad to be rid of. It was supposedly only temporary while he looked for something else, but Emerson was getting used to having him around. She knew he had big aspirations, but Jake and Olivia had suggested offering him the job on a permanent basis. Emerson was still considering it, but she'd take her lumps if he turned her down because he didn't want to put all their eggs in one basket.

"It did," she replied with a grin. The heat of his body staved off the chill of the wintery breeze. "How was your morning?" she asked when they came up for air.

"Good. If the product sells well in all these new channels, it could be a great earner. I think we're in with a potential distribution network in the UK. Opening a European pipeline could double the distillery's revenue."

"Assuming the renovation goes well and on schedule next year," Emerson added. "We won't produce enough without that."

When she'd point-blank refused Connor's offer of personal investment, he'd understood. She needed to do this on her own terms. Instead, she'd gone to the bank and explained the reasons behind her father's loan. They had paid back the loan in full, using funds from the quick sale of their father's house. A friend of Jake's had wanted the house and had offered a fast closing to move in before Christmas. But she'd asked the bank to consider providing her a new loan. She'd shown them production volumes, expansion plans, and with thanks to Connor, a new sales and marketing strategy that would boost income considerably.

And the bank had been impressed with the plan. They were prepared to write the sheet clean, treating Emerson as a new business owner. They'd asked her to come back once the distillery had achieved three months of back-to-back improvement, and they were well on their way. Her plan included expanding the events hall into a new distillery, while the old distillery would be renovated into a larger, multi-functional events hall.

Connor let her go and walked to the roller shutter doors of the warehouse, lowering them to block out the cold flurries fluttering their way onto the concrete floor of the warehouse. "Jake's just shutting everything down, and Olivia is setting up for the wedding tonight."

Emerson thought about the small Christmas Eve party that was a surprise wedding for one of the Denver ice hockey players. She'd offered to work, but Olivia had assured Emerson that she and the team she'd hired had it covered. Still, she'd planned to stay the night at Connor's anyhow, it being Christmas and all. That and the fact that his space was big enough to host both their families for Christmas dinner.

"Is it wrong that I'm so relieved Liv said she didn't need my help?" Emerson asked as they walked toward the offices.

Connor threw his arm over her shoulder. "Is it wrong I'm relieved I get to take you home and make out with you all afternoon?"

Emerson laughed. "You wish. I have things to bake, make, and stuff. And you have things to wrap."

Connor pouted. "I'd rather be unwrapping you."

"Maybe if you get all your chores done, you can get a reward like a good boy."

"Always the negotiator," he muttered.

They grabbed their things from their respective offices. Connor had unofficially moved into the spacious cluttered storage closet down the hallway instead of sharing an office with Liv as Emerson had done. He'd moved Emerson's old desk in there after asking Emerson if it was all right to clear out the space.

On their way out, Emerson checked in on the tasting rooms. Everything was decorated in sprays of flowers and greenery, in white and sage green. It smelled glorious. "Liv," she called out.

"One sec." Olivia clambered from beneath the white tablecloth covering a long bank of tables. "Sorry, needed an extension cable. How does it look?"

Emerson took another look around the room. The wedding planner had done an incredible job of creating the theme, and Liv had been equally successful in helping pull it all together. Round tables stood alongside the windows. The fairy lights outside would really highlight the snow later. On the other side of the room, there was a small dance floor. Discretion had been the name of the game. They'd not been allowed to tell anyone what they were hosting, with the whole distillery held to a nondisclosure agreement. There was a private deal for photographs with a high-end magazine that Emerson hoped would shine the distillery in a positive light. "You've done a wonderful job, Liv. Really. Dad would be amazed by all this."

Liv smiled. "Thanks. I think he would, too."

"Right, I'm heading out. Are you sure I can't help? Connor is still here. He would be good for any and all heavy lifting."

Liv shook her head. "No," she said firmly. "I've got this."

"Well, you know where I am if you need reinforcements tonight. I'll only be—"

"I'm fine, Em. Honestly. Leave this to me."

Emerson took her sister's hand and squeezed it. "Fine. I get it. Break a leg."

By the time she got to the parking lot, Connor had cleared his car of snow and had the engine going to heat up the inside.

"Everything good?" he asked as she slipped inside. The leather seat already felt warm through the denim of her jeans.

"Everything is perfectly fine."

Connor squeezed her knee before driving them home. It was funny how in such a short time she had come to think of their places interchangeably. Especially as the weather changed and there was less for her to do in her garden. It was nice to stay at his place. It was bigger than hers. And she appreciated the view of the Denver skyline. But if she stayed there too long, she got claustrophobic, and needed to get out of the city.

Once inside his home, Connor helped her out of her coat and hung it on the hook by the door. The seasonal lights they'd strung over the balcony on Thanksgiving weekend sparkled, even though snow swirled around them. And when Emerson switched on the lights to the Christmas tree in the corner of the living room, everything began to take on the magical glow of Christmas. She grinned as she recalled the stoic look on Connor's face as they'd tied the tree to the top of his Mercedes to bring it home. They'd decorated it together, and once done, Connor had tugged her down to the floor and taken her on the blue rug, *again*.

"Want to get naked with me?" Connor said, slipping his arms around her waist, nuzzling into her neck.

She turned in his arms. "I was just thinking about the afternoon we decorated the tree. But as truly wonderful as that idea sounds, what I need to do is switch on some Christmas carols and do some baking. Want to help?"

Connor grinned. "If the only goods you're willing to let me eat are your baked goods, then I don't really have a choice."

"As I said earlier, if you're a good boy, I might let you strip me naked and bend me over the kitchen island."

"Oh, can we include flour and sugar? Make a big mess?"

"Only if you promise to vacuum and mop before everyone arrives tomorrow."

"Spoilsport."

Connor let her go and walked to the wine rack. "Pinot?" he asked.

"Perfect." On the kitchen counter were two boxes. One of ingredients, the other of baking utensils. Connor had gotten the turkey and all of the vegetables. He'd picked them up on his way home from the distillery the previous day, while she stayed late at Dyer's to finish off a run with Jake.

"What are we making?" Connor said, placing a glass of wine in front of her.

"Apple pie, obviously. Lemon squares. Rocky Road. Double chocolate chip cookies. A cheesecake. And cheese breadsticks for the charcuterie." She picked up the wine and, after clinking the glass to his, took a sip. "Mmm. That's good."

Connor drank from his glass. "Not as tasty as you."

She playfully slapped his arm. "Stop. You need to focus. If there's no dessert tomorrow, it'll be all your fault."

"You know the stores are still open, Em. I could pop out and get something, then it could be you, me, this bottle of red, and a whole lot of mischief."

Emerson laughed. "Here," she said, handing him the scale. "Make your own mischief by measuring two cups of that." She pointed to the flour. "I'm going to make a start on the crumb base for the cheesecake."

"You realize you're making more types of dessert than there are guests, right?"

For a moment, she paused to think. Her and Connor. Jake and Liv. His mom and Derek, plus his dad. Seven of them. "Wrong. Five desserts plus something savory. And it's Christmas. If you can't have multiple desserts on Christmas, when can you? Wait, can you eat any of this?"

Connor grinned. "I usually eat what I want from Christmas Day to New Year's but work out at least three hours a day, since I'm off work. Gym session, weights, and then focused stretching. Want to join me?"

Emerson shook her head. "I can't imagine anything worse. I'm just going to eat it all and start again on January first."

"One of the many reasons I love you," Connor said, tearing into the bag of flour. Plumes of it went into the air, dusting his stubble and black T-shirt.

She couldn't help but laugh at the shocked look on his face.

"I don't even know how that happened," Connor said, pulling at his T-shirt to get a better look at the damage.

"You could always take it off and bake shirtless," she suggested, helpfully.

Connor raised an eyebrow. "I've been trying to get you naked since we got home. Was that an invitation? Because I'm about to walk straight through it," he said, moving around the island toward her. He pulled his shirt over his head and threw it on the counter.

She made a show of pushing him away, but ultimately let him pull her into his arms. "I like the way you said *home*," she said, softly.

"Want to make it permanent?" he asked. "I know how much being out of the city means to you, but we have the means to keep both places. Here during the week and then your place on the weekends?"

Her heart skipped a beat. The idea of them living together had been something she'd considered, but for some reason she'd always assumed he'd want them to live in his house, which definitely had more space than her home. "In the summer, the garden needs a bit more work."

He kissed the tip of her nose. "Emerson...I don't really care. Here or there. Five nights to two nights, three nights to four. It doesn't matter. Home is where you are, anyway. I just want to make a start on a plan where I get to wake up next to you every morning for the rest of our lives."

Now her heart melted. "I want that, too, Connor. Truly."

She stepped up on her toes, and he bent to meet her, kissing her thoroughly and more deliciously than any of the treats she intended on baking. Unable to resist, she slid her fingertips beneath the waistband of his jeans, reassured by his steady heat.

"If you start that, we're stopping baking," he muttered against her lips.

"You're practically naked, which is highly distracting, so we're stopping baking," she said before whooping as he bent forward and picked her up, his arms holding her tight. "Connor, we do need to finish it later."

"Fine, but we're finishing this negotiation once you're naked and beneath me," he laughed, carrying her into *their* bedroom.

About the Author

Scarlett Cole is a contemporary romance author that calls both Toronto, Canada and Manchester, England home. A born city dweller, she periodically quashes the urge to live in the country by hiking up a mountain to remind herself that living away from people would terrify the pants off her.

She believes everybody deserves their love story to be told and loves her heroes on the rough and rugged side...and usually tall (because she married one of those 6ft 6" men you read about in romance!). She's an A-type personality and Scorpio star sign, so good luck getting her to do anything she doesn't want to.

When she isn't writing, she's happy to talk about hot men and expensive shoes while drinking a cold gin and tonic. Don't bring up olives. As far as Scarlett is concerned, they are the devil's food. As long as you don't bring up olives, she's happy to hear from you any time.

Also by Scarlett Cole

If you enjoyed, LOVE IN NUMBERS, head on over to Scarlett's website to check out her other series:

Second Circle Tattoo Series

Preload Series

Love Over Duty Series

www.scarlettcole.com